Captain Janeway . . .
in her own words!

"When I went into the escape pod, part of my hair had been burned off above the shoulders. When I came out, it was an inch below the shoulder. How much time was that?

I wanted to walk. I tried, but had no idea where 'down' was. My foil poncho crinkled as several strong hands lifted me. My scorched hand moved in a pathetic wave of thanks.

I saw figures over me, humanoid if not human.

'Do you understand me?' one of them asked.

'Yes, I do.' My voice was raspy, smoke-rawed and out of practice.

'I'm Ruvan, chief medic. This is Zell, our second in command.' He turned to Zell and said, 'She has burns over thirty percent of her body, but only four percent are deep damage. I have them treated and compressed. Her legs are the worst. She can walk, but slowly and with help. Another week in that pod and her muscles would have atrophied.'

'At least we found her in time.' Zell said. "She's alive. We're all alive for now. It's good enough."

The first officer turned to me and took a step closer. 'Welcome aboard the *Zingara*. I don't recognize your species. Who are you and where do you com[illegible]?' "

STAR TREK VOYAGER

THE CAPTAIN'S TABLE

BOOK FOUR OF SIX

FIRE SHIP

KATHRYN JANEWAY

AS RECORDED BY DIANE CAREY

THE CAPTAIN'S TABLE CONCEPT BY
JOHN J. ORDOVER AND DEAN WESLEY SMITH

POCKET BOOKS

New York   London   Toronto   Sydney   Tokyo   Singapore

An *Original* Publication of POCKET BOOKS

POCKET BOOKS, a division of Simon & Schuster Inc.
1230 Avenue of the Americas, New York, NY 10020

STAR TREK is a Registered Trademark of
Paramount Pictures.

A VIACOM COMPANY

This book is published by Pocket Books, a division of
Simon & Schuster Inc., under exclusive license from
Paramount Pictures.

ISBN: 0-671-01467-6

First Pocket Books printing July 1998

10 9 8 7 6 5 4 3 2 1

POCKET and colophon are registered trademarks of
Simon & Schuster Inc.

Printed in the U.S.A.

"Naow, about goin' back. Allowin' we could do it, which we can't, you ain't in no fit state to go back to your home, an' *we've* jest come on to the Banks, workin' fer our bread . . . an' with good luck we'll be ashore again somewheres abaout the first weeks o' September."

—Captain Disko Troop
Captains Courageous
by Rudyard Kipling

CHAPTER

1

"AND JUST HOW DID YOU FIND YOUR WAY TO THE CAPTAIN'S Table?" a stout man in oilskins asked her.

"I smelled fire. And trouble."

"Both bad things at sea. Please go on."

Captain Kathryn Janeway sipped at her brandy, then did as she had been asked.

Maybe it was just cabbage stew. Trouble and cooked cabbage smelled a lot alike.

Dark planets always made me uneasy. Humans had sixth, seventh senses. I'd learned to listen.

"This way," I said with an unnecessary beckon.

"Why that way?"

"I don't know."

The narrow street was wet with recent rain, and there was a sense of steam around us. Dim figures came and went from doorways, cloaked and unspeaking. My mind made something of it, but perhaps the downcast eyes and drawn hoods were due only to the night chill. I hoped so, but . . .

"Captain?"

Back to work.

I turned, and tripped on a faulty brick in the street—doors, windows, banners, and signs spun, and so did I. All elbows, a knee—I tried to catch myself, failed—and Tom Paris caught me.

A clumsy captain. That's what every crewman wants to see—his elegant, surefooted, universally competent captain taking a spill on a grimy street.

"Shall we dance, madam?" Paris's college-boy face beamed at me, backlit by a gauzy street lamp.

"Quit grinning, Lieutenant," I snapped. "Starship captains don't trip. And we *never* dance."

He smiled wider and arranged me on my feet, making me ponder courts-martial for a second or two. "I'm sorry, Captain, I just thought your injuries—"

"They're fine."

Another few steps padded away under our feet before I realized that my mood had completely changed. Caution had blended to intrigue. I could no more turn back than fly.

We were heading down an alley that made me think of Old London's back ways, heading toward a corner and another street. I wanted to get there, but caution boiled up a certain restraint. A few seconds wouldn't matter.

A passerby now looked up and nodded greeting. So other moods had changed too?

"This place feels *really* familiar," I mentioned.

"I thought I was imagining it," Paris said. "No place in the Delta Quadrant can possibly look familiar to us, unless we double back on our course—"

"—and we didn't do that," I abbreviated. "This place seems like an old movie to me . . . a Gothic mystery . . . one of those stories with the light in the castle tower and the woman in the diaphanous nightgown running across a moor, casting back a fearful glance—"

Paris bumped his head on a hanging sign. "Looks like a western to me."

Casting him a glare, I said, "Lieutenant, let's get around that corner."

"Aye, aye, Captain."

An unexplained thrill ran down my arms as cobblestones kneaded our soles. Holmes, are you hiding there around the corner? Watson? Wet and foggy, yet cowled in city sounds and people's voices muffled behind shutters. There were no horses' hooves or wagon wheels—this culture was beyond that—but I found myself listening for a clop and clatter. The smoke-yellow streetlamps were electrical but inadequate. I had a feeling not of neglect but purpose. Just a feeling . . . nothing but a feeling . . .

Usually feelings didn't so completely guide me. Usually I depended upon rationality, upon keeping feelings reined hard, for they were inaccurate and undependable. Not how do I feel, but what do I think—that's what guided me, and so far had kept us all alive. Feelings were too susceptible to fears, and fear was a daily diet on this unending mission. And feelings were too sudden.

Even good feelings had been reined in a long time ago. I enjoyed a few things, but always kept control and never let myself enjoy too much. I never went over the top and forgot where we were and why. This kind of restraint, for a human being—a human woman—was unfortunate and even unnatural, but serviceable for me. If I kept my feelings in their place, good and bad, then I could handle the truly awful.

Like these last few days. Truly . . .

Just as I cast off my thoughts as beginning to be a little too Vulcan, I realized the voices we were hearing had gotten notably louder now that Paris and I had rounded the corner. Nothing raucous—just easier to hear, even delineate individuals. Somebody was having a pleasant time. Down the street, there was a rowdier place somewhere.

There were several doorways, each with some kind of hawker's sign swaying gently over it. When had a breeze come up?

I came to the first door on the left, snuggled into a leathery wooden archway by a good meter, and the heavy aged-oak door was propped open by what looked like an iron bootscraper. There was music, and a heady scent of fire and food. My memories stirred and pushed me toward the door.

"Tavern of some kind." I looked up at the dreary wooden sign and the carved letters.

"The Captain's Table . . ."

"Sounds nice," Paris commented.

I peered briefly at the faded paint in the shape of four

stars in each corner of the sign. "Very nice, Tom. But why is it written in English?"

He eyed the sign again. "English . . ."

At a table to my right, voices muttered and drew my attention.

"—two months out of Shanghai when a gale mauled our rudder clean off. We hove to in high seas and sawed planks out of spare spars. For four days we fitted a jury rudder, then piloted with lines and tackles around the Cape."

"Eight thousand miles—a feat of seamanship wizardry for sure, Captain Moodie."

"A compliment, Charlie, from a man who ran the Bora in a steam launch."

"Oh, yeah, me and Rosie could move mountains, give or take them leeches."

As the two men paused, noticing me, I moved on into the pub, leaving them some privacy.

The wooden door wouldn't open without my shoulder involved. The wood was warm from inside, but dank on its surface from the fingers of fog slipping under the archway. I walked down a short corridor that guided me into a left turn, through a second archway with darkened timber and a whiff of sea rot. As I turned, the Captain's Table tavern opened before me.

A warm smoky cloak wrapped my shoulders and took me by the waist like an old friend's arm at a fireside, coddling me into the clublike environment of a country pub. To my left, there was a piano, but no one was playing. Its rectangled rosewood top sprawled like a morning airfield, reflecting incarnated gaslight from sconces on the paisley-papered wall. Before me was a raft of round tables, at the tables were people. Beings. Mostly men, a few women—most looked human but there were some aliens—who sat in wooden armchairs worn to a warm grousefeather brown.

Over there, to the right along the wall was a glossy cherrywood bar with moleskin stools. The age-darkened bar laughed with carved Canterbury Tales–type figures. Over a mirrored backsplash a shelf was crammed with whiskey jugs, ship's decanters, and every manner of bottle. Over the bar and bottles glowered a huge Canadian elk head with a full rack, which threw me for a moment because it was so undeniably of Earth. I looked down at my uniform, expecting to see an English shooting suit. If I looked out a window, would I see hedgerows and pheasants?

I might see England, except that the image would be rippled by the occupant of a majolica bowl on the piano . . . a lizard? At first I thought it was part of the ceramic design on the bowl, but no, it was a real live gecko, a mottled yellow-green chap with two-thirds of a tail, and he was enjoying feasting on the conch fritters in the bowl. I would've warned somebody that a creature had crawled in, except that several people from a table over there were watching the gecko and commenting on the length of its regrowing tail.

A British pub in the Delta Quadrant with conch fritters and a live-in lizard. Hmm . . .

Many of the people glanced up—some nodded, others raised their glasses to me, and still others glanced, then ignored me further. A young man in a cable-knit Irish sweater, with longish ivory hair and a voice like a Druid ghost's, softly greeted me, "Captain."

How did he know?

As I paused and returned his look, I noticed that there was glass crunching under my boot. As the company turned for their own look, a lull in the general movement of the place made me notice what they'd been doing—that several people were scooping up spilled food and righting toppled glasses and chairs. Here and there someone was nursing a bruised face or a bleeding lip. There'd been a fight.

Then a fellow wearing a maroon knit shirt, with a sailing ship and scrolled lettering embroidered on the left side of the chest, nodded and invited, "Welcome aboard, Captain. Relax. We'll have it all cleaned up in no time."

Beside him, a large creature, with a mirrored medallion on his chest and a set of antlers rivaling the elk's on his head, nodded elegantly as the lamplight played on the hollow bones of his face. He was demonic, yes, but still somehow welcoming. I didn't feel threatened at all. Even my instincts were voiceless.

The embroidery on the shirt didn't really surprise me—if a planet had water and wind, there was also some sort of sailing vessel. Common sense of function demanded certain designs, just as telling time and traffic control had a certain universal sense that could be counted upon just about everywhere. There were only so many ways to run an intersection.

But the two who had spoken were clearly human and shouldn't have been in the Delta Quadrant at all. My crew and myself were the only humans in the Delta Quadrant.

I rotated that a couple of times in my mind until I finally didn't believe it at all. *Most* of these people looked very human indeed, though quite a range of types—not unusual for a tavern in a spacelane, in a populated sector with civilized pockets.

"My crew was a mixture of types from all over," someone was saying—a young man's voice, but without the flippancy of youth. I looked at the nearest table and saw several people listening intently to a small-boned young man in a blue jacket with red facing running down the chest. His white neckerchief was loosened, and though he seemed relaxed, he also seemed troubled by his own story.

"The ship wasn't even ours. It was a converted merchantman on loan to us. Many of her timbers had rot in them, and though we possessed forty guns, several of those were inoperative. It was in the afternoon that the enemy closed on us, and the breeze was fading. We would soon be outmatched *and* crippled. On our last move, the enemy's sprit caught our mizzen shrouds—"

"Oh, my," someone uttered, and half the company shuddered with empathy.

The young man nodded somewhat cheerily at this. "Yes, but I lashed it there. Why not? I thought my ship would sink otherwise, and I wanted to fight! So I lashed up to something that would keep me afloat. My enemy's ship."

The table's company laughed in awed appreciation. I nudged a little nearer to keep listening.

"And I got it, by God, I got it," he said, shaking his head in reverie of a rugged moment. "Their shots passed straight through the timbers of our gun deck as if going through a straw mattress. They invited me to surrender before action became a slaughter. They had this odd conception that we didn't have it in us to establish ourselves as a power with which to reckon. But I'd hardly begun. I turned and simply told them such. My crew was so enthused that my riflemen in the tops dispatched the enemy's helmsmen one by one, and then a brisk fellow of mine vaulted the yards and dropped a grenade into the enemy's magazine. Such a roar! Their sails were lit afire!"

"And you were still made off to them?" the fellow in the maroon shirt asked.

I stopped moving forward because I was now listening to the dark-eyed young officer in the blue coat with red facings.

"Oh, yes," he answered. "If they sank, they would drag us down. I had only three guns left, but might as well be shooting. But the other captain's ship was a goner and he soon struck. *Serapis*'s crewmen were well thankful to off-board their vessel, you might well understand. A sinking wreck is bad enough, but a sinking *and* burning wreck soon becomes legend. We unlashed, and off we limped. Our entire gun deck was gone."

An unfamiliar alien standing nearby asked, "So you won? Or you lost?"

The officer craned around for a glance at the question, saw that this creature might be someone who wouldn't or shouldn't already know the answer, and offered, "My opponent's ship was a brand-new warship. Mine was a half-rotted old merchant. My ship sank shortly after his, but his was the costlier loss and we denied the enemy domination of vital commerce and supply lanes."

The young captain took a sip from a horn-shaped mug that looked like pewter. He sank back a bit in his chair and stared at the tabletop, seeing something quite else. "I heard later that the other captain had been made a knight for that action. I told my men that if I ever met him again, by God, I'd make him a lord!"

Everyone laughed again—and so did I—and somebody, a woman, commented, "You're a brat, John."

The young man nodded. "Oh, thank you."

Someone else said, "That's a pretty fair story. Too short, though."

"It seemed rather lengthy at the time. I'll be longer winded from now on."

"Do that. Short stories are for musers, not doers."

For a moment the conversation died down and I heard

other things. Faint music from somewhere, but not from the piano . . . Dueling pistols on a wall plaque, castle torchères, coach lamps, and railroad lanterns, a shelf with little unmatched stone gargoyles, a huge Black Forest cuckoo clock with a trumpeting elk carved on top of flared oak leaves and big pulls in the shapes of pine cones, devil-may-care patrons huddled around the tables like provocateurs in a novel, and a large silver samovar that needed polishing—this place boggled the mind with unexperienced memories. Was I hearing the groan of oak branches and waves against a seawall? The mutter of robber barons plotting in a back room? It was all seductively Victorian, and I felt right at home.

In a fireplace burned real wood, and somehow from it came the earthy aroma of autumn leaves like my grandfather had heaped up and burned outside the big farmhouse every October. He hadn't been a farmer, but he had a good time pretending.

Keeping my voice down, I turned my face just enough to speak over my shoulder to Paris. "This place looks like the *Orient Express* stopped at a Scottish pub in the Adirondacks. This isn't *like* Earth, Tom . . . this *is* Earth." He didn't respond, so I added, "I wonder if there's a back door to home. Somebody here has been to the Alpha Quadrant. Maybe they can show us their shortcut. Give me your tricorder."

I put my hand out, still looking around the pub, but Paris didn't give me his tricorder. Irritated that he could be so stupefied, I swung around to snap him out of it and found that he wasn't behind me anymore.

"Paris?" I called back toward the hooded entrance, but he didn't come out. I went to the archway and looked down the musky corridor to the street door, but he wasn't there.

I turned into the pub again and looked around, taking more care to check each person, each being. A pale-haired man, very thin and not tall, stood at the bar, dominating a group of others who were listening to him. His dark uniform coat, lathered with ribbons and medals, had a high collar and tails, and the right sleeve with its thick cuff was pinned up to the coat's chest—that arm was missing at the shoulder. He certainly wasn't Lieutenant Paris, and neither were any of those around him.

Down the bar a stool or two were some men in naval pilot coats and sea boots. I found myself surfing the walls for a portal back in time, and *way* off in space.

I looked up a set of worn wooden stairs with a spindled railing, but there was no sign of Paris.

Had he gone back to the street? Why would he?

I turned to go out, but someone caught my arm. I looked—a young man, human, five feet eleven, if I reckoned right . . . and if I was Kathryn Janeway, that was a United States Marine uniform. A captain. A flier. He smiled, and there was a very slight gap between his front teeth that gave a homey appearance to his narrow face, with its green eyes slightly downturned at the outside corners.

"Have a seat with us, Captain?" The Marine turned, not letting go of my arm, to a group of people at one of the larger tables, and he gestured to the nearest man. "Josiah, make room for the lady."

"Actually, I've lost track of my crewmate—"

"That's how it works at the Captain's Table," the woman said. "Don't fret over it. He'll be fine."

Annoyed, I peered at her briefly, pausing in the middle of a dozen thoughts and wondering if she were really a captain, as everyone here seemed to be. She wore a simple turtle-necked knit sweater, olive green, with three little crew pins on the collar, too small to read from here. She was unremarkable looking, average in most ways, yet self-satisfied, and had a bemused confidence behind her eyes that said she'd crewed a few voyages. Beside her was a pleasant-faced Vulcan, which pummeled the lingering theory that I was imagining the Alpha Quadrant elements. He had typically Vulcan dark hair, but swept to one side instead of straight across the forehead, and he wore a flare-shouldered velvet robe with a couple of rectangular brooches. Whether rank or ceremony, I couldn't tell. He motioned for me to take the chair they cleared, and the woman in the olive sweater nudged a little birch canoe full of walnuts toward me, showing a flesh-colored fingerless glove on her right hand. Looked like an old injury, but it didn't seem to bother her.

The man called Josiah, older and more grizzled than most others in the knot of patrons at this table, was now standing and offering me his chair. "Right here, madam."

Smoldering aroma of burning leaves . . . the musky scent of old wood . . . the comforting nods and touches of the people around me, the music, the elk head, the paisley wallpaper . . . I felt so much at home that I lowered into the chair in spite of having a crewman now missing.

". . . and that, my friends, is how I come to be sitting here with you, sipping this excellent brandy."

Standing over Janeway, the man called Josiah turned toward the bar and called, "Cap! Shake the reefs out, man! Let's have those mugs here while there's still a beard on the waves!"

She had no idea what that meant, but she liked the sound of it. Her hand didn't go through the table, at least. She lowered herself cautiously because she felt there was still the chance another part of her would go through the chair.

A tall man with white breeches and a double-breasted blue jacket left the clique around the one-armed man at the bar and approached our table. He had a deep voice, uncooperative dark hair, and he was irritatingly proper in his manner. "Captain, welcome to our little secret," he said. "Care for a game of whist?"

"Not right now . . . Captain," she said, daring the obvious while she tried to place his jacket in time and came up with about 1830. Maybe earlier. Noncommittally she added, "Just getting the feel of the place."

"It takes a moment for the logical mind," this tall man said, and pulled another chair up to the table for himself, tapping a set of playing cards on the table, then leaving the stack alone. Nobody else seemed to want to play cards right now, and he didn't seem willing to push.

"There's record of places like this," Janeway mused. "That planet in the Omicron Delta region . . . people see what they feel like seeing. Relive fond memories, great victories—"

"—or make new ones," the Vulcan said. Now the cloud of dimness rose a little more before her eyes, and she noticed that under the sleeveless velvet and satin panels of his ceremonial robe he was wearing a red pullover shirt with a black collar and gold slashes on the cuffs. It looked familiar . . .

In the flood of familiarity and comfort here, she dismissed the nagging hint.

The man who wanted to play cards sat rod-straight opposite her—how could he be sitting and still be standing?—and in the fingers of yellowish lamplight she could now see that his uniform was weathered, even frayed at the shoulders, and there was a little hole on one lapel. This didn't bother the others at the table or short him any of their respect as they turned to him while he spoke, and that told me something about him. So she listened too.

"This place has a mystical characteristic that newcomers find boggling," he said. "Certainly I did. I took the better part of the next voyage to dismiss the Captain's Table to a bad bottle."

"Magic comes hard to the organized mind," the Vulcan said.

Janeway looked at him, a little amazed. Vulcans didn't buy into mysticism any more than she did. Janeway saw in his expression that she was right—he was much more amused than serious. The woman in the olive sweater smiled and nudged the Vulcan as if he were being naughty. What an unlikely couple. They obviously knew each other very well, and she got the idea they always sat together.

"I don't believe in magic," Janeway told them. "There's obviously some bizarre science at work here. I've seen—"

The dark-haired officer's thick brows came down. "You call this science, Your Ladyship?"

She paused, waiting for a laugh at his calling her that, but nobody did laugh. Not even a chuckle. She sensed the lack of humor was something about him more than something about her.

"Once upon a time," she answered, "people thought fire was of the gods. We thought the stars were heaven. Then we made fire for ourselves and went to the stars. We learned there's no true alchemy, no 'magic' that can't be mastered eventually, but just science we haven't figured out yet." She glanced around again and sighed. "It's funny . . . I don't really want to figure this out. It looks like Earth, but . . . it's an Earth I'd make up myself. And that can't be real."

"Real enough, Captain," another voice interrupted. It was the elegant officer with the tailed coat and the medals and the missing arm. He now turned from the clique at the bar, most of whom followed him as he approached our table. "The competent commander takes events as they come and acts upon the dictates of duty."

"Duty often fails to proclaim its requisites before the crucial moment, Your Lordship," the Vulcan said.

The woman in the sweater grimaced and chided, "That's it—lip off to a historic luminary. Brilliant."

"It's 'an' historic," he dashed back fluidly. "Like 'an' horse."

"Or 'an horse's ass.'" The woman looked at me again. "Don't try to figure it out all at once. You'll just end up sitting in a corner making sock monkeys."

The Vulcan made one elegant nod. "I have seven myself."

Janeway squinted at him. Was this all a show by some benevolent traveling theater group?

"I think the captain should tell her first story right now," the woman went on, looking at me again. "No point wading through hot air we've already heard, right? Dive, dive, dive—"

"Perhaps," the Vulcan said to his cocky tablemate, "*you* would like to regale us with one of your tales of grand heroism. The time you sat on the barkentine's deck at dawn, cracking thirty dozen eggs for the crew's breakfast and feeding the drippings to the ship's cat. Or the time you fell off the trader's quarterdeck step while carrying a can of varnish—"

"They were defining moments," the woman nipped.

Janeway was about to politely decline the invitation to relive one of the many tense and disturbing incidents that had happened to her and her ship since the accident that had dropped them in the Delta Quadrant, when yet another blast of incongruity appeared at the entry arch.

Pushing to her feet, Janeway hissed, "That's a Cardassian!"

Her arms were clutched from both sides and she was pulled back into my chair.

"A Cardassian *captain,*" the Vulcan said. "All captains are given entry here."

Trying to get the pulse of this place, she buried what she really wanted to say and instead pointed out, "That can be its own kind of problem. It's one thing to club with other captains. It's something else to ask captains to club with those who have attacked our people and killed our shipmates."

They all fell silent at her words. They eyed the Cardassian just as Janeway did. Had each of them seen an enemy captain in this place? Had that been the cause of the bar fight they were now pushing out of the way?

The fact that they didn't argue with her was revealing. They were captains. Loyalties, emotions, and a sense of purpose tended to run deep among those who had held in their charge the lives of others, in such intimate conditions as a vessel. And more, many here must have defended innocents from various aggressors—Janeway saw that in their eyes right now and heard it in their silence. None of them wanted to tell her she was wrong.

Given entry, he had said. Not *were welcome.*

Suddenly Janeway thought this place a lot more interesting.

"Did you get another command, Captain Jones?" the Vulcan asked the man who had told the story.

"Yes," John said, and his gaze fell to his own hands cupped around his mug. "Yes . . . but one is most definitely not the same as another."

"That's hard on the heart, I know, John," the woman said to the man who had told the tale. "To move on to another ship after the one you love is destroyed."

Janeway added, "Somehow we find it in ourselves to move on if we have to."

"Have you 'had to,' Captain?" the Vulcan asked, his hazel eyes gleaming almost mischievously.

Janeway nodded.

"Go ahead," John invited, pushing a frothing mug toward her as several were delivered to the table. "Tell your tale."

Black spirits and white, red spirits and gray,
   mingle, mingle, mingle, that you mingle may . . .
By the pricking of my thumbs,
   something wicked this way comes.

               Shakespeare, *Macbeth,* Act IV, Scene i

CHAPTER

2

"CAPTAIN! MY LEGS ARE ON FIRE!"

And it *hurt*—

Confused by pain, distracted by the scratched crack of my own voice, I pounded my thighs with raw hands and called again for the captain in the smoke.

No answer, no answer . . . no one handing a fire extinguisher to me through the black cloud.

Pain was the immediate thing driving me crazy—I gasped a mindless wish to let go and float on.

Fight it or die . . . *fight it.*

"*Voyager,* this is Janeway! I know how to take down those ships! Do you copy!"

No answer. No response better than the crackle of static. Some kind of blanketing—

"Captain!" I called again over my shoulder, into the stifling heat of the tour craft.

Still no answer from the captain, no noise in fact other than the snap of destruction, the hiss of escaping atmosphere, and the slap of my hands on my own legs, and these were more like punctuations to the silence than noise in

17

themselves. Yet I listened to them as if clinging to the last thread of a rope over a cliff.

No answer from the captain . . . was there anything worse on a ship?

Ship—only a touring craft, four meters by three, deployed from a larger vessel that now was only an exploded hulk to which we dared not return. A significant portion of its hull material was splattering through space at us, a hailstorm of hot knives, bits of metal impaling our craft's thin shell—*Pok! Pok!* And now as we lay on the butcher block, fire had broken out.

And on my ship, there was no answer from their captain either. Why wasn't I there? Why had I left? I had to get back. They couldn't do without me, they needed me—

There they were, locked in that damned spacedock!

I could just see my ship, shrouded by the massive girders of the low-slung spacedock, smothered in a gout of smoke and fire and destruction over the terraformed asteroid we had thought was such a great find. Have any of you ever experienced that kind of frustration? Usually we're on our ships when trouble comes, you know, at the first sign of it, we hurry right back to our bridges and alert our crews. Can you imagine what it was like for me? No warning, no hint of trouble coming, and I was off board when it came? All I could think of was my crew, scrambling to muster for action without their captain on board.

Yes, I can see that a couple of you know what that's like. Later, if you want, I could sure use a little commiseration. Would you tell me your stories of what happened to your ship when you couldn't get to it?

My ship hadn't been at red alert, or even yellow alert, and sure hadn't expected to be in the middle of an attack. Power was depleted, repairs were under way, half the ship was taken apart and being worked on. My ship . . . my crew . . . our whole world . . .

"*Voyager!* The enemy's power consumption curve is way off! It's got to be their shields! It's a bluff! Are you reading me!"

A puff of acidic breath from the little craft's helm panel choked off my cries. The electrical system—must be shattered. There was no light now except a single wide beam suffering through the forward viewport, gasping harder than I was. My scorched hands beat at embers on my legs. I crawled aft, my knees shuddering in weakness and pain. My fingers shivered to the left, the right—he had to be here somewhere. How could he be missing in four by three meters? Were my hands numb? Was I touching him and not even realizing it?

I pounded the commbadge on my chest, but would that work any better than the tough short-range comm on this tour vehicle? Down was down.

One more try, if I could just breathe—

"Their shields are limited to one band! That's why they seem so powerful! Find the frequency and shift your weapons phase! Are you reading me! Chakotay! Paris! Can you hear me! Recalibrate!"

Artificial gravity . . . slipping. I was now crawling along a wall. The deck was against my elbow suddenly, my left elbow. Was I still crawling aft? The burning carpet competed with me for the air that was left.

I waved frantically at the smoke and wiped off part of the side viewport, just enough to look out through my stinging eyes and witness hell unleashed on the innocent. Several ships were hovering over the populated areas, cutting away at the skin of the colony. The destruction of the settlement on the Iscoy Asteroid.

It boiled me in pure rage. The Iscoy had been hospitable to a fault. Unfortunately, this touring me around was the fault.

I'd allowed this to happen. I'd let myself fall into a state of relaxation. The ship was in much needed spacedock, being tended by her own crew and others we trusted, everyone was resting, well fed, happy, and I'd let myself suspend vigilance for a few hours. Now this.

The attack had come out of nowhere—no warning—I'd seen the same thing a dozen times, but not like this. The other times, we'd been out in open space, with room to maneuver, ready for action, not lulled and resting like this. The ship hadn't been in spacedock for some time. It had felt so good at first to settle her in there, with technicians other than ours, and the smiling faces of people willing to help. The Iscoy were country-inn hospitable. I liked the Iscoy. They liked us. They had a nice tidy spacedock and they'd welcomed us to it. They'd even invited us to stay with them if we wanted to abandon our struggle to get home. They'd thrown a thank-you luncheon in my honor, to thank me for letting them help us, no less, and now I was here, halfway to no place, screaming my head off into a vacuum.

The menacing ships were a gaggle of confiscated vessels from a bunch of cultures I didn't recognize. At least, it looked that way. No two were the same design. They'd come in, put up some damnable shields, and started cutting up everything in sight on and around the Iscoy Asteroid. A million Iscoy settlers, and my crew. Sitting ducks.

"Chakotay!" I hammered at the controls, now buried to my wrists in cottony smoke. "We can stop them with one wide burst! Chakotay, are you reading me!"

I pressed my nose to the viewport and looked from my cloudy cave out into clear space, and there I saw the spacedock, with my ship and my crew and the Iscoy technicians helping us out. I witnessed the largest menacing ship cut into the spacedock grid, saw the girders dissolve like sticks, saw the magnetic clamps shudder as they tried to let go of the ship's primary and secondary hulls.

Several more of the Menace crowded their ships against the insectlike girders and opened fire. My ship tried to fire back—a few feeble shots out of the dampening field that naturally surrounded a metal structure with power generating through it. The spacedock itself was becoming a trap.

Looking through a simple hole with just my bare eyes, I saw my ship tip up on her side. Then came a great cloud of evulsion behind her, beneath her. Her long cetacean hull was clamped tight to that spacedock and began to slide with it like a slab falling from a rock, the entire contraption, ship and dock, grinding toward the smoldering asteroid. If they couldn't compensate, natural gravity would take over.

Then, the nightmare parted, and hell came from its maw. As the ship slipped from the spacedock, a blinding ball of light erupted, forcing me to look away. When once again I could blink out the tiny port, I was met with the sight of white-hot metal shards spinning in every direction, like a flower opening without anything in the middle.

Without anything because the middle had just destroyed itself.

My lips parted to murmur my anguish, but nothing came out. I knew a warp reactor core detonation when I saw one.

My eyes should have been protected. I shouldn't have been looking. I shouldn't have had to see the death of everything I had been living for.

Relegated to mere spectator, I watched the demolition of my vessel and my crewmates. I'd seen something no member of any crew wants to watch. And I was too far away to help or to die with them.

The carpet beside me broke into flames. I tried to turn away with some grace but fell to one knee instead. My long hair caught the tip of a flame and ignited. *Sssszzzzzzt*—it lit like a fuse! Why did I wear it so damned long anyway?

I slapped at the ends of my hair madly, with only my hands to put out the fire. Human hair burned like flash paper, and if I didn't stop it, my scalp would be next. Halfway across my shoulder, I squeezed out the last burning bit. Now my hands were worse off as I tried to keep feeling along. I wanted to look outside again, but if I didn't get out of here soon, the smoke would kill me. I dropped to my hands and knees.

My left palm came down on a blade—I yanked back, suddenly dizzy with a whole new pain. Blood drained down my wrist into the stiff hot fabric of my sleeve, giving my blistered skin an odd kind of relief. I had cut myself on a piece of the Iscoy ship we'd come from. It had come to claim us the hard way. I couldn't remember its name.

Was there a life-pod in this thing? There had to be. Where, where . . . aft? Below?

I hunched my back and gagged my throat raw of the bitter electrical smoke, sucking enough oxygen out of the poisoned capsule to struggle another meter aft. There, I found the captain.

Crushed into a storage cubby, thrown there by the impact of his ship's explosion so nearby, he was stiff, coiled with spasms. I called to him again and again, pulled on his arms, his legs, the ridge of leaf-shaped spines down his back—what kind of stego-evolution is that? Air conditioning?

No use for them now. His burned uniform virtually fell apart in my hands, just as mine was curling off my body, leaving scorched skin beneath. I grabbed one of his arms and a spinal fin and dragged him aft. When he came free of the cubby, I rolled him at the oddest of angles along the starboard wall.

Part of the light faded when our craft rolled away from the sun's meager comfort. We were moving, constantly moving, without power but pushed on our uncontrolled way by the explosion of the larger ship.

Where were the enemy ships? Would they come after a vessel this small? Did they know the captain was on board? Did they know I was here too?

Hot . . . hot . . . Sweat sheeted my face, wrecked my grip, got in my mouth, and made me spit. I pulled him, I dragged him, I dragged myself.

Then one thing went right. The aft part of the cabin was already waiting for us. The hatch to the escape pod was already open. Some kind of automatic safety feature. A little ventilator whirred madly, trying to keep the smoke mostly back in the main part of the craft. Like me, it was failing.

For a galling moment the captain's spine ridge caught on one of the impaling bits of metal poking through the craft's shuddering skin, and another convulsion stiffened his body in my cramping hands.

Casting one glance back toward the main viewport, I took my last glimpse of open space before committing myself to the pod, and there I saw a piece of gray hull streaking by, tumbling—a nacelle and part of the support strut, barely recognizable, covered with sparking damage and charred hull fabric.

I wanted to go forward again and look, try to find some figment of proof that I hadn't seen what I knew I had, but this touring craft was floating death if I didn't leave immediately. There was so little oxygen left, the escape pod would quickly exhaust itself trying to fill the poisoned cavity.

I was crawling into a coffin.

* * *

Shifting the captain's coiled body into the pod, I retrieved his feet from the entryway before feeling around for the controls. There had to be a button, a latch, something; it had to be simple, nobody would design anything complicated. Where was it?

I started pounding my fist on the sides of the pod, my eyes watering, blind, stinging. It had to be here.

As my lungs tightened to intolerance, I demanded rationality long enough to pound the curved wall in a pattern. I started at my own scorched legs and drove my fists in a straight line from my knees to behind me, then moved out six inches and repeated the pattern, mowing the lawn up to my side, over my head—

A sucking sound startled me. The hatch slid shut and the pod pressurized. Warning lights flashed through the murk on both sides of my head, hurting my eyes and making me feel insane.

Hostile sector. How could we have known?

I was *supposed* to know. I was supposed to have that special instinct. But intuition had failed. Usually I could forgive myself, but not this time. We were too tired from our own disaster. I'd let myself get tired. Experience had been dulled. I'd told myself the worst was over. I'd allowed myself a moment's peace.

Now this, now this.

Don't think about it, not yet, keep concentrating, survive, survive. One thing at a time. One small thing, then the next. Launch the pod.

I pounded again at the place that had shut the hatch. The release had to be in the same area. Nobody would design anything else. Anything different would be harder, and nobody in his right mind would design a safety feature to be complex. It was the same from culture to culture. Technological cultures found those things out early. Some things had to be the same, had to be common sense, or people would die all over the place.

I kept pounding. It *had* to be there! We were now a bug on the back of a run-over mole and we had to get off.

Something clicked. I heard it, but my hand was too numb to feel anything. A tremendous crack threw me against the bulkhead behind me. Just luck I was sitting in the right direction and ended up with a backache instead of a concussion.

Gravity changed. The pod had its own. I fell and landed on my side, half on top of the captain . . . Up wasn't where it had been a moment ago.

Silly visiting dignitary couldn't even find the floor.

We were loose! The artificial gravity bobbled momentarily and left me with a nauseated stomach as the pod tumbled through space, jolting in collision after collision with flotsam from the destroyed ships out there.

A faint little pink utility light came on, providing at least a sense of . . . no, it didn't provide much. At least I wasn't sitting in a black box. Now I was sitting in a hot murky haze. Even looking at my own tarnished body and alien captain's crumpled form was better than utter darkness.

How many enemy ships? Enough to bother coming after a two-man escape pod shooting past them?

I hugged my stinging legs, bit my lip against the pain, and waited to be blown to bits. Sometimes that's all there is— the last few seconds of waiting. Sometimes the ship disappears under you, and all you can do is take a deep breath. I'd heard that somewhere . . . some captain . . .

My hand drifted from my knee to the area in front of me. The alien captain shuddered once under my searching touch, then went suddenly and ominously still. The ventilator whirred madly, thinning the black haze to a gray veil. My eyes burned as I blinked and squeezed, trying to see the Iscoy captain's face.

His gentle face, his soft amber eyes with the double-slit pupils, his welcoming nod, and that snaky excuse for a smile had broken through the first twinge of alienness that came naturally to everyone, even the vaunted me. As my uniform smoldered against my skin, the fibers melting and sizzling, I drifted into a replay of the first greetings with the Iscoy, just four days ago. I wondered if my demeanor had been pleasant for him when I beamed onto his ship, declaring myself leader of a powerful troupe willing to trade. Had I seemed arrogant? Hard? Had I seemed a cold woman unable to mellow?

He hadn't seemed to take me that way.

Dredging up a flake of sense, I began peeling off my uniform. In my preoccupation with surviving, I hadn't realized my clothes were a garden of embers and I was still being scorched. Once the uniform lay on the curved deck of this purposeful bathtub, I stomped out the embers and tried to snuff the smoldering so it didn't eat any of the precious oxygen in here. Now I sat in only my underwear, a pathetic shell-colored chemise that brought little comfort. At least I wasn't so hot anymore.

The half-melted fabric of my uniform almost fell apart as I peeled the last of it off my legs, taking golfball-sized patches of skin with it. Curled, crispy fibers plucked at the melted skin and some stayed embedded in my legs. I needed treatment . . . I'd forgotten how much burns hurt.

I'd never been burned this badly before. Half my body was numb, the other half itching and sizzling. Was I in shock?

If it had been anyone but me, I'd have known what to do. For myself, I couldn't think. For long minutes I hugged my knees, blurring in and out of moaning consciousness, roused periodically by a loud thud on the hull as we crashed through the debris field from the attack outside. Were they still fighting? Or was it over now? Had the good guys won? I was blind, deaf, mute in here, grasping at the pitiful remains of my experience and imagination to figure out what was happening.

I knew what I'd seen. The boiling seltzer of warp core rupture. A ship blowing up.

A muffled whir inside the bulkhead stirred my mind after a while. Was this pod under power? Yes, there was a tiny engine of some sort keeping the pod stable, probably powering little thrusters. Made some sense . . . Power to get away from whatever calamity had caused the pathetic occupants to launch in the first place. It probably had a limit. After a while, the pod would be adrift.

Uniform . . . still smoldering somehow, eating oxygen. I shook myself into action and pushed at the clump of fabric with one boot. Where was the airlock? Oh, there—

I found the airlock release, opened the narrow hatch, shoved the uniform inside.

Oh—my commbadge!

Somewhere inside the hot fabric . . . there. I pulled off the small delta shield gold pin and clipped it to my chemise.

After a moment or two of guilty reflection, I rolled the Iscoy captain's body inside, also. Tears blurred my eyes as I felt the lingering warmth in his body, but I knew death when I saw it, when I could feel it. Awful, ugly responsibility, to consign the commander of another ship afloat without a proper burial, but I knew—we all knew—it might come to this. Dying was one of the clauses in the contract with deep space.

I didn't know whether or not his ship was still out there. He was gone. My ship was gone, and I was still here. Neither of us could go down with our ships. A terrible tragic thing.

"I'm sorry," I croaked to him. A miserable good-bye.

Don't look at me like that, Captain Cressy. You know about burial at sea. It's the same for us in space. All right, then, shall I go on?

Thanks.

A *clack*, a vacuum sucking noise, a second *clack* as the outer port closed again, and it was over for him. Now I had the whole dim bathtub to myself. Carefully I stretched out my legs, flinching at the crack of my own skin. I had to stretch out, or my muscles would contract permanently. Patches of skin on my thighs and calves cracked like cardboard as I extended my knees.

I closed my eyes and drifted through waves of agony. The tears for the captain drained down my hot face, drawing his memory upon my cheeks until I knew that I would never forget him. He had wanted so much to be back on his own ship when the attack came. How horrible it had been for both of us when we lost contact with our vessels.

Contact . . . I touched the commbadge on my chemise.

"Janeway to *Voyager* . . . do you copy?"

My head clunked back against the pod's inner skin. I waited for an answer.

Did this pod have a locator signal? If so, it must be automatic, because there was no control panel in here. Just the airlock, the hatch . . . What was this cubby hole? A survival kit! Of course! Food, liquid, maybe medical supplies?

Only the anticipation of some relief from the burns roused me from my sweaty fatigue. I fumbled for the commbadge again. Lucky I'd remembered it. In this state of smoke inhalation and pain I might've pushed it out the airlock with the uniform and my Iscoy friend.

"*Voyager*, this is Janeway . . . I'm in a survival pod. Location unknown . . . The captain is dead. If you can read me, please try to respond . . . I've got severe burns . . ."

Were any of my people left out there to hear a call? Any friendly ears to listen?

In my experienced mind I knew better. I'd seen the magnetic clamps shudder, trying to let my ship go when the big strike came. They hadn't been abandoning the ship. They'd been rushing to battlestations and been destroyed trying. Pride encroached upon my misery.

Suddenly the whole pod shook around me. Had I been hit?

I crawled to my knees and looked at the overworked control panel and tried to remember what the Iscoy captain had told me about the readouts on these panels. Warp speed!

This escape pod was hyperlight! Some kind of mini–anti-matter reactor core!

Not a bad idea, for an outpost so far away from the Iscoy homeworld, now that I thought about it. A non–warp pod wouldn't get anywhere. A warp pod might have a chance.

How fast was I going? Warp one? Two? That would be the max, in something this size. In fact, this pod might have only a warp surge reactor, with a time limit.

I had no way to know. It was saving my life but keeping me completely uninformed. At warp speed, even warp one, I might have a chance to be rescued by somebody other than the victorious menace out there.

If I had a chance to live, then I had to make myself survive. I started digging through the small cubbies and panels.

Food packets, dehydrated . . . a thermal foil blanket . . . hydrating capsules . . . medical kit. I wanted all of that, but mostly I wanted the med kit.

My hands shook as I lathered some kind of ointment over my arms and legs and my right hip, where the burns were worst. I didn't even know for sure if this stuff was for burns, because I couldn't read the alien writing on the tube, probably meant for fleas' chipped scales or something, but any ointment in a storm.

The little ventilation system worked frantically, and the pod was clearing now, allowing me to see in the flush of the pink utility light. As my eyes cleared, I flinched at a completely unexpected sight—an alien face looking at me through the haze.

I flinched like a schoolgirl and almost lashed out. Then it came to me that I was looking at some kind of video screen. It had no frame or hint of its existence until the screen actually came on. It was on now.

I was staring into the face of the enemy. They were communicating with me somehow, or perhaps only broadcasting a wide-range message to the conquered Iscoy, and this pod was picking it up. As I fought for rationality through my fury and fear, that became more likely. The square screen flinched and flickered—there was apparently damage to my box of survival—and there was no sound. The alien's mouth was moving. He was speaking. I heard nothing.

His face might have been beautiful in another circumstance, statuesque right down to its color, a glowing quartz violet. He was humanoid—not a surprise for advanced beings, since the basic form was so efficient and adaptable, and why was I thinking about this right now?—and his eyes were like a horse's eyes, big chestnuts set in soft round browbones. He had hair—a mass of pure white silky spools, like a decorated shower cap. Simple knit clothing, also white. He was like a mythological being, a lilac angel. He gazed and nodded and warned in silence from the pod's screen. And I hated him to his dirty murdering innards.

He and his kind were demons out of the night. They were slaughtering my crew and our new friends. I glared in pure despise at him as the screen fritzed and blinked, starving itself of power so I could survive. He became uglier and uglier as every moment of my utter helplessness came by.

I loathed him. I determined to loathe him forever. I wanted revenge. He was the Menace. He and all his kind.

Just as the hunger for revenge took a good grip on my

warrior soul, the screen fizzled and winked out. Even my enemy's company had been company. Now I was completely alone.

Alone and wanting very much to fight. Life was cruel.

And now I was cold. The sweat was evaporating in the ventilation and I was covered with moist ointment. I hoped the ointment had a sterilizing compound in it. That might save me from infection, the real menace with burns.

Menace . . . violet skin, chestnut eyes, white hair, white clothes. I would never forget.

The chill of the pod's inner skin drew the heat out of my body—something I had wanted very much a few minutes ago.

I decided against swallowing anything in the med kit. Alien medication could just as easily make me grow feathers as do any good. What was this? Some kind of syringe. Antibiotics, maybe?

Or something else. Something more desperate, more final? If I were stocking a survival craft, would I offer a final solution?

No, I didn't think I would, but somebody else might. Space was cruel. Ways out were valuable.

I set the syringe in the med kit and promised myself to use it if the time came. How many weeks would I give myself?

Stay alive. Remember the Menace. Revenge and warning. Turn back the conqueror tide. Those were good reasons to stay alive. My teeth gritted with determination.

The copper-colored thermal foil blanket fit around me well enough but didn't stay in place unless I held it, and my hands hurt. I used a scalpel in the med kit to cut a slit in the middle of the brown foil, then pulled it over my head like a poncho and hoped the foil would keep me from going further into shock. I curled up inside my tiny tent and gave in to the pain, the drowsiness. The foil was crunchy and uncomforting, but it gave me something I very much needed right now.

A chance to rest, with a chance to wake up.

Wake up and fight.

CHAPTER

3

"OPEN IT."

"It's partially opened already. Jammed at the hinge—heavy damage on the outer skin. I don't recognize these marks."

"I don't know. Get the torches. Ruvan, are you reading life in there?"

"One heartbeat."

"Someone tell Quen."

"I'll go."

English . . . the words were like music.

No. No one speaks English in the Delta Quadrant except you and yours. It's the commbadge working.

I had no idea how long I'd huddled in the survival capsule. Hours had eventually blurred into days, and days became uncountable. I had no way to count, no way to measure time, except to watch my burned-off hair get longer. The days were a blend of boredom and pain, and many times I found myself gazing in mute challenge at the little syringe that might have life inside or death. It became a grim game. Would I win, or would it?

There was the other game too, the trick of extending my

misery by rationing the dry food and the hydrating capsules. I rationed myself almost to starvation, and the challenge itself kept me going. Bones pushed outward against my thinning skin as I dotted ointment on my burns day after day.

When I went into the pod, part of my hair had been burned off above the shoulders. When I came out, it was an inch below the shoulder. How much time was that?

I thought I heard a bump. Then the airlock made its sucking noise, and hands were reaching for me.

Angels were reaching into the pod, drawing me out . . . beautiful people with glowing brown hair and light eyes, skin like hand lotion. I felt so dirty against them . . .

I wanted to walk. I tried, but had no idea where "down" was. My foil poncho crinkled and laughed as several strong hands lifted me. Dignity suffered greatly. What a sight I must be as they carried me away. I twisted my neck to look around at the sorry little pod that had saved my life. My scorched hand moved in a pathetic wave good-bye, thanks.

I saw figures over me, humanoid if not human, no outward spines or webs or bony formations. Just ordinary human forms with human faces, except for the coloring. Pale skin, hair in the dark greens and browns, and light eyes. And they weren't all the same, I began to notice. Some eyes were green, some amber, some pink. And their hair was different shades of forest green and umber. At least it was in the dim light here. By the time they laid me on the cot in their idea of sickbay, I'd collected lots of faces.

None of them seemed threatening, but I might be beyond that. A certain numbness sets in after a while, and it takes fear along with it. I just watched the goings-on. People dressed in dull clothing did things to my wounds, ran analytical tools over my body, then gave me injections with needle syringes similar to my little friend in the pod. These people didn't look like doctors or nurses. In fact, they didn't look any different from the crewmen who had pulled me out of the pod. I expected medical teamers to be dressed differently from everyone else.

And none appeared to be women. Was I imagining that?

Were they just unfamiliar and I wasn't noticing the right things?

No women at all . . .

The lighting in this area was low, and the team had to work with hand-held lights or lights attached to their uniforms, if these casual-looking clothes were indeed a uniform. The medical team didn't say much, except to agree from moment to moment on how to treat me, so I didn't say much either. Winced a lot, but didn't say much. Treatment of burns was almost as much fun as the burns themselves.

Once my wounds were dressed—these people had experience with fire—they fed me a thick warm liquid. What I wanted was a porterhouse steak, au gratin potatoes, and glazed baby carrots, but they were probably smart not to dare my weakened body with solid food.

And they didn't change my clothes or alter my appearance, except to sterilize my wounds for treatment. Why did they keep it so dim in here?

The doctor was a young man who reminded me of Tom Paris, except with lighter eyes and hair the color of the nocturnal sea; in certain light it was actually blue. He clicked off his utility light and raised my cot to a sitting position. Then he punched a signal button on panel and said, "She's ready."

"I'll be right there."

A simple comm system. Good. Something I could recognize. That was one. If I could get to a thousand, maybe things would work out.

I didn't bother to ask the doctor any questions. On my ship, I wouldn't have let the Doctor answer anything in this situation, so I waited.

The door opened—not an automatic sliding panel, but a swinging hatch with a handle—and a wide-shouldered young man stepped into the sickbay. He had skin like butter and eyes almost the same color, but his wavy hair was the color of morning drizzle, not gray, but more into the silver blues. The pigmentation of these people was truly a fantasy, like a child had picked the colors for the painting—no rules. He wore a utility vest with several pockets, woolly trousers, and soft shoes.

"Do you understand me?" the young doctor asked.

"Yes, I do." My voice was raspy, smoke-rawed, and out of practice.

"I'm Ruvan, chief medic. This is Zell, our second in command." He turned to Zell and said, "She has burns over thirty percent of her body, but only four percent are deep damage. I have them treated and compressed. Her legs are the worst. She can walk, but slowly and with help. In fact, that would be a good thing. Another week in that pod, and her muscles would have retracted into atrophy. Would've been terrible, Zell, just terrible—"

"At least we found her in time." Zell gave the sensitive young medic a brotherly grip at the base of his neck, actually comforting him right there in front of a stranger. "Sit down and rest, Ruvan. You haven't been off your feet since yesterday. She's alive. We're all alive for now. It's good enough."

Through aching eyes I watched the two young men curiously. They acted more like family than crew. I suddenly felt very lucky, but there was something gray and fatalistic about their attitude.

The first officer turned to me and took a step closer. "Welcome aboard the *Zingara*. Our captain wants to see you."

"And I have things to tell him," I responded, letting them ease me to my feet—oh, my legs weren't happy at all with this. "There's something very powerful out there and I think it's coming this way—"

"You can tell the captain."

I clamped my mouth shut. No point wasting breath.

Zingara, Zingara. Pretty name for a ship . . .

The two men held me straight as I shuffled toward the doorlike hatchway. I didn't resist the help. There was no point in being prideful and ending up on my face, right?

At the door, I paused. "I should clean up before I meet your captain, shouldn't I?"

Zell shook his head. "He wants to look at you as you are, the way you came aboard. Afterward, you can clean and change your clothing."

"Makes sense."

"We have nothing new, but you can have ours. All we have is men's clothes, but—"

I offered him a thankful gaze. "I'll be honored to wear the clothing of those who rescued me."

He smiled but didn't say more. I wouldn't have said anything, either, if I'd been the first officer here.

They walked me through a narrow corridor and out a hatch in a transverse bulkhead, which turned out to be a portal to the large main deck. The wide underdeck of their ship had no corridors as I knew them, but instead was a broad open area. Crewmen were doing their jobs on an open platform that ran from beam end to beam end without partition. This deck seemed to be more or less in the middle, for I could see vertical hatchways with ladders that led up from here, and down from here. Most of the activity seemed to be down.

Curious eyes combed over me from every angle. They were a handsome but tattered lot, with the unpredictable coloring of Ruvan and Zell—hair in the muted greens, blues, grays, some lighter, and skin from gold to peach. Their hair was of various lengths, though mostly as if there were no barber on board and they trimmed their own or each other's, with a knife, with a machete. Handsome, shaggy, but in a child's drawing sort of way.

All were young, all male, all thin and . . . chilly. Most of them wore elbow-length shoulder capes, mismatched, no particular color, and many wore fingerless gloves. These weren't uniforms, because nothing was standardized. They just wanted to keep warm. I thought it had been just me, in this depleted condition, but this ship *was* cool.

And dim as a cloudy day. The crew worked by what I would've called utility lights, little bare bulbs of various colors that seemed piecemeal in their organization, and larger worklights set on the deck, powered by extension cords and umbilical cables skittered all over the place.

There was damage here, some of it heavy. Had they already encountered the Menace? Was my warning a needless one? Did they already know what was coming?

The crew paused in their work as I shuffled by. I looked at them and they at me, knowing we were completely odd-looking to each other. Some of them were working alone. Others were helping each other, holding tools, lifting mechanisms, sweating and struggling together. They had to assist each other because almost every one of them, I noticed, had some kind of injury. Some limbs were splinted, others bandaged, and some of the crew simply limped to show their troubles. They'd been through something, and been through it very recently. They were a mess.

Almost everywhere I looked, except for the deck we were walking on, the ship's inner skin was coated with little squares of colors ranging from ruby to orchid, mostly opaque or metallic, each slightly more than an inch across. These squares patched the innards of the ship above me and to the sides. Some of them were off, lying in neat boxes on the deck, and behind them were the guts of the ship, embedded right into the walls. There were little squares on the curved walls that obviously formed the shape of the ship, on the ceilings, in the archways—they were everywhere except where the crew had to walk to get to them. As Zell and Ruvan ushered me past one of the holes in the deck, I looked down the ladder to where more crew were working, and saw more sheets of squares. The whole ship seemed to be packed with them.

The rest of the technology looked about a hundred years behind mine. On the other hand, some of these mechanisms I didn't recognize at all. Possibly the technology wasn't just *behind* mine on a time scale, but sideways somehow as well. That happened now and then, even though most things had to be developed with a certain background supporting the inventions . . . Oh, well, my thoughts were drifting. Always the engineer, under what was left of my skin.

And another odd thing—as we passed working crewmen, both Ruvan and Zell paused here and there to check work or wounds, and during these little stops they touched hands with their comrades. Not the whole hand, like a handshake, but just a brief grip of fingers, or even just a brush of fingertips. I was reminded of the origins of the handshake on Earth: warriors approaching each other and gripping sword hands as an assurance that neither would go for the blade while they talked. This must be something like that, an old and culturally ingrained method of reassurance to each other. It struck me as kind of nice among these shaggy and obviously toil-hardened young men.

"Right here," Zell said, and eased me through a double-wide main hatchway in what my spacefarer's sense told me was the forward section of the ship. This was like an old-fashioned forecastle, crew quarters in the smallest area of the ship, with narrow quarters that had two bunks each, rather cluttered and lived-in. They looked average, just what anyone would've expected, except that most of the bunks had a blanket of some kind of fur. Might have been synthetic, but I doubted that. Looked like rabbit fur. In spite of an initial surge of disapproval, the warm comfort was too inviting to resist.

Zell led me to the farthest forward of these cabins. Before we went in, he turned to Ruvan. "I'll take her from here. You go and sit down in a quiet corner and eat something."

Ruvan smiled sadly. "I wish you would stop giving medical suggestions."

"It's not a suggestion," Zell told him. "It's an order."

"Mmm . . . all right." Ruvan reluctantly left us and headed back through the main deck. The last I saw of the worried young doctor was a glimpse of his hair in a work light as he knelt at someone's side to check a wound.

"This is Quen," Zell said, "our captain."

We stepped inside the cabin, which had only one bunk and a small desk. There, the captain sat hovering over his work.

The captain was another good-looking young man, with mushroom skin and soft shoulder-length hair the exact color of Scotch pine needles. What a storybook character he might've made, something out of a twentienth-century fantasy novel, except that through his good looks, he also seemed tired and overburdened. He didn't look up from a clutter of square metallic plates on his desk as I approached and forced myself not to lean on anything. Still feeling as if I'd been beaten with clubs, I also forced myself to wait a few seconds.

Finally he handed two of the metallic plates to Zell, and looked up at me. His expression changed to surprise—though we were basically similar, clearly I wasn't one of his species or any other that he recognized. I'd seen that look before.

Beyond that, what a sight I must have been. My legs were wrapped in Ruvan's compress dressings, my foil poncho was crinkled and cockeyed, and my hair—may the gods of cosmetics save us from this. Since part of it had been burned off, the right side was longer than the left side, as if I'd put a bad wig on crooked.

I gave him a moment to understand that the tattered mess he was looking at might not be the real me. Then I spoke up. A plaintive "It's dark in here" was the first thing out of my mouth. It should have been "thanks" but I wasn't in full control of my mouth.

"We conserve energy," he answered, without looking up. "Lights take energy. Zell, what did Ruvan say about her?"

"She's hurt, but she'll live. And if we don't get Ruvan some relief soon, I think his head's going to explode or he'll start bleeding from the eyes or his hair'll curl—"

"I know, I know . . . There isn't anybody to help him right now, Zell. The tiles have to be tended and the engine repairs are more important than medical. With the last find taken, that means more rationing until we can take another one. I don't have any spare hands. He'll just have to explode or curl up."

Zell smiled. These people had good smiles.

Now Quen leaned back and was abruptly stopped by a hard wince. His eyes snapped shut and he gripped his left arm near the shoulder. Zell stepped closer and firmly massaged what was obviously a recent injury to his captain's shoulder. Quen winced again but relaxed some. Neither of them seemed bothered to be showing either their familiarity or their weaknesses to a stranger.

After a moment Quen nodded to Zell and waved him off, then looked at me with clearer eyes. "So . . . who are you?"

Finally!

"My name is Kathryn Janeway."

"Do you want us to call you that?"

"Why not?"

"A little long for trouble, isn't it?"

I smiled. He had a point. "Well, you call me what you like. Spacefarers have to adjust, don't they?"

Something about that sentence bothered them.

"You're not . . . anything we recognize," Quen prodded. "You're not Berm, or Peliorine, Tauma, Omian—"

"We call ourselves Terrans. Humans, more generically.

We call our species 'Homo sapiens.' What do your people call themselves, Captain?"

He glanced briefly at Zell again; what did those looks mean? "We're citizens of the Republic of Penza, on the planet Om. We call ourselves 'men' . . . 'people,' 'survivors,' 'Omian' . . ."

He seemed at a loss for what I was getting at.

I nodded. "Some things don't translate well. I've traveled many solar systems and the expanse of interstellar space and met many cultures. I understand."

He narrowed his eyes in obvious doubt. "Interstellar space . . . How are you understanding us if you're from so far away?"

Slipping my hand down the neck hole of my thermal sheet, I pulled off my commbadge and handed it to him.

He turned the small gold shield over and over in his fingers. "It translates?"

"Within a certain radius, yes."

"It's so small . . ." He peered closely at the commbadge and held it for Zell to see.

"If I hadn't pulled her out of the pod myself," Zell murmured, "I'd say she was a TCA agent, with something like this. If we could figure this out . . ."

"I know," Quen cut him off, but his tone was wishful and hungry.

Just as I began to fear for ever getting my precious little helper back, Quen simply handed it to me.

"It could help you?" I asked. "And you're just giving it back?"

Quen's brows drew together. "It's yours, not ours."

My recuperating fingers cramped slightly as I took the commbadge back and pinned it on the neck hole of my poncho.

"Your injuries have been treated?" he asked. "You're feeling all right?"

"Yes, and thank you for your doctor's help. I'm sure I was nearing the end of my rope when your rescue team found me."

"What were you doing in the pod?"

"Surviving," I said bluntly. "I was negotiating with the

Iscoy when they were attacked by a mismatched fleet with a power curve that didn't make sense. But I recognized the pattern. It was an attacking fleet inflicting a total-destruction maneuver. It completely wiped out the Iscoy outpost."

"Iscoy?"

"You've never heard of them?"

"No."

"That's odd. If the pod was low-warp, the Iscoy Asteroid can't be all that far from here at cruising speed—"

"And there was an attack, you say?" Quen persisted.

"Not just an attack, Captain. A slaughter. I saw the weakness of their battle plan, but I saw it too late. I was off my ship. I tried to broadcast how to fight the Menace, but communications systems were being blanketed somehow. The Menace knew that if we talked to each other, we'd figure them out. They came in—" My hands begin to shake with deeply knotted emotion. "—and they put the entire Iscoy settlement to the torch. There was no warning, they took no prisoners, they refused to contact us with terms, they were completely heartless, soulless, they ignored cries for surrender or mercy—"

"You say you *saw* your ship destroyed? You're sure you saw this?"

His directness pulled me up short and made me realize where my tone of voice was going. I took a long breath and forced myself to calm down. "I saw the spacedock disintegrate. I saw a core explosion; I've seen them before. We were murdered, and we didn't even know why. Captain Quen, something is on its way . . . and we'd better be ready when it gets here."

"This thing that's coming . . . is it coming from the Berm and Kavapent routes?"

Uh-oh.

"I've never heard of those," I admitted.

"You were on the Kavapent route when we found you," Zell challenged. "You must've come in through the Berm Cloud. How did this ship of yours avoid the sands?"

What could I say? I had no answers. I'd come in blind.

"I'm new to this sector." Best I could do.

Quen watched me with an acute analytical gaze. "What ship were you traveling on?" he asked instead.

"It's a starship," I said, deliberately being a shade lofty. "The *U.S.S. Voyager.*"

"A what?" Zell asked.

"It's a fifteen-deck, seven-hundred-thousand-metric-ton light cruiser, registry number NCC 74656, Starfleet authorization, the defense and exploration agency of the United Federation of Planets. Currently exploring the Delta Quadrant. We were displaced by some kind of anomaly over which we had no control. We were trying to get home but were *very* far away—"

I paused because my legs were starting to hurt as Ruvan's anesthetic wore down, and also because both Quen and Zell were staring at me through the strangest doubts and worries. Had they picked up a lunatic?

Zell squinted and murmured, "Fifteen decks . . ."

Quen quieted him with a glance, then peered at me again. "You were a passenger? A traveler?"

My shoulders, slumped with cramped muscles, squared a little. "Neither. I'm the captain."

At this, Quen paused and passed his hand across his open lips. He held still briefly, deciding whether he had boarded a liar or a loon. He and Zell exchanged a suppressed glance that drove me crazy with frustration.

Quen pressed his lips flat, thinking. After a moment, he added, "No, uh . . . proof of this . . ."

Despite my injured legs, I managed to cock my hips and make a sorry motion to my foil poncho. "Well, not *on* me."

He shifted his injured arm. "If you're a captain, how long does it take at full speed to get from the largest sector star to the smallest?"

A legitimate question. Anyone in charge of a ship would have to know that, the simplest of area details, visible from multimillions of miles to anyone with the most basic of telescopic equipment.

Quickly I yanked up a shabby image of the star charts we'd made as we approached the Iscoy Asteroid and decided I just might know that one.

"At full hyperlight?" I asked.

"Yes."

"I'd estimate that would take my ship . . . about four days at maximum nonemergency warp speed."

The two young men looked at me as if I'd just grown green hair. Quen shifted his position to stretch a leg, but he was concentrating on what I'd just told him, adding it up. Finally he said, "It's a four-*month* journey with a light kick."

That's what comes from assuming. I shrugged. "Then your top speed is less than mine, that's all. Or your measure of time is different."

Zell heaved a doubtful breath and drawled, "No one's top light kick is better than Quen's."

Not getting anywhere on this tack, I decided to redirect the conversation.

"What's a light kick?"

"We use storage cells to funnel solar energy into our hyperlight batteries and provide the kick of ignition up to light-speed."

My engineer's head started clicking. "Storage cells . . . you must mean some kind of capacitor."

Without committing himself, he continued, "Then the fusion engine takes over, and we can travel from star to star. One charge, one kick. If we get stalled in the interstellar void, we could suddenly be years away from home."

"I know the feeling."

"Power streams from the star to the skin of the ship, into the cell tiles, and we get the kick. Once we're kicked up to light-speed, the fusion engines can keep it up."

"But you can't initiate the warping process without solar collection?"

"Of course not," Zell said. "To build a fusion engine that could cold-start a light kick would take ten thousand times the mass of our engines. We can't go around towing a planet-sized fusion engine. It would take the resources of a million cities."

"You've never visited interstellar space, then?"

"Not willingly," Quen murmured. "And luckily, not us personally. We've heard of ships being stalled. The rescue process is almost a suicide mission itself. Some freelancers do it, but it takes just about half a lifetime."

"Besides," Zell added, "there's nothing in the void. Explorers have gone out and looked. They're gone half a lifetime, then they come back and tell us there's nothing there but dust. And they've been gone all that time just for dust. Nobody goes anymore. Not on purpose."

"Have you tried generational ships?" I shifted my legs, determined to stay upright long enough to plumb the culture that would be part of my life for . . . how long?

"There's no such thing as a perfect seal," Zell explained. "Everything leaks eventually. Even a cubic inch of loss a day means you're out of air eventually. If there's no air when you get where you're going, then you wake up dead."

With his slender hand again covering his mouth, Quen began shaking with amusement at his first officer's explanation. Laughing! In the middle of all this damage, with his own injuries still hurting, and after picking up a half-dead lunatic in a pod, he could still laugh!

I actually envied him.

With some halfhearted effort, he regained control of himself and straightened in his seat.

"Well," he asked, rather slowly, "what do you want?"

Here it came. A long steady breath . . . hold it a minute—

"I'm requesting you to take me back to my ship. If they're not destroyed, I've got to tell them how to defeat the Menace. I figured it out, but I was too late. I can make it worth your while in many ways."

"You said you saw your ship being destroyed," Quen reminded. He wanted clarity. Couldn't blame him for that.

I tilted my head and sounded like a scolding mother. "You must know nothing in a battle is that definite. I might be lying to myself. I *saw* the spacedock disintegrate and what looked like a warp core explosion . . . but I can't let that be my last try."

Zell picked up a small folding stool and moved it toward me. "Do you want to sit?"

"No!" I knocked the stool away. "Some of my crew might have survived! They might have salvaged sections of the ship. I can't just assume they're all gone. I have to see for myself and do an objective assessment. You *have* to take me there!"

Quen shared another glance with Zell—not one that cut me much slack for sanity—then came the hard question. "Where?"

"If you follow the stellar pattern directly across the red nebula at the narrowest point and broadcast a beacon I can encode for you, the Iscoy should be able to pick us up."

"Which spaceroad marker pattern?"

"I don't know anything about the markers around here."

"Did you notice any signals?"

"I was blind inside the pod."

"What about before you were in the pod?"

"No . . . I wasn't paying much attention. We had . . . an escort."

Not going well at all. Try again. "All you have to do is follow the stellar pattern in a direct line from the direction my pod came from. There wouldn't have been any deviation from a direct path—"

"We know which stars are in that direction," Quen told me. "The nearest one is a six-month journey."

"Six months . . ." I faltered momentarily, wondering if my translator were making his idea of a week into mine as it usually did, and if that meant I'd been drifting for at least that long. Was he talking about light-speed, and how high? What was his maximum light-speed with this kicking business?

Details, details. I was still having trouble thinking, adding up the trigonometry, the variants—

Going back to basics seemed like something they hadn't thought about in a long, long time. No surprise, there. This ship didn't strike me as a teaching vessel.

"What kind of power does your science use for hyperlight?" Quen asked. His calming tone brought me back to some self-control.

"Our hyperlight-speed," I began, "is fueled by matter/antimatter reaction, ignited by passing certain waves through dilithium crystals. We can generate an independent ignition any time we want to."

"Any time . . . Can you show us how to do it?"

I sighed at this, knew it was coming.

"Captain," I said, "I could be the best engineer in Star Fleet, and if I go back two hundred years in technology, I can't build a warp engine without the infrastructure that builds its million components. No matter what I tell you, you can't build warp drive without support. I can't say, 'Get me stone knives and bear skins, and I'll build you a warp drive.' But I can improve your systems to recover faster when you do fall out of warp. I might be able to help you eventually figure out a battery ignition system so you won't be slaves to solar energy. You won't have to live in a handful of forts with nothing but desert between. Our technology is generations beyond what I see out there on your deck, and so was the Iscoy's. My science skipped this jumping phase altogether. We know how to upgrade you to self-contained ignition. That would be worth your trouble, wouldn't it?"

I was careful to watch every word I said. I didn't want to make promises I couldn't keep. I was sworn not to violate the Prime Directive by providing unknown races with advanced technology. Even races with their own crude warp drive were covered until a decision was made by the Federation council. But if they could get me to *Voyager*, or any of her crew, then it was worth some prevarication. I'd find some way to reward them.

He watched me through weighted eyes but didn't offer any answer at all. Though my soliloquy had some elements of fascination to them, they looked at each other again—one of *those* glances.

"Well?" I prodded.

Seconds trucked by. My legs ached. My raw knuckles itched. The foil poncho had long ago lost its crinkle and now brushed pitifully against the edge of Quen's desk. Noise from the main deck outside interrupted us as somebody dropped something that went clattering abeam. None of us looked.

Finally, Quen sighed. His brows were drawn with an infuriating pity for me.

Zell shifted his weight in the most damnably clear universal body language I'd seen in a month.

"Nothing has fifteen decks," he uttered.

Damn, was I in trouble.

Their suspicion was both aggravating and understandable. Unable to avoid a tincture of desperation in my voice, I demanded, "What can I do to make you believe me?"

Quen seemed genuinely regretful, and in spite of my anger I couldn't help but empathize with him. "You don't know about the Berm and Kavapent," he said. "You don't know the marker patterns, signals, or spaceroads in this sector. You don't know about light kicks. Everyone who pilots any kind of ship knows those things. Every captain."

He didn't need to spell it for me. I felt my face harden and my glare turn fierce.

"You're not going to take me back?" I challenged. "You won't even try?"

"It would be against my pledge," he said with obvious conviction. "I have an obligation to my crew. If we make a light kick, and there's no star there—"

With one hand pressing on his desk, I leaned forward. "You won't need any solar power, Captain Quen, I told you. The Iscoy have the technology you need, and if any of my people survived, we have it, too. You'll get it. Your capacitors can be charged directly off a warp core. It's a ten-minute process! All you have to do is take me there!"

Only after it was too late did I realize my teeth were gritted and my fists clenched. From their point of view, I couldn't blame them. How did they know I hadn't been put off some other ship because I was nuts? Because my injuries were too extensive? Because I was some kind of danger? What was the past of this strange rubbish they'd scooped up? How long should I rave before they slapped me in their version of a padded cell and fed me applesauce? I realized my tune had better change quickly, or I would risk being put off the ship as some kind of spacesick Jonah.

And my plans would have to change, too. Quickly.

"All right, Captain," I began, gauging my tone like organ keys. "I don't want to be trouble or get in the way. I'll work my passage until we can come to an agreement. You can bunk me with one of the other women."

Seeming surprised at that last part, Quen looked at me quizzically. "There aren't any other women."

Oops—more trouble in River City.

"Your crew is all-male?"

He shrugged. "I've . . . never heard of anything else."

"Really? Then I'll bunk wherever you have room for me," I offered. "I'll do whatever work you have. Show me your engine room."

With both hands Quen brushed his shaggy emerald hair away from his drawn forehead, and frowned. "I don't like putting a woman to work. I'd rather send you—"

Before he finished that thought, I broke in. "I can assist your engineers significantly. My technical abilities can boost your power levels, your speed, and probably efficiency. I'll outwork anybody. I'll earn my place in your crew. Don't put me off until you give me a chance. I'm willing to trade improvements for a light kick as soon as you feel fully compensated."

Starfleet officer, sure. But I could haggle like Ferengi at a flea market.

Quen watched me as if waiting for me to break down and weep that it was all a pack of lies and I was playing some kind of game. That it was all a sorority prank. That I was really a princess pulling a fast one. I think I could've told him anything but the truth, and he'd have been relieved. After all, he already had the truth.

"If we try to contact a transport," Zell suggested, "we'll be giving up the salvage. Sasaquon or Oran is in the area. They'll move in on us."

"We couldn't go yet if we wanted to," Quen confirmed. "Don't worry. She'll just have to wait."

I had no idea what that really meant, but I got the idea that the situation they were in was buying me time. My mind raced briefly with plans, plots, ideas, and the long-range goal. The Menace was coming. I had to be ready. I had to make these people ready.

"Get clothes for her," Quen said. He started writing with some kind of stylus on one of the metal plates. I didn't know what those were, but this one had something to do with me. A log entry, maybe. Or recorded orders. "Assign her a bunk. Put her to work."

He handed the plate to Zell, who pocketed it in his vest.

"You," Zell told him then, "lie down for a while."

He plucked the stylus out of Quen's hand, then scooped up all the plates Quen had been working on.

"But I'm not finished," Quen protested. "Give me those back!"

"No."

"I want to get those out of the way before—"

"Bunk. You. Now."

Quen glowered at him. "Zell, I told you to quit giving me orders."

The first officer leaned over him and glared. "It's not an order. It's a threat."

He stuffed the metal plates into the hip pocket on his utility vest, as if to close the subject of Quen's doing any more work right now. He hoisted the fur blanket from Quen's bunk behind the desk and dumped it over his captain's head, leaving Quen sitting there, buried and chuckling.

Odd.

The crossroads before us was dim and disturbing as Zell ushered me out of the forecastle area and back to the main deck. He paused at a wall of lockers midships on the transverse bulkhead and opened one. From this he pulled a fur blanket, a small pillow, and two brown sheets, and from another cubby he pulled some clothes.

"If you'll show me to your engine room," I offered, "I can begin improvements right away. As soon as my hands and legs heal more, I'll be able to—"

"You're not going to the engines. You're going to work the tiles."

"But I can improve your—"

"We'll see later what you can do." His tone wasn't exactly patronizing, but it wasn't exactly encouraging either as he added, "Everybody starts at the tiles. Here are some clean clothes. We don't have any women's clothes—"

"That's all right."

I shook out the folded gear and discovered a simple pair of brown trousers that looked and felt like buckskin, an eggplant-colored knitted sweater with a thick cowl neck, and one of the shoulder capes that many of these men were also wearing. Apparently they put as little energy into heating as they could get away with and still function. It was chilly in here, but not enough to cause condensation. They seemed comfortable enough, probably because they'd grown accustomed to the chill. At least, I hoped so because that meant there was a chance in hell frozen over that I'd get used to it too. This was livably cool, as were the leaf-dropping crispy autumn days back home, but my shivering betrayed how spoiled I'd become to the warm and roomy accommodations on board my starship.

"Nobody here has feet as small as yours," Zell said, looking down at my boots. "I hope your mucks are good enough."

"They're just fine. I think my feet are the only part of me that didn't get cut, bruised, or burned."

"That's lucky."

Right there in front of the crew and the gods of luck and everybody, he helped me slip the trousers on over my bandaged legs. I'd gotten used to a captain's privileged privacy over the past few years, but there wasn't time for that. With a huff of relief I peeled off the crumpled foil poncho, and instantly every crewman on the long main deck turned away and suddenly got very interested in his work—not what I might've expected from the shipload of young men with no women on board.

"Your crew is very chivalrous," I mentioned, standing there in buckskin trousers and my silk chemise.

"What's that mean?" Zell asked, also conspicuously *not* looking at me.

"Polite."

Because my wrists were still stiff, he helped me pull the sweater on, then he fastened the clay-and-black checkered capelet over my shoulders. Felt like blanket fleece. Looked like Robin Hood. All I needed was a haircut.

"After you clean up and rest and Ruvan says you can work, you'll start over here."

Zell led me to the beam slightly forward of midships. He stooped and picked up a small tool with a scrubbing brush on one end and a pointed metal hook on the other. He handed this to me unceremoniously.

"The tool of your trade."

"It's a toothbrush," I said.

"It's a reamer," he corrected.

"What do I do with it?"

"Ream." He pointed at the bulkhead, which was encrusted from footboard to ceiling to the other side of the ship with those little metallic squares. "These are our cell tiles. They store energy, and when we need the energy they drain in an instant—"

"Capacitors. Giving you your power surge for the kick."

"And other things. Some of them are used for power flow on our fusion engines, our sensing probes—other things. It's complicated. Your job will be to ream out the crust that gets in between the tiles, keep the tiles absolutely clean and polished, and make sure they're fitted evenly and attached securely—"

I swung around to face him and almost twisted my leg off. "Are you telling me I'm a deck swab?"

He paused, then shrugged. "No . . . you're a tile reamer."

"But I'm a fully qualified and licensed chief engineer!"

"Not here you're not. Everybody starts at the tiles. I started there, Quen started there—"

Suddenly looking at months of working my way up to any real influence, I shook the little brush in his face and charged, "You don't have time for this! The Menace is coming!"

He gazed at me briefly with infuriating pity. "We'll keep a lookout."

"So did the Iscoy!"

"Zell!" one of the men at a side-mounted control stanchion called suddenly, and we both turned. "We've got approach!"

Zell took two steps toward the control stanchion, and was instantly thrown hard to his left by a jolt that rocked the whole ship. The *Zingara* heaved under us, actually leaving my feet by a couple of inches. I ended up on one knee, with the rest of the crew scrambling around me purposefully.

Frustration rocked through me as I realized I had no idea what to do or where to go, or even how to get out of the way and avoid making a nuisance of myself. Were we under attack? Had the Menace come sooner than even I expected?

Shoving to his feet and plunging to the control stanchion, Zell looked at the monitors and confirmed what was going on. He looked up and rasped out his order.

"Raid! Emergency posts!"

CHAPTER
4

QUEN APPEARED LIKE A PISTOL SHOT FROM THE FORECASTLE
hatchway, dragging his fur blanket caught on one boot. He
came in so fast, in fact, that I barely saw the transition
between when he wasn't here and when he was.

"Who is it?" he demanded.

Kind of an odd question—

"Sasaquon!" Zell answered. "Angle two-six over the
prad."

All the crewmen had instantly jumped to their feet. On a
Starfleet ship, when there was trouble, most people went to
a post. There was no command chair or central arena on
this deck, yet I got the idea that the general area with the
helm was their version of a bridge. The helm was a standing
console with one crewman manning it, which meant it was
probably exclusively navigation and speed duty. Weapons,
sensors, everything else must be somewhere other than that
console. But where?

This empty, desperate feeling I had—it was nightmarish.
I was a captain, but here I was nobody. A third wheel, a
dunsel, with no idea what to do or how to help, or even what
was going on. I should've been grateful for the crash course,

50

but that was hard to appreciate while hanging here, completely impotent in the middle of trouble.

Standing near the helm officer, but not touching the helm itself, Quen ordered, "Hurry up, Vince, get us a corridor groove on standard trajectory. Othien, mark the racker and take weapons."

"The rod level is still down, Quen," Zell called, then he dropped into the lower deck through the big companionway right in the middle of the main deck.

I didn't understand their jargon, and obviously my commbadge didn't have a reference point from which to translate those words, so they just came through as the sounds Quen and Zell were making in their own language. Rod level, prad, corridor groove—I wanted to know what all that meant. I wanted to participate! I wasn't just a bird sitting in a cage, was I? I could help, but I didn't know how!

A few more lights popped on, all red ones, over control consoles where the crewmen now clustered around the perimeter of the deck. So their ocular physiology was like mine—red lights let us see what we were doing without forcing the pupils to contract. In the midst of my uselessness and confusion, it was good to find one thing I recognized.

Quen turned to one of his crewmen who was manning a panel of some kind aft of the helm. "Massus, let's have a full view."

"Full view." The crewman named Massus fed several metal plates like those I'd seen Quen working on into slots in his panel, paused, corrected something, then cranked a central lever all the way down.

The simple exchange showed me that repetition of orders had found its way into this culture too. Made sense. Clarity, control, understanding—

What in hell!

"Oh, my—" I choked, crouching in shock and looking around, overhead, to the sides.

It was as if the top half of *Zingara* had dissolved! We might as well be on an open-decked vessel in the middle of an ocean, with other vessels wheeling around us! Beautiful!

Beautiful, yes, but suddenly terrifying! We were virtually standing out in space! For a moment I actually held my breath, expecting all the oxygen to be gone. It took a firm shake of the senses to realize that this was some kind of artificial projection through the tiled inner skin that allowed Quen and his crew to see everything that was going on outside the ship, with the exception of directly below. What a great idea!

There's air . . . you're breathing . . . it's all right . . . you can breathe . . . out . . . out . . . out . . . let's go for an in . . .

I put my hand up, pressing it to the black sheet of space beside me; I could still feel the tiles, though I couldn't see them.

And, beyond my scraped fingers, this space was beautiful! I'd been used to looking through portals that had definite frames, or at the big bridge viewscreen aboard *Voyager*. Until now I hadn't realized how separate that view had been. This way, I was actually out in space, as if gazing at a mountain range from a canoe on a lake!

While feeling like I was about to exhale myself to death, I looked around and saw that a row of scanner readout screens had flickered to life below the disappear line. Most of them made no sense to me—no, that one did! Angle of vessel incline. One down. Forty or fifty to go. Oh—I got air!

Understand, Captains, those of you who work on an ocean, this was as if you jumped off your ships and ended up under water—or for us space captains, ended up outside our ships without a pressure suit—and suddenly realized you can still breathe. What a shock! What I was seeing just didn't link up to being able to inhale and function.

Convincing myself to behave as I might on a holodeck, that what I saw above me was a scanner illusion, a fabrication of the real thing, I pulled myself to my feet so I could see past the "rail," craned my neck, and peered out into open space,

Space here was indeed magnificent, crammed full of nebulae, bright sparkle clusters, a disturbingly close asteroid belt, and not much farther away an entire planet with a thick green atmosphere, a heavily watered surface, and frozen poles. To the other side was a fan of peacock-tail formations of chromatic gas-charged rings with dust plumes, as if someone had plucked the bird's feathers and laid them on a tabletop. For a moment the incomparable natural beauty caught my breath in my throat. I stared like an idiot. Until another shot rocked us—that woke me up.

To overcome the initial shock of what I was seeing, I retreated quickly to the logic of mathematics and engineering and clung to the anchor of figuring out this technology. It would never work unless these people had, like Starfleet, the ability to computer-magnify selected images. A ship passing close, say, fifty kilometers, would never be seen by the naked eye without help. We just hadn't evolved in space, so our senses were useless without machines adjusting things for our pathetic abilities. Good thing the machines needed us to design and build them, or they might get cocky.

The other ship, now wheeling past us from abaft to abeam on the port side, was relatively simple in configuration. It had a time-tried spaceborne design—functional and roughly cigar shaped with no appendages except weapons and broadcast arrays. The shape of the vessel presented the slimmest possible target at almost any angle except directly above and below. That explained why the intruder was staying on a level plane with *Zingara*. This added to the image of our moving about on an ocean's surface. Since Quen made no attempts to dodge under or over the other ship, I got the idea *Zingara* was a similar design.

And similarly banged up? That ship out there was patched and weathered as if it had been through a meteor shower and barely got out. Parts of the hull didn't match other parts, and sections were painted differently, as if made out of junk parts from other ships, and there were patches on top of other patches, creating a crazy quilt of a hull. Yet it looked strong—the repairs were tough and heavy, with thick welding strips visible even from here.

Beneath me the hull vibrated as powerful sublight engines revved to life. I winced—I knew a cold-start when I heard it. *Zingara* surged into a wheeling motion that countered the other ship's movements and forced them off their vector. The other ship corrected and started on a modified path downward from our plane, heeling to keep its slimmest profile to us.

"Sasaquon's moving to wing position, Quen," the crewman next to me informed.

"Don't let them get between us and the prize," Quen said. He wasn't responding, but passing an order to his helmsman, who immediately adjusted his controls, which included a joystick arrangement—probably thruster control.

"Absolutely quaint," I muttered, but after a moment of watching I recalled instead the retractable columns and yokes that once upon a time had been used to steer airplanes. As I watched *Zingara* being maneuvered, and the *Sasaquon* moving out there, my eyes scanned past a monitor that came on-line a few steps forward of me. I forced myself to watch it, to get used to it, to figure out what I was seeing. Three blue shapes in schematic, obviously vessels, flickering, changing position—

"I get it . . . ships in relation to each other . . ." The croak of my realization drew a look from the crewman manning that monitor.

He pointed at the shapes on the crackly screen. "This is *Sasaquon*. This is us. And this shape here is the prize we're defending. It's a derelict minesweeper. It's below the vid line right now."

"Thanks," I said, and scooted closer.

The third ship was below us, and clearly in pieces, like a wreck on the ocean floor, except that in space it was held together by some kind of tethers. At first it seemed the tethers might be inner cables that hadn't snapped. Then I changed my mind and concluded that someone had deliberately tied the pieces of the wreck together to keep them from drifting apart.

"I'm sorry you have to see this," he told me then.

"No—it's very interesting. I'm Kathryn Janeway."

"Lucas." He took a moment from his work to brush fingers with me. As he turned briefly, the blue form on his scanner reflected on his brown capelet and yellow hair, and I don't mean "blond."

"We have that name in my culture too," I mentioned. "Some people shorten it to Luke."

"That would work," he said. "Yours is long. You should shorten it for trouble. Duck down, please."

He pulled me to a crouch and looked over my head at the circling *Sasaquon*, then adjusted his scanner to compensate for speed.

"Did you shorten yours?" I asked.

"Everyone does. We have very long names."

"Then you'd better call me Janeway. There's not much of a way to shorten it. Jay . . . Jane . . ."

"What about the other one?" Lucas spoke as casually as if we weren't in a defensive maneuver, but carefully worked his equipment and kept his eye on *Sasaquon*.

"Well," I began, trying to be polite, "there are ways to shorten Kathryn. I've never done it. Kathy, Katie, Kate, Kay—"

"Kay is good. Short. Pardon me—" He reached past me and tapped some of the metallic squares near my elbow.

I noticed that he had no knobs, pressure panels, switches, or keys, but was running his fingers horizontally, vertically, or diagonally along some of these squares to adjust the picture on the scanner. The screen itself wasn't a screen at all, but dozens of these squares with each one broadcasting a fraction of the whole picture. A couple of them were "out," making little holes in the scene. This was a darn cute technology and I wanted in on it.

Later.

"What's your job here, Lucas?"

"Right now I'm keeping visual positions of everything in the challenge area. Usually, I map space."

"You're a stellar cartographer?"

"Usually. I also—"

As he started to say more, the sky above us blew to white—a hit on the hull directly above the midship section! Though only an illusion of what was going on outside, a shell had just exploded against the skin of the ship and we had seen it without any obstacles to our view, as if fireworks had exploded ten feet over our heads and sparkled over a glass ceiling. I flinched and ducked as the sparks rained and dissipated into a halo.

"It's all right," Lucas said. "We can take it for a while."

I made myself understand, with some effort, that what I was seeing was actually happening on the other side of an invisible ceiling.

Steeling myself in case we were hit again above the vid line, I asked, "Can you show me what *Zingara* looks like?"

Without answering, Lucas touched a square. Nothing

happened. He corrected to another square, and the scanner screen changed. The three vessels suddenly took on a photographic realism. A miniature identical of *Sasaquon* veered past a clear image of *Zingara*. Quickly I added up the ships' similarities and differences. *Zingara* was somewhat more boat-shaped, possibly to accommodate her "vid" line, which for us created an illusion of a weather deck here, while the moving ship on the screen still had its decktops on. Mounted upon those tops were recognizable king posts with loading cranes, a rotating crane, and low-slung turret guns and cannons, but no living decks. All those, apparently, were down here on this level and below. Out forward was a barge bow with cushioned fenders for pushing, and aft was a stern transom that looked as if it might open and make a ramp. A fairly sensible working ship, able to defend itself. Like most ships, it wore its purpose on its sleeve.

The other ship was roughly the same basic shape, but its sheer line was broken with stacked housings amidships. It also had cranes, but all four of those were rotating cranes—no, there was one gantry crane mounted on the underbelly. The movements of the two ships looked like the *Monitor* and the *Merrimack* lumbering about in Hampton Roads.

From the CGI, with no frame of reference, I had no way of knowing the length of these vessels. Wait a minute—yes, I did. I had myself and these men standing around me. Turning, I eyeballed the distance from the forecastle transverse bulkhead to its correspondent aft and tried to remember walking it, even on bad legs. Maybe four hundred feet?

The steps might be wrong, but I thought the measurement was close. How far had I walked to get from that transverse bulkhead to Quen's cabin? Forty more feet?

Double that, add it up—*Zingara* bargained to be about five hundred feet overall, maybe five-fifty. A good, strong, serviceable tug size, not too big to turn tightly, not too small to have muscle. Made sense.

I compared my judgments with the CGI version of the ship, at the points where the hull started tapering toward the bow, and where it tapered toward its stern, and decided I was right—the two big transverse bulkheads were the markers for the midship section. That looked right, given my estimate of this deck with the other measurements. Well, I had to do something with my time while we were being fired on, didn't I?

"Why are they firing on us, Lucas?" I asked.

"They want to keep us from our claim."

"You mean that hulk out there?"

"Yes."

"Whose was it to begin with?"

"It was Shan. Derelict in the war."

Not much help.

"You just had a war and you're a salvage crew? How do you decide—"

My question was cut off by a hard hit forward of us from *Sasaquon*. The shots weren't like the long streaks of phaser bolts or the bloom of photon torpedoes. These shots were propellants of some sort, actual projectile weapons, not contained energy. As the *Sasaquon* fired and *Zingara* fired back, I could actually see solid projectiles spin across the space between us, and see the impact on the hulls, and over our heads on the vision of space, as if there were a glass ceiling over us. Impact and explosion. These weren't just solid iron like cannonballs. They were some kind of ballistic missile with a tracer stream. They wiggled toward us on a deadly trajectory, struck, and detonated.

Shots from *Zingara* did the same to *Sasaquon*. Both ships wobbled in the wash of enormous power and thrust as Quen's crew tried to work *Zingara* between the other ship and the wreck. How was the return fire handled? I didn't hear the captain giving orders to fire. That was how it was done on a starship—weapons officer taking specific orders to fire from the command officer, with the exception of "fire at will."

Had "fire at will" been given here?

I looked at Quen. He wasn't watching the big picture overhead. Instead he was huddled over a patch of squares with another crewman on the starboard side. Why wasn't he paying attention? Zell was belowdecks in the engine area, unable to handle command. Why wasn't Quen doing a captain's job?

Somebody was doing the shooting. Which of these men were the gunners? Or were the gunners not on this deck at all? Were they below? Or were they actually in the gun turrets?

Easy to solve.

"Lucas, who's handling the weapons?"

"Turretmasters," he answered.

"Aren't they waiting for orders?"

He looked at me, perplexed. "Orders? To shoot at Sasaquon? Nobody needs orders for that."

"Aren't you depleting your firepower with inefficient shots? The angles aren't coordinated with the ship's movements! Isn't somebody orchestrating the general activity?"

He squinted at me briefly, as if I'd asked him why his captain had green hair. "Everybody knows what to do," he said, perplexed and trying not to be rude to the dummy next to him.

Quen now straightened and watched as we slid downward and to the starboard, until we ran abeam of *Sasaquon*. He watched the other ship, but gave not a single maneuver order. Instead, he mildly spoke to a few of the crewmen here and there.

"Mark the rackers," he said. "Adjust the ergo stull and keep your corridor clear. Don't get fouled. Massus, cope the rod level."

"I'm watching it," Massus answered without turning. "It's not holding steady."

"Send the curry cards down to Zell so he can keep up the measure."

"All right."

No *yes, sir,* as I would have demanded. The lack of protocol and formality grated on me. Some things didn't translate, so I didn't even try to understand the technical jargon yet, but I knew inefficiency when I saw it. Why wasn't anyone barking orders? Why weren't suggestions rushing across the crew?

In the middle of my criticisms, the enemy angled across our bow and got off a good shot directly at the left side of my forehead. Rationality hit the wind and I ducked. When I looked up, a quarter of the ceiling was blinking between here and not here. Quen and his crew watched it, wheeling

underneath the jagged patch of reappearing upper bulkhead.

Zell appeared halfway up out of the companionway and
craned at the reappeared section. Quen knelt by the companionway hole, spoke to Zell. Together they made some
kind of decision, and Zell disappeared again. They left the
ceiling as it was, partly there and partly gone. No one that I
could see made any attempt to fix the damage so there
would again be an unimpaired view of space.

"I can't see the *Sasaquon*," I uttered, more or less
thinking aloud. "Are they deliberately trying to impair our
view? Is that why they're firing on the upper hull?"

Lucas was only half listening as he adjusted his screen,
which was apparently the only mechanical visual reference
to ships' positions. "'The' *Sasaquon?*"

"Yes, that ship. The *Sasaquon.*"

"Oh. Sasaquon isn't the ship. Sasaquon is the captain
over there. The ship is the *Aragore.*"

"You refer to your enemies by the captain's name?"

"Don't you?"

"Not really . . . that's a good detail not to get wrong. We
put the names of our ships on the outside hull. What if you
don't know the captain's name?"

"We know anyone who would attack us."

I shifted my aching legs and mumbled, "Like hell you
do . . ."

Luckily, rather than add to a bad situation, my words
were lost in a timely explosion on the lower decks. A ball of
smoke piled out of the companionway. With it came a gout
of choking crewmen, including Zell. Many of them staggered aside, and still more could barely walk. The rancorous
smoke reached me just as I realized it was poisonous. I
clapped a hand over my mouth and nose just in time to
avoid a deep breath.

"Vents!" the second in command called, sending others
running to select controls.

Quen helped Zell to his feet. "What happened?"

"Racker leaks," Zell gagged, waving at the smoke. It was
clearing fast—and a good thing, that. "We had a choke
catch, and then a . . . low-grade . . ."

He doubled over, clearing his lungs. Around them, a

dozen crewmen were coiled on the deck, choking and seized up. Several had burned hands and scorched clothing.

Quen was damnably patient; I wouldn't have been. Low-grade what! What!

"Rod level drop," Zell finished.

"He's got us, then." Quen turned his tired eyes to the fracturing view of the enemy ship, just as the overhead bulkheads flickered back into existence.

"Quen, losing thruster control!" the helmsman called. "I can't hold against the pull."

"Steer right. Somebody get a window."

What pull? Gravitation from something? Were we too near a planet? He couldn't mean the wreck, could he?

I stood up and craned to see this area of space, to know what was going on, but as I looked upward, wide spans of damage in the panels flickered, reappeared, and shut out the vision of open space. We were once again in the shoebox. The overhead areas of the *Zingara* now showed patches of fracture, burns, and overloads. There must be a lot of mechanics packed up there, in order to provide a bulkhead-to-bulkhead computer-generated view of space beyond it, and also to carry ship's general systems. I was sure regular systems flowed through there; no fighting ship could afford such a big area to be devoted only to a viewscreen.

Steer right? Away from the wreck? Away from the one thing that could give us cover and a chance to win?

"Are you giving up?" I called.

To my left, Lucas flinched visibly and stared at me, but I was looking at Quen and Zell. They both blinked at me, and so did most of the crew—those who could still stand, anyway.

Then the most amazing thing happened. Zell turned his back. He faced Quen, and together they went to speak to Massus and two others over there in the aft corner, where the poison smoke was thinnest.

"Captain!" Angrily I pushed to my feet and stepped right over two recovering crewmen. "You can't actually be—"

Somebody hooked a hand in my elbow and whipped me around so fast that the words were snatched from my lips and I got a bad suck of that foul air.

Lucas and another crewman had me by both arms. I

twisted against them and threw over my shoulder, "Captain, there's got to be more you can do!"

By now they'd hustled me to the far forward end of the shoebox, way down the deck from Quen and Zell.

Lucas pushed me into a corner and held me there while the other crewman stood back and watched, as if to let me know I couldn't get away from both of them.

"Don't bother Quen, Kay," Lucas warned. "We've lost the prize. Look at the crew—there's too much injury to keep on. Our vid is down, there's a rod level leak—"

"That doesn't mean you should give up," I said. "What kind of message is that to send to Sasaquon?"

"Sasaquon isn't like the others. He'll kill us."

Furious, I shook off his grip. "I don't understand the stakes here! What are you people doing? Is this a salvage operation, or are you invading somebody's claim, or what?!"

"We're not invading; it's a legitimate claim. Sasaquon's stealing what we need to surv—"

"Then why don't you defend what's yours?"

"We're too broken down now." He glanced at the other crewman who was guarding me, a lanky boy with scraggly brown hair and a gap between his front teeth.

"Use that wreck for cover!"

He and his friend stared at me, mouths agape, obviously with no answer for anger that seemed to make no sense to them.

"We can't move closer to the wreck," Lucas said, amazed that I would even suggest it.

But why was it amazing? Why!

"There are ways to fight, don't you know that?" I challenged. "Don't you people know anything about tactics? Don't you have tricks? Reserves?"

Lucas put his hands up to quiet me. "Do you want to be locked in a bunk?

For this he got a sock in the shoulder from a pointy fist. "I've just watched my ship get blown to pieces, and I'm not going to do it again. Both of you stand down!"

Though the punch didn't faze him, he was certainly stunned. He and Gap were actually afraid of me!

Intimidation worked in my favor as I shoved them both out of the way. Stalking back—all right, limping—toward the helm deck, I stocked up the half-dozen points I was going to make when Quen had no choice but to listen to me, which would be right now.

Coordinate maneuvers with firepower. Create a distraction. Bluff. Use the wreck for cover. After all, it's already a wreck!

What! A burly crewman with fuzzy rust hair done in a face-frame of braids had me by the wrist. I glared into his pale surly face as he said, "Don't bother Quen. We don't do that."

"Who are you?" I demanded.

"I'm Vince, the deck boss. Don't bother the captain."

"But I'm a captain too!"

"On board one day and you're a captain." He shoved me back. "Quen and Zell will handle the ship."

"You've got to trust me!"

He arched over me like a birch bending in a storm. "We don't *know* you!"

Lucas appeared at my side and squeezed between us, breaking Vince's grip on my arm. "Don't hit her, Vince!"

"I wasn't going to hit her!" the big deck boss snarled. "Get her out of the way!"

Nobody had to push me—the ship took care of that when it pitched up onto its starboard side and we all went crashing. I landed on top of the deck boss, and Lucas landed on top of me. There we were held as if by magnets through a surge of unseen power.

I dug my way out from under Vince's meaty leg and tried to see what was happening. Zell had disappeared completely under a wash of cables and equipment, and Quen was clawing his way up a deck that at this angle was virtually a wall.

At the aft transverse bulkhead, Massus held tightly on to a handgrip and shouted over the whine.

"We're caught in the Sands!"

CHAPTER
5

"SURGE THE COMPENSATORS!"

"They're oversurged already."

"Then bleed 'em!"

Orders fell like crackling leaves all around me. The weight of Vince and Lucas rose from me, and I was free to crawl along the tilted deck, maddened by the whine of straining engines and sizzling electronics, half of which were breaking and the other half crackling back to life as hasty repairs were made in every corner of the struggling *Zingara*.

I thought the ship must be finished, wallowing on such a tilt, groaning like an old scarecrow whose bones of wood and clothes of rags had begun to crack and shred in unkind wind. And there was nothing I could do about it, nothing I knew to do, no control that would recognize my touch, no way to know what had caught us or how to get out of its grip. The blind helplessness of the survival pod had been better than this poison helplessness and ignorance of what was happening and how to correct it.

The top half of the ship flickered, and part of the viewscreen came back on—which meant that jagged sections of the tile-encrusted bulkhead up there actually "disappeared," showing us a vision of what was happening out there. Now I saw what the problem was: Those peacock plumes of space matter and dust were now engulfing us in a sinister blue-green wash, sucking us deeper into the fans of energy. The Sands!

Instantly I realized I'd been wrong about the peacock plumes. They weren't just spewing dust left over from some ancient cataclysm. They were some kind of energy surge, with gravity sucking us in toward a collapsed or collapsing core. I'd completely misread what I'd seen. Quen's action to move away from the wreck was the right one, but even that had been too late to avoid the gravity wash. The ship was too weak to fight the pull into the Sands, so certainly it would now be too weak to claw its way out.

Did they have tractor beams? Could they latch on to something and take a purchase? At least hold themselves in place until repairs could be made? I hadn't heard anything like that. These ships didn't look as if they might be rigged for energy traction, not with all those cranes and booms and hauling hardware.

The ship around us screamed until I thought my brain would burst, engines relentlessly thrusting against the wave-like suction of the beautiful and deadly Sands. Like the giant eye in a peacock's feathers, the moon-sized center of this plume gorged itself on *Zingara*, washing against our hull with great arms of blue-green energy, as if we were being shoved again and again by ocean surf.

I'd never seen anything like this and didn't have any idea of how to fight it, though I struggled to come up with some wild plan to save the ship. As the crew scrambled around me, and the ship fought to put its own internal gravity back somewhere near upright so we could at least walk, the cold reality hit me that it wasn't my place to save the ship. I could have thirty ideas, but these people weren't interested in hearing them and would stand between me and Quen when I tried to tell him what I thought. No power, no influence, no one listening to me. No reputation, no rank, no confidence in me . . . I had nothing to offer that anyone here wanted. The weight of impotence almost crushed my chest.

"Look!"

It was Lucas, pointing furiously at an open part of the partial view above and to our sides.

I pulled myself to his side and looked out with my smoke-stung eyes. "Another ship!"

"It's Oran," Lucas gasped.

"Friend or foe?" I asked.

Through a glint of hope, he admitted, "That depends."

The new ship pulled out swiftly from behind a shimmering cloud and angled not toward us, but across our bow at an angle. At first I was irritated that the newcomers weren't rushing to our aid, then realized that they were steering clear of the surging Sands.

And those were some surges, if I was seeing right and measuring right. The peacock plumes were flowing and heaving back and forth against whatever gravitational power made them go, surging out and back by scores of kilometers, and they could easily strike out and capture a ship, which is probably what had happened to us. So the ship out there, Oran's ship, was smart to give way.

Why were they here? To help us or take advantage of our trouble?

Quen appeared between me and Lucas, gauged the distance of Oran's ship, its attitude, speed, and seemed also to be trying to guess its intent.

"Zell!" he called without turning.

"Down here." A voice, from somewhere below.

"Are the extenders up?"

"Yes, up."

"Go ahead and cast the harpoon cables. Hurry, hurry."

"Firing."

"Don't make him come to us."

"I won't, I'm casting. Vince! Get down here!"

Now Quen turned to the helmsman. "Keep the thrust up. Don't let us slip any more than we already have."

I pointed at another part of the jagged-edged view. "Here comes Sasaquon!"

Everyone around me looked where I was pointing, to Sasaquon's ship corkscrewing across our beam, firing salvos the whole way.

"Must be desperate," Quen muttered.

Though I didn't take it as a joke, several of the crew

around me indulged in a gallows chuckle as they scrambled back to their posts and fought to compensate now not only for the suction of the Sands but the missiles hitting us.

Electrical damage sizzled through the systems around me and everything was suddenly hot with uninsulated energy. The view around us flickered, altered, some patches of tiles losing their ability to show us what was happening in space and others gaining it back, so that the view was inconstant and patchy.

What would Oran do? As the new ship wheeled in the distance, I still couldn't read intent in its motions.

Zingara jumped in place suddenly, and two cables fired outward from our lower hull, spooling into space between Sasaquon and Oran's ship as they came closer and closer to each other. Like a drowning swimmer being pulled under by a riptide, we had stuck a hand up to the surface and now hoped somebody would grab that hand.

Someone might just as easily slap it and push us under. Sasaquon was trying. Oran—an unknown factor.

I suddenly wanted my own viewscreen from *Voyager* in front of me. I wanted access to strong sensors and far-reaching communication, to order a view of Sasaquon himself so I could look in his eyes and know his face, memorize his expressions, and so he could see the determination in my eyes. I'd always cherished that face-to-face option with my opponents.

"Lucas!"

He was clinging to a handgrip with one hand and fingering tiles with the other, feeding information that scrolled across the scanner portion of tiles in front of him. I clasped another handgrip and squinted at the screen. A faulty image of our ship, Sasaquon's, and Oran's jockeyed with the giant fan of energy from the Sands, showing *Zingara* clawing against the generated wash of the plume, very artificial and somehow just as scary as the real thing visible in patches above and to the sides of us.

How strange!—it struck me again—to just look up and out as if the top half of the ship had opened up like the top of a box! Or the top of the coffin . . . The next few moments would tell. My teeth gritted so hard with frustration that I thought they'd crack.

"Lucas, can you show me what Sasaquon looks like?"

"What?" he called over the maddening whine of engines. "You want what?"

"I want to see Sasaquon!"

"Oh . . . now?"

"Yes!"

If I could've done it myself, I would have. The tile technology was a completely mystery, and I vowed to learn it as quickly as possible so I could get things for myself. He had to do two things at once to fulfill my request, but he did it and I was suddenly looking at a fuzzy picture of a strikingly handsome man, older than Quen, silver-haired with a good trim cut, with a ruddy complexion and dark eyes. Though his coloring was closer to human than any I'd seen yet, I could tell he was one of Quen's race. Something about the bone structure I was already getting used to. He wore the same kind of clothing as Quen's crew, except that the ragged shoulder capes were missing and Sasaquon wore instead a bright red vest. Though he seemed more like a businessman or an ambassador than a warrior, there was something effectively sinister in his appearance simply because I knew he was the one out there attacking us, trying to push us into the Sands.

The photo was some kind of communications record; though there was no sound, he was apparently just talking, not fighting, giving me the idea this had been recorded sometime in the recent past. Behind Sasaquon, crew members passed by wearing the same red vest and looking markedly healthier than Quen's crew. I resolved to ask about that later. Why were the enemy better dressed and better fed?

"What about Oran?"

"There's no time for this!" Lucas gasped. "We have to get out of the Sands! I have work to do!"

"All right, do it," I told him. There was really nothing I could do except stay out of the way.

As the ship shook and shuddered around me, I forced myself to concentrate on what Lucas did with the tiles and what the scanner screen made of them. A selection appeared on the screen with a bunch of little ships in profile, each on four tiles. So the four tiles were option files. He picked the ship that looked like Oran's, and the screen filled with the one ship. It made sense. I loved that it made sense. That meant I could learn all of this if I just had the time before we got crushed or smeared against a solid core somewhere at the hub of the Sands.

In the middle of near-disaster, I thought to myself, Great! Give me twenty minutes before I die, and I'll learn this stuff!

"He's almost got them!" Lucas called.

"I've almost got it!" Voices from the crew shouted back. "Just a few more seconds!"

"Just another second . . ." Unable to affect what was going on in space, I fixated upon learning how to work the tile scanner and find out what Oran looked like. Now that Sasaquon's stylish and elegant appearance was burned into my memory, I wanted to know who and what else I might be up against. Know your friends, know your enemies, know yourself. Simple, simple—

Suddenly a jolt took the deck out from under me. I spun away from my scanner and missed the handgrip as I grabbed for it. The scanner flickered and changed to another menu, confused that I had left it without instruction, and I threw out one pathetic grasp toward the sorry tiles as I rolled away.

"What happened!" I shouted over the scrambling of the crew and the abrupt howl of the engines.

Nobody bothered to answer me, though several cast me surprised glances. Overhead, the view of space flashed and changed again as parts of the panorama changed back into bulkhead and other parts of the bulkhead flickered and changed to the outside view, which ironically was directly above my head as I ended up flat on my back, nestled under a coil of extension cord—and there, straight out in space, the two working cables that had gone out from our hull had been successfully captured by Oran's ship. They were going to pull us out of the Sands!

Friend or foe? Friend!

"And we need one!" I shoved the coil off my legs and clawed to my knees, crawling under two other crewmen who were stumbling around me. Heartened for the first time in weeks, I watched as Oran's ship fired on Sasaquon, and the turret guns of *Zingara* also fired in spite of our predicament.

The combination of missiles from both ships drove Sasaquon to vector away and stop firing on us, at least for the moment.

Just before I was about to shout for action, demand we take advantage of the moment, Quen came out of an electrical cloud on the starboard side, dropped to one knee, and shouted down into the deck well, "Haul in!"

I heard Zell shout an answer, unintelligible under a squall of surging auxiliary power. This power was a different sound from the main engines, and I tried to identify it and what it was doing; soon enough I understood that this was some kind of donkey engine reeling in those tow cables. Oran's ship was providing us with anchorage, and we were hauling ourselves out of the Sands by reeling our own cables back in. *Zingara* was showcasing her nature as a working industrial ship.

"Haul . . . haul!" I encouraged, murmuring to the ship itself. I saturated my mind with the wonderful illusion of Oran's ship getting closer, though it was actually *Zingara* that was moving.

The color of hostile space filtered slowly from the surging aquamarine blue to the more comforting velvet black as we drew ourselves slowly out of the Sands. The pumping of the donkey engine took on a sensible regular pulse, though it was roaring almost as loudly as the ship's main engines and the power thrusters. There was at least a sense to the sound, a purposeful rhythm that said progress was being made.

In the distance, Sasaquon's ship wallowed, struggling, and flashed, with damage inflicted by the combined shots from us and Oran, but experience told me the respite wouldn't last if we didn't get out of here and fast. I was experienced enough with hostility in space to know that there were few buffers, few really good second chances that didn't somehow make things worse without a great deal of quick creativity, and I didn't know whether these people had that.

"It's working," Lucas uttered, his voice rough. His fear showed clearly now as I looked at his young face and his buttery hair flecked with dirt from the shattered panels above us.

His glint of hope caught me and I stopped looking for a

picture of Oran, instead let myself be enthralled by the sight over the starboard rail. One ship, pendent against the blackness, helping another out of spaceborne quicksand—this was the best part of intelligent life, my favorite part, something I'd seen too seldom in the Delta Quadrant. I found myself hungering for the simple code of ethics employed so widely and freely in the Alpha Quadrant, established early on by the expansion of the Federation. Suddenly I wanted to go home more than ever.

Quen pulled himself along the slanted deck to peer over Lucas's shoulder at the proximity scanner. "How do we look?"

"Almost there," Lucas said, without committing himself with numbers.

Quen turned and called, "Resi, how's the helm feel?"

The young man at the helm, stiff-legged and breathing hard with tension, nodded, shrugged, and choked out, "I'm getting something back."

"Good," Quen gasped back. "I hadn't planned to die till the day after tomorrow."

He gazed out at the spectacle of Sasaquon's ship moving off, out of firing range, probably to duck away for repairs.

Possibly, if we had done enough damage, we'd have a buffer zone to repair our own ship before we came up against the efficient Sasaquon and his red-vested crew again. If only I understood why these people were fighting! Should I even be on the side of the people whose ship I was riding? I didn't have any idea whose team I should cheer for. Sasaquon had attacked us while we were down and damaged, of course, but some rules of war allowed for that perfectly honorably, and did I really dare judge before knowing the history of these people and what was going on?

I had to be on Quen's side for the moment, because that's where my life was and I had to fight for my own life. Whether that would hold, I'd have to see.

As he hovered near me, watching his ship slowly crawl out of the brilliant muck of space trouble, I watched the crease of his intelligent eyes and tried to see the hidden, ravaged youth under the fatigue and burdens he bore. His complexion was dusky, his eyes pouched. His hair, pine-colored, dirty, and dull, was the tired stuff of an overworked person who didn't take good-enough care of himself. There was great relief in his face, but his brow was still creased with worry. Did he think we might not make it?

At any other time I'd have blurted out the question. Not now, though, for I was learning that my voice, on this ship, wasn't so welcome as I was used to.

Was I spoiled by command? Could that be true? Had there been somebody belowdecks on *Voyager* whom I had stopped hearing?

If only I could go back and ask . . .

Abruptly the throbbing belligerence of the donkey engines fell off to a low rumble. Something had changed. The strain was gone. The Sands had released their hold on *Zingara*. Under us the deck heaved, then fell slightly, then came to an even keel. Compensators had found their center, and we could move again without hanging on or losing equilibrium. The difference was quite a physical surprise, like quickly getting up out of a rushing river.

"Quen." Zell appeared, just from the neck up, in the deck well. "We're clear."

"Keep the thrusters going. I want a buffer zone."

"Right."

"Send Vince back up here."

"Vince!"

Quen glanced at me as he turned back toward the view of Oran's ship. He said nothing to me, yet I knew he had in that instant registered my presence, my expression, my reaction, whether I looked afraid or not.

"Quen," Massus called from his place behind the helm, "Oran's releasing our cables. Should I reel in?"

"As quickly as you can," Quen confirmed. "Resi, steer us back toward the wreck, but go in an arch and follow the curve of the Sands so we don't get caught again. Protect the wreck, though."

"Protect it?" I blurted. "From what?"

He didn't answer me, and I almost shouted my question again, except that something about his manner silenced me. He gave me no more than the slightest glance as he concentrated hard on what was happening to his ship and the other two vessels. He was still worried. Why? We'd gotten out of the trouble, hadn't we? What was he still afraid of?

"Here he comes," Lucas said, riveted to his scanner just below where Quen and I were peering out into space.

Quen stepped back a few paces and to his right, away from me. There, he brushed some tiles with his fingertips and stood back again. A set of dark tiles glowed to life, and on came a vision of another ship's interior, another crew, and a helm similar to *Zingara*'s. That ship also was encrusted with tiles. So the general technology was the same, despite the fact that Oran's ship wasn't configured much like *Zingara* on the outside.

A young man who could easily have been in this crew, such were his looks and his clothing, appeared on the tiles. "You're going to have to move," he said bluntly, without the slightest protocol or formality.

"Get Oran, Jara," Quen responded, his voice suddenly brusk.

"Fine."

The man on the screen made a quick motion and stepped out of the screen. Another man appeared, taller, stronger, with coloring similar to Quen's, except that his hair was darker and almost into the navy blues, with glossy accents that were nearly black, and cut shorter.

"Are you out?" Oran asked. *"We can't see too well from here."*

Quen nodded. "Yes, and thank you."

"You're going to have to move out of our way now."

"We'll defend it."

"You don't have the power. We've been starving for a month. We'll take what we can. I'm sorry."

Quen simply nodded again. "Sorry too."

The tiles went dark. Briefly Quen gazed at the dark patch that a moment ago had shown the other captain's face. He rubbed his face, squeezed his tired eyes shut for a few seconds, then pressed both hands to his head as if to hold it on.

"Mmmm . . ." he complained inarticulately. With his eyes still closed, he stomped one foot on the deck. "Zell?"

From below: "What!"

"Get ready."

"Aw! Why can't two things in a row go right?"

"I don't know," Quen uttered. "Massus!"

"I know, I know," the other crewman said without turning.

I looked back there at Massus and, instinctively, all at once, got the idea that he corresponded with the on-bridge engineering office on Starfleet ships. Suddenly things made a little more sense.

Then the sense stopped. A bright white light appeared on the hull of our rescuer's vessel, then another and another. The lights bloomed wider, and at their centers were solid red dots—missiles!

Oran was firing on us!

CHAPTER
6

"I DON'T UNDERSTAND! THEY JUST SAVED US! THEY PULLED US out! They drove off Sasaquon! Why are they firing on us?"

"Later!"

A powerful voice sounded at my side, and two big hands shoved me physically to the side and down out of the way.

I twisted around to see who was manhandling me. Vince, the deck boss, whatever that meant, was back on the main deck, keeping me aside and barking orders to the others. His rusty hair was flecked with insulation and metal shavings—so there was damage below too.

Ducking lower than his grip, I squirmed away from him, and he instantly paid no more attention to me. Somehow I felt less insulted this time and cooperated by staying down and back. They had their hands full, and I didn't know how to help. Thrusting myself into the middle of the problem wouldn't do anything to solve it, and I should've known that from the start. I'd figure all this out, some way or other, I'd add up all that was around me, what I'd heard and seen, balance the inconsistencies, and pick at the technology until the curtains lifted. I'd do it myself, get my answers, and figure out what to do—later.

A flickering memory from my earliest days aboard Starfleet ships came sniggering back: what it was like to have people on board who didn't know what was going on but always tried to push themselves into the middle of things. I'd always hated that and taken solace in Starfleet crews with darned few civilian visitors crowding the bridge at critical moments.

Was that it? Was I spoiled? I'd come into Starfleet through all the right channels, always knowing the rules and understanding what was happening around me. Today I had been thrown into a situation I didn't understand, with a technology I didn't understand, and was being fired upon by people who had just saved my life.

Before I even finished that thought, the ship virtually dissolved around me. The vision of space overhead and to my sides disappeared and was replaced once again by the shoebox of tiled bulkheads, now draining cables and conduits and pieces of hardware, spitting sparks and spewing smoke. I ducked to keep my hair from catching fire again, and saw Quen slam to the deck, driven down by a double explosion directly over his head.

Dazed by the blast, he started to sluggishly roll over, waving at the sprinkle of ship guts spilling all over him, then threw one arm over his head. At first the motion confused me, but almost in the same instant I saw that he was protecting himself from a meter-wide piece of the ceiling material dangling from one fraying cable. He'd be killed if it fell!

I pushed away from the bulkhead where I was huddling and made a wild jump toward the hanging piece just as the cable parted. My left forearm and shoulder rammed the piece in midair and drove it only about two feet forward, but that was enough to miss Quen as the heavy material crashed to the deck and skidded against the forward side of the helm.

Surging forward on momentum and the fact that I was in a clumsy mood, I tripped on Quen's sprawled form and landed on one knee beside him. He reached out and caught my arm, keeping me from tumbling down the deck well, and together we struggled up.

"Are you hurt?" I asked, rasping through a cloud of insulation dust.

Leaning against the chunk of his ship that had almost crushed him, Quen pressed one hand to the back of his head, and another hand to his lower back. "I'll have to be hurt later. Thanks for the quick action; I'd have a hard time running the ship, cut in half."

His joke took me by surprise. "Well, yes . . ."

"Stand aside in case any more comes down."

Supporting himself from step to step, he moved away from me. More and more hits from Oran's ship, unremitting hits, hits without pause, missile after missile, until frustration soaked me as if I'd been dunked in a pond. This relentless attack was even more determined than Sasaquon's selective shots and maneuvers. Quen and his gasping crew fought back, less valiantly than I might've hoped, finally accepting their inability—or was it unwillingness— to fight hard enough to win or to die fighting.

Die? Did I want to die fighting for a hulk in space? There must be more to it, some value I didn't understand yet. They said they'd just had a war; was it really over, or were they lying to me? For the moment, I had to take the situation's word that the wreck out there was worth fighting for.

"Veer off!" Quen finally ordered to Vince, who had taken over the helm. "Give it to him. Lucas, signal that we're breaking battle."

"Hmm," I muttered. "Guess it's not worth a fight."

"After all this . . ." Lucas grimaced in misery, coughed, and turned to follow orders. "Now we starve . . ."

As soon as *Zingara*'s attitude changed, Oran's ship stopped firing on us. At least we had that. Sasaquon had kept firing even after we were caught in the Sands. The vessel around us struggled and crackled, with damage running through most of its systems. Injured crewmen gasped and struggled. Ruvan had appeared and picked his way from injury to injury. At last! Something I could do!

I pushed aside a jumbled coil of worklights and cords, and made my way to the nearest injured crewman. The man was barely breathing as I pulled him out of the way. I found a rag and pressed it to the wound on his neck. Rust-colored blood . . . about the color of Vince's hair. Different from humans, but not as different as Vulcans or Cardassians. Somehow the color was reassuring, silly as that was.

The deep-boned shuddering of *Zingara* gave way to a sick crackle as the old industrial vessel limped away from the wreck she had been defending. The doctor, Ruvan, stumbled to me and with a frightened and gratified glance took over stanching the dangerous wound of his shipmate. I managed a smile, trying to reassure him that things might start going better. That was my job as a commanding . . .

Pushing to my feet, I wiped bloody hands on my trousers, introducing stains of endangered life to the filth of a damaged ship, and made my way across the thirty or so feet to the helm.

"Vince," I began.

The big deck boss didn't even notice me, involved as he was in steering the ship, with a certain anger in his motions, handling two or three jobs at a time rather than just the helm as he should've been, and barking orders at crewmen through the smoke and sparks.

"Vince!"

"What do you want?"

"I'm going to help Ruvan triage the wounded."

"Do what to them?"

"Sort them for treatment. I know something about first aid and I can help."

"Fine. Go help."

"But if I do a good job," I said, "I want something from you when this is over."

"You *want* something from me? What do you want from me?"

Putting my hand on the helm console, I knitted myself to the ship and made a commitment that thirty minutes ago had been unthinkable.

"I want you to train me," I told him. "I'm going to learn how to run this ship."

The better part of a day went by before the *Zingara* settled down and the wounded were stabilized. Poor Ruvan nearly collapsed from exhaustion, trying to treat everybody on board, every injury, new and old. I did my best to help him, but my hands and legs were still bandaged, and there was a limit to my usefulness as a nurse.

I was just covering up a shocky young engineer when Vince appeared at my side and gruffly said, "Quen wants to talk to you."

"About time. Where is he?"

"In his quarters."

"You want to escort me or shall I just go on my own?"

The sarcasm was lost on him. Vince simply pointed forward and said, "You know where it is."

"I certainly do."

"When you come back," he said, "report to me."

Good. Now I could tell Quen I was sure I could help. All I needed was a few weeks of training to learn their engineering.

All this went through my head as I made my way across the half-wrecked deck to the forward bulkhead and to Quen's quarters. Mental lists of what I would say first, middle, and last scrolled through my mind. Wrapped up in my thoughts, I stepped right inside the captain's tiny quarters without even knocking.

Quen sat on the edge of his bunk, not at his desk, and he was speaking to Lucas, whose face flickered on one of the little tile screens. He noticed me but didn't break his communication.

"Go ahead, if you can put us through. I know he wants to talk to me," he said. "He's been trying all day. Can you make the connection?"

"I think I can do it now," Lucas said. *"They're being pretty cheap with the power down deck. I'll try to bleed off a little."*

The screen wobbled briefly, went dark, came light again, and struggled to focus on another face: dark navy hair, familiar bone structure—

Oran! I thought, stepping closer. Are you in communication with him? With the enemy?

"Quen?" our enemy on the screen began. *"I'm glad to see you. When we couldn't make contact, I got worried . . . You look exhausted."*

"I'm glad to see you too," Quen responded, his voice rough with fatigue. "I'm not exhausted. I'm just dusty. The tiles are dirty, too. You're not getting a good picture."

"Who's that with you?"

Quen glanced at me. "We picked up a rescue pod. This woman was in it."

"A woman? In space, here?"

"She's not from here," Quen said wearily. "Sorry we couldn't get your messages earlier. We're trashed over here."

On the flickering screen, Oran frowned. *"I heard you were hurt. Are you?"*

"No, no . . . just the same old aches."

"You're a bad liar," Oran told him. *"Listen to me now. I can trade the wreck in right away and arrange an air drop. You could pick it up on the other side of Lucarta Cluster, and no one will know."*

Quen moved his stiff shoulders. "Too big a risk for you. Sasaquon would find out. He's got eyes everywhere. And it's against your Pledge. I won't let you do that, Oran. We'll see to ourselves. I think we can make basic repairs in a month or so . . . but we've lost our rod level controls, and for that I need replacement parts. We're also down on fuel, and the forward top tiles are almost all fried."

Incredulous, I watched all this, but kept my mouth shut—and that took some doing. He was telling Oran details that could be useful to an enemy. Indignation gave a little way to curiosity. Somehow this all had to make sense eventually. The pieces of this dizzy puzzle would come together or I would simply force them into place. These two men, these enemies, spoke to each other with a strange warmth, even devotion. And only hours ago they had cut into each other's hulls!

"Have you got enough food?" Oran asked.

"Yes, plenty, no problem," Quen told him. "We made a good trade last month. Still living on it."

On the screen, Oran's expression was undisguised misery. He knew, and so did I, that Quen was lying.

Oran shifted his weight, forcing the screen to bobble to keep him in the middle. *"I don't like leaving you out here."*

"We'll have another chance. I have to go now."

"Take care, will you?"

"Don't worry."

Without any further words, Quen simply reached for the

tiles and brushed them with his fingertips. The picture of Oran went dark, leaving only the dull brushed metallic tile squares now pretending to be a wall.

Quen pressed his hands to his face, rubbed his eyes, then drew a deep breath and turned to me. "I know," he said. "Oran's our enemy, and you don't know what's going on."

"No, I don't," I told him. "That was critical information you gave Oran. You people have the strangest chivalry I've ever seen. Are these your enemies or not?"

"They're . . . our competitors."

"They tried to kill us."

"After they pulled us from the Sands," he clarified.

"And I don't understand that. Were they trying to give us a fair chance?"

Quen stretched one leg and winced, then rested back on his bunk, prompted on one elbow. "Oran had to fire on us until he could take the prize. He owes it to his crew, just as I owe mine."

"Why would you give him crucial information?"

"Why not? The battle's over. They won. They won't fight anymore."

"That's very naive of you, Captain," I said with a little shake of my head. "If it profits him to defeat you, eventually he *will* take advantage of any information he has."

"Not this."

"Why not? Why do you say that?"

"Because Oran's my brother."

Stunned, as he obviously expected, I sank back and leaned against a small ledge on the bulkhead. "Your brother. You don't mean that figuratively? You had the same parents?"

He nodded. "I used to steal his candy."

"And the relationship's amicable?" I pressed. "His attempts to help were genuine?"

"He'd still try to help us if I didn't stop him. So you don't have to worry about Oran. I'll do what I have to do for my ship and mates to survive. Oran's under the same obligation."

"What about Sasaquon?"

"He's . . . hard to understand sometimes. He'll kill us if he gets the chance."

"Then why didn't you accept Oran's offer of help?"

"Oran knows I can't accept. He's my brother and I don't want him compromised in the eyes of his crew. He's just torn between his Pledge and his brother." Quen flexed his shoulders again and sighed. "You're new here. There's a lot you don't know. Give yourself time to understand—"

"Yes, I'll understand everything eventually, but you have a very confusing operation going here. I know you think I've got some kind of space madness and you're treating me like a charity case. You just don't believe me, and I guess I can't blame you. After all, I can't suddenly develop transwarp for you. I could describe it, but you don't have the infrastructure to build it. I can make little improvements within your technological ability, but the question is . . . *should* I?"

"What do you mean, 'should' you?"

"My fleet swears to a directive that we won't interfere in developing cultures, but that starts to get vague once a culture discovers hyperlight travel. We can't explore *and* quarantine ourselves at the same time. We can't stand guard over a future that hasn't happened, or we'd never pull a drowning child out of a lake. I don't know what to do, really. Why should I care? You don't even believe me. Probably I wouldn't believe me, either."

My words trailed off as I realized I'd started to ramble, let my thoughts fall out of my head like seeds from a gourd.

Uneasily, Quen gazed at me, wondering just how crazy I really was. "Well, we don't know you . . ."

"No, you don't know me, but . . . damn it!" Frustration put a peak on my tone and I quickly fought for control.

"You don't know the roads," he said quietly, "you don't know the markers or lines, you talk about technology that can't possibly work, you want us to go somewhere without knowing how we'll get back . . . and you want us to treat you like a captain?"

I folded my arms and shook my head. "Sounds silly, I suppose."

"Well, far-fetched. This story about being 'thrown' so far from your home and trying to get back there . . . I've never heard of anything like that. And this civilization you say was attacked, we've never heard of them either."

"The Iscoy," I said, irritated. "They were decent people,

incredibly helpful and welcoming. I didn't make them up, Captain. They lent us their spacedock, their materials, and even said that if we tired of our journey we could live with them. 'Stay with us,' they said, just like that. I'd be a liar if I said I wasn't tempted. A home for my crew, the warmth of a sun . . . but we're Starfleet officers and we belong in the Federation. We have a sworn duty to report what we know and take what we've learned back to the civilization that gave us our lives, our careers, and a ship to take us to the stars. We have as much obligation to them as to our families. The ship wasn't our personal plaything to possess and enjoy. It was an investment by the people of the Federation and we owe them. It's not just our desire to get home, it's our duty."

Yes, perhaps I was just venting, but it felt good to say all this to him. Maybe he would sense some trace of truth in my heartfelt words. So I let myself ramble. Often the truth spills from a toppled barrel.

His expression suggested a captain's empathy. He seemed to hear something in my tirade that the commander of a ship would understand. At least, if he didn't believe me entirely, he believed me a little bit.

Sensing it was time to throw him a bone of cooperation, I tried to appear more relaxed and cooperative by unfolding my arms and simply rubbing my aching fingers. "In light of that, I appreciate that you finally agreed to talk to me."

At this, Quen paused, got to his feet, and winced again at whatever was hurting him.

"Only to assure you," he began, "that hopefully within a month, two at the most, you'll be put off the ship."

Sharply I pushed away from the bulkhead. "Why! Why would you put me off?"

He gazed at me, both disturbed and confused by my reaction. "We have to find a place to trade for air. When we do, we'll make connections for you to go to a planet or an outpost where you can be comfortable and your injuries can—"

"But *why?*"

"Why . . ." Quen scratched his head, ruffled his hair out of his eyes, and frowned. "Women don't belong in space. We don't have women on our ships."

"Look, Captain," I began sharply, "I understand what your people believe, but I'm trained for space and I want to stay out here!"

"Already, some of our more suspicious men want you put off *Zingara* before anything happens to you, and I'm sorry to have brought you onto a ship that might be doomed. If we can't get air and supplies, we might be finished. If a woman died on my ship, I couldn't live with myself."

"Why didn't you accept Oran's help, then?" I asked again. "If things are that bad?"

"We can't join up. That would constitute a confederation. It's against the laws, and we always defend the laws. I just wanted to promise you that we would try to get you off as soon as possible. Until then, and we're sorry about this too, but you'll have to do some work."

My hands shook with bottled indignation and the cold realization that I could be in big trouble. The idea of being put off the ship terrified me. I'd come here hoping to be a hero, finally able to show how much I knew, tell them what they were doing wrong, show them how to fight. Instead, I was in the way, I was a woman, I was going to be put off. Stranded on some planet? Put off into a culture where I'd be the alien woman at the end of the block? Someday I'd graduate to being the weird old lady alien at the end of the block? No, thanks!

And I was very possibly the only person in the quadrant who knew how to defeat the Menace. What about that? I'd been in the wrong place at the wrong time, with the right knowledge to interpret what I was seeing, and I was being told there would be no chance for me to act upon it. When the Menace came, I'd be planet-locked.

My chin tucked as I tried to control my tone. "Captain, I already asked to be trained. Vince is going to train me."

"Train you?"

"Yes. I'm a Starfleet-licensed senior warp engineer. If Vince or somebody can familiarize me with your—"

"Vince already said you were getting in the way out there today."

That didn't do anything for my tone.

"In the way!" I erupted. "Was I 'in the way' when I saved your life?"

He shrugged and conceded with a nod. "No, that was very nice and quick of you."

"Nice and *quick . . ."*

"But you can't stay. We can't devote the resources to training you for the down decks because you won't be here to use what you learn. The crew would be very distracted by a woman on board all the time. They'd be looking out for you too much."

"I don't need looking after!"

"That wouldn't matter," he said quietly. The empathy in his face was absolutely enraging. "I'm sorry . . . I don't want *Zingara* to be the ship where a woman died. You're not staying. You've got a month. Maybe two. I hope just one."

CHAPTER
7

MENIAL WORK. PETTY, MENIAL WORK. THE DULLEST, MOST repetitive, most numbing task on this entire vessel fell to me. Me, the captain of a Federation starship, a qualified senior engineer, a top-scoring graduate of Starfleet Academy, with an enviable service record and socks older than most of these boys, and I was scraping tiles.

Things settled down quickly, out of necessity. The damage was being slowly repaired, and every day Ruvan scurried about like a mad hare, trying to treat the wounded. Nobody spoke much. Nobody complained at all. They joked some.

They wouldn't even let me repair the circuits behind the tiles. My job was to repair the tiles, clean the tiles, scrape the adhesive, ream the grout. The tiles were energy capacitors that stored solar power like batteries that emptied themselves in an instant, but there was more to them. They also served somehow as pixels in the huge virtual-space viewscreen and in smaller groups as scanner screens. As I worked on them, I became less and less sure that they were made of metal, though they looked metallic. They *felt* ceramic, but I came to doubt that too. They were made out of some kind of amalgam or composite. Some were beveled. Others had squared-off edges. My tools were the toothbrush, its reaming pick on the other end, a file, an adhesive neutralizer, a polishing gel, a shammy cloth, and creeping mental paralysis.

Hour by hour, day by day, I figured out that their idea of time was a little different from mine, but not unmanageable. Their idea of a day rounded out to my idea of thirty hours—comfortable with a little adjustment for sleeping. Their idea of a week was about the same as mine, and a month was a few days longer.

In actual function, I got *more* sleep than I was used to. The working day, though, was much longer. They ran two watches instead of three, and there was no real "off" time. We just worked all the time we weren't sleeping. There was certainly plenty to do.

Scrape, scrape, flake, flake, ream . . . sharpen, bevel . . . and the tiles weren't the same color, either. These in front of me were opalescent, pearly. Those over my shoulder were drab blue-gray. The only consistency was their size and the fact that they encrusted most of the interior of the *Zingara*. They had to be kept clean of crust, moisture, dust, and adhesive swell, or energy could bleed off—and polished, or they wouldn't show their pixel in focus.

I felt like I was doing somebody's fingernails. Ten thousand times.

Scrape, file, buff, buff, scrape, pick—

"Daughter of a Starfleet *admiral* . . . top of my *class* . . . Departmental Award in warp *physics* . . . used to have tidy *hair* . . . look at me *now* . . ."

One month, maybe two. I had one month to get out of this sector somehow. Or one month to show these people that I was worth having around. I fought to remember who put me in this position in the first place: the Menace. Mental calculations, guesses, bits of information, and mathematical voodoo kept nagging at me, telling me this: Given the kinds of methods I saw used by an aggressor civilization against the Iscoy, added up with the scarcity of large settlements in this sector, the Menace would eventually come here. Sooner or later, they would chew their way across the Quadrant, heading toward Quen's people because—what a target! They didn't have a clue how to fight!

A pair of boots appeared beside me—Zell, picking at the bulkhead beside me. As I scooted out of his way, I noticed that Quen was standing there too. Quen watched as his first officer twisted a couple of toggles and pulled open an access drum. Swallowing the pretty obvious annoyance that they thought I was now talking to myself and answering too, I listened to their conversation about the engineering. Making sense of their technical jargon through a translator had its limitations, so I was careful also to watch, to see which components they were pointing to and what they called them and what they said.

My stomach crawled as I listened—not because of anything they said or did, but because I realized I was learning a technology that might be in my future. I didn't want to admit that, to commit to this space, this life. Sitting here listening, etching into my memory a new technology, made me complicit in my own isolation.

I had a few suggestions but kept them to myself. Why should they listen to me? Why should they believe my stories? I didn't look like a captain, that was for sure. I didn't know anything about this space, the channels or markers, couldn't tell a warning from a nav beacon. I might be a spy or a Jonah. A lunatic. They were all uneasy around me, not used to having women around. Quen had put me to work because I was a mouth to feed and I should work my passage, and also, I knew, to help stave off suspicion.

Scrape . . . pick, pick . . . buff . . .

"Why don't you let your women and children into space?"

The question just popped out. Had to get this started somehow.

The two looked at each other with that "Is she crazy?" expression I was getting used to.

"We would never do that," Quen ultimately said. "It would be disrespectful."

His brows drew as he eyed me for reaction. He was disgusted that I'd even suggested it and was wondering what kind of people I came from. I was wondering the same about them, but also had to admit I'd misjudged their reasons for all-male crews.

"Life is hard and ugly in space," Quen continued when I didn't respond. "Women shouldn't have to see it."

Zell picked at a spool-shaped component in the thing they were working on and added, "I would never want my mother to see it."

"What if your mother wants to see it?" I asked.

"She wouldn't," he snapped back.

Quen finished, "I've never known a woman who wanted this kind of existence."

Whether they were deliberately giving me a dig, I couldn't really tell . . . No, I didn't think so. Though I watched carefully for indications that they were sending me a sideward insult, nothing surfaced but their contempt for the way they were forced to live. No point arguing the feminist case. After all, this wasn't my culture. Sooner or later I would find my way back to the Iscoy and chase the wild chance that anybody from my crew survived the Menace attack. Then we'd continue our voyage back to the Alpha Quadrant, back to home, where we fit in.

"If this life is so unsatisfying," I asked, "why stay yourselves?"

"We have to stay."

Continuing to scrape, pick, and buff, I decided to backtrack a little as long as they were held captive by the work they were doing, and press for a few answers.

"Because you lost your war?"

"Who told you that?" Zell blurted.

Quen motioned him silent. "Lost? We won."

I stopped working. "You certainly have a peculiar definition of victory. What did you fight for? The right to squabble over salvage with Sasaquon and Oran? Are you telling me *they* lost?"

"No, they won too," Zell said. "We were all on the same side."

"Well, you're going to have to explain that one."

Dumbfounded by this ill-informed dolt they'd picked up, the two men eyed me, then each other again. I thought they were going to tell me to find out for myself, bother somebody else, don't disturb the command team, but Quen shrugged and told Zell, "If she's going to be here, she deserves to know. Make it short."

Insulted that he wasn't going to take the time to explain himself, I cast Quen my best disapproving glower as he pushed to his feet and climbed across a scatter of tools and cables, then disappeared into the lower deck well.

When I turned back, Zell was giving me a series of annoyed glances as he worked. He didn't want to talk to me. How infuriating! On my ship, I, the captain, would've taken the time to explain our situation to the lowliest of deckhands, and certainly to a rescued wayfarer. What kind of people were these?

"Well?" I prodded. "You have your orders, right?"

Unhappily, he huffed, "Keep working." Then he began: "The Assembly had to fight a war on the planet and in space with the Assosa Shan."

"Another planet?"

"No, it's the western continent on our planet. They wanted to absorb our nation into theirs again, using some ancient land claim as an excuse. We used to be part of them, but our forefathers fought for independence three centuries ago and established our own continental government."

"Sounds familiar. Sorry—go ahead."

"The Assembly had no fighting ships, so they hired all the private ships around and gave us the right to fight as official ships of war."

"Like privateers," I murmured.

He shrugged. "Whatever that means."

"It means a government issuing raiding rights to private ships during wartime."

"Well . . . that's it. What was that word again?"

"Privateers."

"That's a good word for it."

"What's your word for it."

"Our word for ourselves, you mean?"

"Yes."

"We're warranters."

"Warranters. That sounds almost the same as privateers. A warrant . . . letters of marque . . . a license to raid given by the current authority, right?"

Zell pondered all this, and I was struck by his apparent care and desire to get the story straight. Ultimately he decided, "Uh . . . I guess that's it."

"You won this war?" I pressed on.

"We won and their government collapsed. The Assembly absorbed them, and suddenly there were billions more people who had come from a destroyed nation, all scrambling to survive. I don't know how to explain this to you . . . We were being oppressed and we threw the oppressors off. Now we have to take care of their people too."

Zell paused now and stopped working, as if he couldn't do two things at once and explaining this to me in short form took all his concentration. I didn't say anything. Better he have the chance to organize his thoughts.

"After the war, the Assembly government was unstable," he said. "While we were trying to recover, the people we fought to get into power fell out of power, and a council of citizens came into power just long enough to stabilize everything. It's called the TCA. Temporary Civilian Authority."

"Uh-oh . . ." I stopped working and gave him a suspicious glare of understanding. "I don't like the sound of that. Just how long has this temporary authority been 'temporary'?"

Zell sniffed and wiped a greasy hand on his shirt. "Six years."

"Six years? You've been out here, like this, for *six years?* Six years is not temporary!"

He dived back into his work, and I could see that my words annoyed him.

I urged him to keep filling me in. "If you won the war, why don't you just go home?"

"After we won the war for them, the new Assembly didn't know what to do with us. They owe us payment for years of loyal service. They went into truce with the other hemisphere and mutually declared us on our own."

"Because they didn't want to pay you? Sounds like your 'new' government is corrupt."

"I don't know," he said morosely. "They aren't . . . living like we thought they would. They aren't using the principles we fought for."

"And you've been supporting yourselves by salvaging the wrecks from the war?"

"We're trying to survive until things change again. We scrupulously obey the laws because we don't want to turn into real pirates. If we start breaking laws, the Assembly can make their actions seem legitimate. Eventually things will change. Bad people will cycle out of power. It always happens . . . sooner or later . . ."

"Unfortunately it's usually later and after a lot of damage. 'Do your best and hope things change' doesn't usually work in the long run. Why can't you just go home?"

"Go home and live unfree? We face a prison sentence for not coming in, and after that's served, we'll be assigned to a farm or a factory, and be fed, and be given a cubicle to live in. That's not what we fought for. We won't go and be oppressed. If we can't live as free individuals, we won't go back. Everything we fought for will be given up."

"You mean they won't kill you, but you'll live as serfs?"

Zell twitched as if he'd suddenly developed a rash. Clearly he didn't like even reminding himself of these unfortunate facts. "The only way we can live as free individuals is in space. So this is our life now."

"Mmm," I uttered. " 'Live free or die.' "

He looked up. "What?"

"The state slogan of, uh . . . New Hampshire. 'Live free or die.' "

A mirthless chuckle huffed from him. "I like that."

"I've always liked it too," I told him, letting my solicitousness for their problem show through. "Sounds like your new leaders are setting the warranters up against each other."

His brow drew tight as my words galvanized thoughts that he didn't like hearing. "And passing laws that keep us from banding together."

"Like what?" I asked. "What kind of legal language could stipulate that?"

"Easy. If we join together in a common purpose, it constitutes a hostile confederation."

"Oh, yes—Quen mentioned that, but I didn't know what he meant. That does sound like the paranoid afterglow of a war."

"None of the captains would break the Pledge to his own crew. So we have to fight each other. We can barely keep our own crews and families alive. Especially now that Oran's got the salvage rights to that prize. That wreck would've fed us for half a year."

From across the deck, Massus interrupted, "Doesn't mean he can keep them."

And several of the men laughed as they relentlessly worked. Zell smiled and shared a glance with them.

"Can't you at least help each other in little ways?" I pestered. "Medical supplies, food?"

"Can't. If you do, you've broken the Pledge to your own crew."

"If you're so desperate," I asked carefully, "why did you rescue me, knowing you might end up with another mouth to feed?"

"Good question!" Vince's roar tumbled up from just inside the deck well.

Damn it! He was in a perfect position to eavesdrop down there!

Everybody laughed—except me. Then, after a moment and many relatively friendly glances from the crew, I did feel a smile creep over my dissatisfaction with all this.

"Most of us rescue survivors in good faith," Zell went on. "It's part of the Pledge."

"This Pledge . . . it bonds you to your ship and shipmates, but not to other ships?"

He paused, then agreed, "Basically. It bonds us to our ships and shipmates *first*. It also bonds us to the law we fought to defend."

"Laws like the one that says you're forming a hostile confederation if you help each other?"

He only nodded. Apparently he thought this was a raw deal.

I agreed. "That's why Quen and his brother are forced to compete and can't join forces?"

"They fought side by side for years. Now they have to fight each other, even kill each other, to keep their crews alive. We're all obliged to do anything we can to keep our ships and crews going. We're the last light of freedom . . ." His voice trailed off as he cranked on a tool and grimaced with the effort. "It's getting harder. But, if we band together, the TCA has authorized itself to confiscate our homes and arrest our women and children. As it is now, if we stay separate, they leave our wives and mothers alone."

"So you're forced into a situation where you have to compete to survive, like tribes in a desert. Or a pride of lions."

"Right. We have to compete."

"Why not go somewhere else? Take your families, make a light jump, find yourselves a comfortable planet somewhere, and settle it. Start over with—"

My words trailed out. The rest of the nearby crew had stopped working and were gazing at me with peculiar expressions of deep feeling. Their eyes, their silence, stopped me. Suddenly I felt bad about asking.

I held up a solicitous hand. "I'm sorry. Of all people, I should know . . . home is home. It's the civilization your fathers and mothers built, the one you want to fight for and keep on a good track . . . the one where you have a common heritage and a common future. There's something to that. I didn't mean to diminish it."

Contempt burned in Zell's eyes. "Enough talking. You'll learn what you need to know later. We have work to do."

Turning back to my tiles, I forced myself to accept that. While I was used to getting answers when I needed them, the message was seeping through my command skull that I wasn't the top of the totem pole anymore and couldn't just demand attention.

As Zell started down the deck well, I threw one more request over my shoulder. "I do have one more question."

Up to his shoulders in the well, he paused. "What's that?"

"Does anybody on this ship know how to give a haircut?"

Now I had the ducks lined up. There'd been a war on a planet with a spacefaring culture, so some of the war had lopped out into space. The salvagers were hired as privateers, "warranters," basically a makeshift navy, licensed to harass enemy shipping. But these were merchant guys, not soldiers. From what I'd seen, they'd developed a few basic tactics, but nothing like the training I'd received at Starfleet Academy or in my years in the service of starships. All the myriad tactics from hand-to-hand combat to space-battle strategic maneuvers were at my fingertips. For years I'd studied the history of warfare for two reasons, to avoid the mistakes and imitate the victories. These people had none of that training, nothing to call upon. They were merchant seamen trying to do what soldiers should do. They weren't soldiers. They didn't know how to *think* like soldiers.

And the corrupt new government was taking advantage of that. In my very few off-hours, I snuggled up with a tile screen and found my way through their basic recent history, and found some curious facts. These people had fought for certain principles of decency and rule of law, but after the war, during the time of upheaval that follows any total collapse, the leaders they'd fought for had been shoved out and nothing less than the old monarchy had wafted itself back into power. They had suspended the working government on the excuse of taking strong action to hold the Assembly together. I suspected from the news releases available that for six years the victory had been betrayed and the old monarchy was busy galvanizing itself while pretending to be temporary. The "Temporary Civilian Authority" was neither of those adjectives.

So here I was, trapped in a culture at least a hundred years behind my technology, where I recognized some things, but most were not up to my level, where warp two was the top speed, and scanners and sensors were weak by my standards. It was as if I'd been dropped on a Quaker farm with an idea of how an airplane might someday work but no way to build it. And I knew the big airplanes were out there and coming this way.

These thoughts I kept to myself. Neither Quen nor any of his crew really saw the scope of what could happen. There didn't seem to be anything like this in their history. They had no experience with government subversion except in theory. Certainly it was all over Earth's history, and I'd seen this kind of betrayal happen several times in the Alpha Quadrant at large—Klingons, Cardassians, Orions. If it hadn't happened in this sector, maybe they just didn't know what could occur. Maybe they really were naive.

I wasn't going for a degree in history, and truth be told, I didn't care that much. My immediate goal was to understand enough about the situation to get myself out of it. I was in trouble. I had a month to change things. How could I possibly do that? I couldn't gain authority on this ship in a month . . . not past Zell and Vince, and certainly not past Quen.

So I scraped tiles and waited for my chance.

After a week or so, in fact, the strangest thing began happening to me—I got custodial about the damned tiles. I'd never really done deckhand work, and there was something therapeutic about this nonmental activity. I had used my hands for study, entertainment, art, interest, play, but rarely for ordinary everyday work. It started to matter to me that the tiles were clean, well reamed, properly filed, polished, and bonded back into place evenly. As I worked, I was slowly reducing myself from the artisan of overview I'd always been to the detail craftsman I'd never been. Before long, the most important thing became my tiles. Pride rested in the tile I'd just buffed. Challenge existed in the dirty one next to it. Satisfaction came in the nods and pats of approval from my shipmates . . . and then, the most ego-fluffing moment of all—two of the crew came over to me and asked me how I was getting the bevel so even, and how to do their tiles better! What a great feeling!

What a strange and unexpected gift, this peace of purpose . . . I'd never dropped down in my career. I'd only gone up. And started fairly high at that—fresh out of Starfleet Academy with credentials that put me above the noncoms on any ship. I was instantly part of any command team around me. I'd never vacuumed a corridor or worked the ship's laundry. For a long time I'd enjoyed the inflexibility of command, and now I was down in the decidedly elastic saddle of lower deck work. I had to be more buoyant than ever before. It had been a long time since I'd taken an order.

How strange it was to force myself not to care about duties that didn't involve me. Why were those two engineers hurrying? What was Quen talking to Vince about? Who was going to recalibrate that system over there? Why were we changing course? Suddenly I didn't have to listen to every conversation. The decisions weren't mine anymore. Here, sitting on the ignoble deck, scraping, reaming, picking, I was learning to be a crewman again.

Something else too . . . It was a relief, somehow. For the first time in years, I wasn't the one making the big decisions. I couldn't influence what was going on around me. So I concentrated on my tiles, and my mind began slowly to shut down and rest.

With the therapy of menial work, the quiet and peace of doing something with my hands instead of my brain, creeping comprehension stole in. The ship, my *Voyager*, was really gone. Destroyed, blown up, utterly out of reach. All the delusions that my former crew somehow might've gotten away finally came to land in the vacuum left by this new peace. Until now I had made myself believe, however fleetingly, that the *Voyager* escaped from the Menace attack and was on its way toward home.

Slowly, as I scraped and polished, reality crept in. The faces of Chakotay, Paris, Seven, Tuvok, and all my crewmates began to swim past me as if waving good-bye. I knew what I'd seen. My goal was gone. Over. I was more than forty years old and wouldn't survive to see the Federation in my lifetime, not without a ship and crew who also wanted to go there, unique in our mutual dependence simply because we had no one else upon whom to depend.

Things were as bad as I could imagine. My ship was destroyed, my crew dead. I had failed to protect them, and failed again to go down with them. The adventure of our lifetimes had cost our lives.

Except for me . . . the captain who failed to go down with her ship. I didn't want to be alive anymore.

What I lacked was the courage to do away with myself. Instead, I scraped tiles and mourned. Probably I should be comforted that they died quickly, together, weren't left to watch each other suffer . . . I never knew it could be so shriveling to have nothing to live for.

I'd never given in to depression in my life. There had always been choices and chances, alternatives, tricks. Not this time. What did I have now to distract me? Not even dreams of the ship gone on its way without me. No images of my crew gone off on adventures to cheer and envy. All that remained to me was grim awareness that all my satisfactions to date had been fraudulent. Darkening in sorrow and nursing bitterness about *Voyager*, I became acutely aware of the curious glances from Quen's crew. Why did I feel their eyes like hidden creatures in a forest? Why did I hear their voices like crickets snapping silent the second I looked?

Damn everything! This was unmindful torture and I was doing it to myself! I was giving in to the sick awareness that I was probably the only human being left in the Delta Quadrant. Throw in a dash of guilt at having survived, spice with humility, and mix thoroughly. Bake on a deep dark deck until ripe and oozing.

Oh, I had to do better than this!

Instantly lightning flashed in my head and I knew what my problem was. Since I'd crawled into that rescue pod, I'd been trailing the events that happened around me. I had to get ahead of this game! I had to start *leading* events somehow. The key to that machine—shake off the quavering doubts of grief and ream, scrape, pick, and polish better than anybody ever had in the history of tile capacitors. That was the way to get ahead! Make yourself more valuable than the job you're doing. If you're going to swab a deck, make it the best-swabbed deck ever!

I went after the tiles as if they were my children, my salvation. I became the tile police. I buffed my assigned units, then took the initiative and went after places nobody else was tending. The interior of the ship actually started to glow a little, the tiles were so clean and even. There were no more dusty niches. Rewards came in the form of grudging respect and those nods of approval from my shipmates, and even from Vince—once.

There wasn't much time or energy for self-congratulation. We were heavily damaged. Food, power, water, everything was being rationed. After some days, when real hunger bit into my guts, I absorbed the true depth of Quen's struggle for survival. Losing the wreck to Oran deprived *Zingara* of a way to sustain itself in the immediate future. Medical supplies were very low too. Ruvan did not possess either the skills or resources of our medical program on *Voyager,* nor did he have the computer-calm objectivity of our Doctor. Ruvan was a bag of emotion and suffered greatly with each of his patients. When I looked at him, I saw a distraught kid, practically an intern, generally self-taught and trying to swim up a waterfall.

As I explored the ship and figured things out, I discovered that *Zingara* was about fifty feet longer that I'd first estimated, and below the main deck there was not just one engineering deck, but an engineering deck and a trying-out deck. On that lowest deck was a whole factory for processing salvage. A wreck could be pulled up to *Zingara*'s beam and very efficiently stripped, recycled down to its base metals, and stored as separate components, which could then be traded to anyone who needed those specific parts, metals, plastics, electronics, or anything else that could be salvaged.

We were saved from immediate extinction by discovery of a rather small free-roaming satellite left over from the war, no longer in any use, which we pounced on with relish, tried out, and sold to a passing broker of apparently dubious connections. This gave us enough supplies to struggle forward for a few more weeks, and it also gave me a chance to watch Quen's crew process a find.

The trying-out process was much quicker and less risky than towing a wreck some great distance to a place where it could be parted and brokered, and of course the wrecks were much more valuable already processed and parted out. I found myself wishing I could see it in full operation, with a big wreck.

No chance for that now; we'd lost our big wreck and apparently they were rare. Oran had possession and all the profits. If these people could find some way to band together, they could not only survive but flourish. They were holding scrupulously to a set of rules and laws, hoping to hold the upper hand someday, at which point they could also possess dignity and honor. If they lived that long.

Yes, the wrecks would be thinning out if this were the way of life for six years after a war. There could only be so many, after all. What would Quen and his crew, and the other warranters and their crews, do after all the wrecks were gone?

And what would an ill-starred expatriate do then? What would I do?

CHAPTER
8

"HE'S BACK! HE FOUND US!"

"We've got an approach!"

"Where's Quen?"

"Othien, wake him up!"

"We're not ready . . . we're not ready . . ."

"Too bad Sasaquon didn't ask if we were ready. Get Quen!"

"Get this junk off the deck!"

"Are you at the scanners?"

"No, I've got to finish the jeklights!"

"Who's at the scanners?"

"Somebody come here with a hex shank and put this conduit back together!"

"They're firing!"

"Turn the ship! He's got us broadside if we don't turn!"

"What angle do you want?"

"Head-on!"

"Whose mucks are piled up on the compensator lid? Get these out of here!"

"The harpoon gunners aren't ready for head-on. We won't be able to aim."

"Secure the kick panel on the control stanchion, or somebody's going to get electrocuted."

"Vid's not up."

"Can somebody get over to these scanners, please? Because we're about to die. Morning, Quen."

"What's happening?"

"We're about to get killed."

"Before breakfast? Never mind the kick panel, Resi, just steer the ship. Don't step in that lube jelly. Angle nine over the prad and bleed the compensators while we have the chance. How close is he? What's his angle?"

Absolute chaos. I couldn't believe what I was seeing. They'd known all along that they were in a dangerous situation, depleted and damaged, yet they'd lulled themselves into a quiet recuperation and weren't prepared at all for what now knocked at our door. Sasaquon was coming back, probably before all his damage was repaired, just so he could get a jump on us while we were still weakened.

And here I crouched, holding my tile toothbrush and looking over a sea of cables and tools and tripping crewmen. The deck roiled under us as we took hits from Sasaquon's missile cannons. He'd gotten the jump on us and we were taking fast initial damage on the outer hull. Even as the off-duty crew tumbled out of their bunks and the watch team scrambled for their posts, emergency lights and warnings flashed all over the main deck tiles. Sparks flew everywhere, inflicting nasty little burns and breaking concentration all over the deck.

Near the aft transverse bulkhead, Quen pressed his hand against the helm stanchion to favor his injuries, not bothering to hide the strain and muscle tension of old-fashioned pain. He had too much on his mind and could hide only so much. Right now fear would have to be the hidden thing and pain would have to just show.

On the tile scanners that did manage to struggle to pictures, various images of Sasaquon's ship *Aragore* and our *Zingara* jockeyed for position, crowded into awkward maneuvers by the proximity of the crackling, rock-strewn Lucarta Cluster to our port side and something called Tauma, a lava flow of ancient but active gas eruptions, boiling below us.

They were either good cover or we were trapped—I couldn't tell which yet.

Thud.

"He's got a harpoon hook on us!"

Lucas's desperate cry rose above a bitter crashing sound that vibrated right up through my boots and into my bones. I stumbled to his side and looked at the tile scanner directly in front of him.

On the tiles was a computer generated representation of our ship, lumbering in space and turning on an invisible spit. A nasty-looking claw hook had embedded in *Zingara's* side. Around us, as the thrusters heaved, the ship let out an *oof* at the piercing of her lung. Now a sinister string on the picture twisted through space, linking us to the powerful *Aragore*. On the ship-positional screen the cable was only a thread, but on the nearby analysis screen a cross-section of the cable showed a strong braided inner core, and a fully served outer sheath. Extrapolating the size of everything I saw, I guessed the cable was probably as big around as I was and, oh, a little tougher.

"What's he doing?" I demanded. "Why is he trying to take us under tow?"

Picking at the screens, trying to focus the tiles, Lucas panted through a grip of pure fear.

"If he gets a shock line on us, he can coat the ship with racker waves. Numb our nervous systems with it. You've never felt anything like it. I hate it! It's like your head is dying and your arms and legs are already dead. He'll be able to tow us over a zone limit and claim he caught us there. That violates the Assembly's edict about—"

"Never mind! I get the picture."

Now, don't forget I was still suffering in plenty of ways. My arms and legs hadn't entirely healed and were itching like bugs under the wrappings, half my mind lingered with the Menace, with the Iscoy victims who I been forced to abandon, and I didn't know enough about this ship to jump in and do something drastic. Certainly the moment Sasaquon attacked I dropped the tile tools and at least started pulling the cords and parts aside so the crew could move around without ending up flat on their faces, netted by the trash of maintenance. It gave me something to do while I tried to think of something better.

Sure, I could've dropped through the deck well and started tampering with the engines, trying to boost power, redirect energy to the weapons and thrusters. Certainly I knew enough about physics and mechanics to help down there, but what good would it do to try? The engineers would gawk at me and shove me out of the way and demand what I was doing, and I didn't have time to explain or prove one damned thing.

I couldn't take them help; Othien had it now, though he seemed baffled by the maneuver Quen had ordered.

"Get insulated!" Quen called suddenly. "Don't touch anything! Othien, let go of the yoke!"

Did he see something I'd missed?

Pushing to my feet, I shouted, "Captain! What do you mean, don't touch anything! You're taking the crew away from their controls? Giving up the helm? Why!"

"Shut up!" Zell boomed as he crawled out of the well and vaulted over the railing. "You don't know what we're up against! Quit interrupting us!"

Stomping down the deck toward him, I put my nose right under his and glared up there. "I know you weren't prepared for what could happen and now you're in more trouble than you have to be, I sure know that! Why don't you shut down that processing station below and concentrate on your battle capabilities! It's a little late now, isn't it?"

"Woman!"

Oh, wonderful—Vince.

"Get back from the command deck! Leave Quen alone! Back in your place!"

I whirled to meet him as he thunked toward me. "My place? What am I, a parrot out of a cage? I can help you, if you'd just *let* me!"

Boom—another hit got us so squarely amidships on the upper hull that I felt like something had landed on my head. The deck-length vid system was down, so we couldn't see a damned thing through the overhead or abeam tiles. No more big window. Just the shoebox. We were really broken.

Quen pressed between us and shouted over the whine of

the ship around us. "Insulate! Vince, you're standing in a puddle. Get one of your crew to buffer the starboard jeklights. Kay, this isn't the time."

Pure fury numbed my whole brain. I hated him for being calm and being right. My head started buzzing such as no anger had buzzed it before. My hands and feet tingled and my spine stiffened. What a time to have a dizzy flash.

Caught up in a rush of emotion that was obviously overcoming me, I stepped back to let Quen run his ship.

I *tried* to step back.

My feet wouldn't go.

Before me, Quen's face was turned upward toward the useless overview screen, which was showing him nothing. Why was he looking up there? There was nothing to—

His arms flared out at his sides, and a strangled gasp bolted from his throat. His silky grove green hair actually stood away from his face as his knees buckled and he dropped straight down before me, crashing into Zell as the first officer slammed sidelong to the deck.

Even with my muscles seized and my hands sizzling before me, I managed to turn enough to see fifty or more crewmen in the grip of this shipwide spasm. They were all falling . . . writhing . . . faces knotted in grimaces of pain and seizure. Some kind of neuralizer had them by the raw nerves.

What was that nerve thing Lucas had mentioned? Why wasn't I falling down?

Through the terrible freeze, I realized I still had some control. I was now the only person on the deck—probably on the ship—still standing. Why? If Sasaquon could zap the ship with some kind of energetic umbilical, why wasn't I down and out, too?

Human . . . I was human. For a moment I'd forgotten that I was an alien here. Of course their weapons would be organized to debilitate their own people, their own physiology. Oh, if only I could think. My nerve endings were in a grinder.

So I was the only person on *Zingara* left standing. Now what? Handle the ship and the engines and the weapons all alone? Run an offensive by myself?

The crew writhed at my feet and all around me in a

pathetic carpet of twisting bodies. They weren't unconscious and my heart ached to see them in such torment. Pivoting weakly on one heel, I looked around and noticed that the interior of the ship was actually glowing with a graveyardish sulfur glow—the tiles!

My tiles! Whatever Sasaquon was hitting us with, the energy was coming right through our own capacitors! And I'd cleaned them and made sure they would work!

Damn it, I hated cooperating with the enemy.

This had to stop. We were under tow, the crew was down, the ship was in spasm, my feet were numb, and I was mad.

Though I couldn't feel my feet, I had some sensation in my knees. Cranking my neck downward, I managed to look at the deck, at my knees, and through massive concentration I made one leg move. Then the other. Through the foggy buzz in my head, I forced myself to concentrate on moving. Luckily, I was already facing the right direction.

Pressing both hands to my head, I held my brains in place and blocked some of the screaming electrical whine and shuffled toward the deck well. There it was . . . a lightly railed open hole in the deck, leading down through the engine room to the hold and the main service loading hatch.

There it was, a big hole . . . I shuffled toward it and forced down the stomach-wrenching caution that usually stops people from throwing themselves down a shaft. My feet scratched forward until there was no more deck, and the well opened before me. I plunged full-length into the well, barely missing getting my head smashed by the other edge, because I had no control to curl up but just fell forward like a bottle toppling over.

Where was I? Had I impaled myself on an engine mount? Would a pool of blood appear on the deck, inches from my face? My cheek was pressed to the deck. One arm was pinned beneath me.

I had to get up, get to my knees. Crawl . . .

The cluttered engine deck lay before me, an obstacle course for a person whose head was twisting off. Between me and the loading dock were two dozen more shuddering bodies of crewmen. As I picked my way past them, over them, my innards cranked with awareness of how many of them I'd come to know fairly well. When had that happened? We worked together, ate together; they accepted me in spite of their questioning glances, they had cared for me and tended my wounds, they hadn't locked me up. I wanted to help them . . . assure them, fix all this—

A flash of white metal caught my eye through the yellow glow from the tile-encrusted bulkheads. The pod! My survival pod! My little bathtub of salvation!

There it was, stowed safely inside the loading airlock, being saved for salvage or emergency use or whatever a thrifty culture might need. I had to get inside.

Wait, wait—first get the remote airlock control. I know I saw one last time I was down here. There it was, on its wall mount. At last! One thing in its place!

The cool white metal of the pod's hatch cuff was cool and vibrating slightly with Sasaquon's energy assault.

I tumbled inside the pod and landed curled up with my shoulder tucked under me and had to squeeze out of that and get my head in the right direction. Where were my hands?

Oh—here was one. I needed only one.

The controls were still working. The pod's airtight hatch rolled shut, giving me a brief but poignant memory of the Iscoy captain's body, burned and crumpled beside me. I ached as if remembering a severed limb and trying to use it.

A brief suction hurt my ears as the pod pressurized, but suddenly the ringing freeze of Sasaquon's neuralizer released me and my arms and legs started to come back. The pod was insulating me somehow—well, there were no tiles in here, were there? Nothing to conduct the debilitating energy surge. The tiny utility light clicked on, faintly illuminating the inside of the pod.

In icy fingers I cradled the airlock remote and picked at the squares of the control panel. Outside the pod, there was a distinct *chunk* as the airlock slid shut, protecting the engine room from the vacuum of space. All that remained was to key the outer hatchway and let the pod roll out, free of *Zingara*.

I put my hand on the launch control, a last cryptic sentence rattled out of my throat.

"This is the time."

* * *

"Come on . . . come on, grab me . . . come on, pull me in . . . here I am . . . grab me . . ."

What were they thinking on *Zingara?* Through the neuralizing zapper Sasaquon was using even now to fry the brains of those boys, were Quen and his crew thinking I had abandoned them? That I was a coward and getting away just because my physiology was different enough to let me move through the deep fryer?

I should've brought a weapon.

Come to think of it, I'd never seen a hand weapon of any kind on *Zingara.* Not a weapons locker, not even a stunner that could be used as a hand-to-hand defensive or offensive instrument. I should've brought a rigger's knife.

As I lay in the pod, waiting, I got an almost-comical mental picture of plunging over the rail of the *Aragore* with one of those pirate-story belaying pins in my teeth. At the moment, I'd have tried it.

What could I use? I wouldn't have the element of surprise on my side, even if this worked at all. There had to be something in here—a sharp edge of metal or even the heel of my boot? I could break a nose with that if I had to.

What indignity—I was winging through space in my steel ball, unable to control where I was going, counting on the actions of an enemy I did not know, being cursed as a coward by the people I did know. Charming.

All at once a sledgehammer hit me and I was over on my face, pressed to the curved side of the pod as if stapled there. A tractor beam! Or a cable, or something!

"I counted on that!" My rasping voice boomed inside the steel shell.

The pod was being winched in—toward the *Aragore!*

"I knew it! I knew you couldn't let me go! Sasaquon, I already know how you think! Here I come . . . keep bringing me in, just keep doing it . . . I'm almost ready . . ."

Talking to myself. There was progress.

Would they know I was here? Could they scan for life signs? Maybe, but I didn't know how soon or at what proximity. I'd have to assume they'd know I was here.

Where was that emergency medical kit? Where was the pressure adjustment?

There were a couple things in my favor. Primarily, I was a

woman. They wouldn't expect much. Finally the chromosome quirk was proving useful.

Somehow I had to get that neuralizer turned off first, even if it were the only thing I accomplished.

But it couldn't be the only thing, because Sasaquon could always turn it back on. I had no way of knowing how long Quen and the crew could take that kind of torture. Sasaquon didn't care if they died, and who could know how long before their lungs shut down or they had internal damage?

From the medical kit I took a metal splint and jammed it into the hatch handle, so no one could open the door before I was ready. And I almost was.

Standard PSI arrangement, perfectly understandable, basically the same for your run-of-the-mill spacefaring technology. Very simple: adjust the interior pressure . . . more . . . more . . . turn the dial up . . . ouch . . . more, increasing the PSI inside. My eyes started to throb, my ears to ache and ring. Two atmospheres, three . . . my ears popped . . . three and a half . . . four . . . oh, boy . . .

A hard bump from outside declared that my little crucible had been successfully captured. I'd been reeled in and was being boated by Sasaquon. Ow . . .

No matter how much it hurts, don't jump the gun—let *them* open the pod.

Straps! Strap in—I had to get strapped to the pod's superstructure, or I'd be blown out the door when it finally opened. This pressure would pop the pod like a champagne bottle and I'd be the foam. Strap in . . . Where were the damned straps?

Ah, in a drawer. Good place for the safety straps. Inside something, completely out of sight, where they have to be searched for. Genius. Over the shoulders, buckle the chest belt, tie the free end of the belt to the . . . the thing keeping the hatch handle—splint, it was a splint. My head pounded so hard, I could hear it.

A metallic scraping noise. I was being hauled in. The last few seconds of docking were spent steeping myself in the idea of doing what I had to do, hardening myself to destroy what I had to destroy, even to kill whomever I had to kill to protect my ship and crew.

My ship . . . *my ship* . . .

God, my head hurt. My ears rang and rang. Quen and the other boys, caught in that neuralizer, suffering. They seemed like children to me, the Lost Boys trying to figure out how to fly.

Just as I had been the only one to survive the Menace attack, I was the only one who could maneuver through the neuralizer, and now this chance for action fell to me and I wouldn't give up my chance. Sometimes chances came by only once.

Somebody was rattling on the door! The hatch handle was shifting against the metal splint! Now, now!

I yanked on the belt that was tied to the splint. The splint jumped, danced, and popped out from the handle. The hatch blew open on its heavy hinges with a great sudden *crack!* My torso slammed forward against the safety straps. My arms and legs flew outward, my shaggy hair sprayed forward and recoiled against my face, and my neck got a good wrenching. The straps cut into my ribs with a sharp snap, and just as abruptly the whole deck equalized. A gush of warm air surged back into the pod and embraced me. I hadn't been warm in so long!

Just as I was yanked nearly out of my skin, all the loose gear in the pod, from the med kit to mini-scanners and tools Quen's crew were using to analyze the mechanics, went surging out the hatch and spattered one of Sasaquon's guards, whose faces I saw as only brief flashes in that first instant.

As I unstrapped myself, feeling bruises rise on my ribs and pelvis, I glared out into what looked like the lower decks of Sasaquon's ship, and at three burly guards sprawled on the deck, unconscious, maybe dead. The cannon of pressure had done its job exactly as I'd planned. Good for me because I really needed something to go my way.

The lady's luck wouldn't hold for long. The noise of the pressure release had probably been heard all over the ship. I had to move—both legs, kid—and crack out of here.

I staggered out of the pod into a well-lit airlock vestibule, my head still throbbing, most of my body sprained, and pawed at the collapsed guards' red utility vests. Nothing,

nothing, ah! Was this palm-sized oblong box a weapon? It did have nice finger grooves molded into its housing, for a much bigger hand, which meant exactly nothing yet.

I took it anyway and veered down the nearest corridor. No bearings at all. A security team could just as easily come pounding toward me from the direction I was heading.

The first chance I got, I angled deeper into the ship, toward the throb of engines. The chances of a security team coming from the power center were less than from the crew decks. While stumbling along, trying to get my feet to work again, I also tried to figure out this box I'd taken off the dead guard. I hoped it was a weapon, but mostly it looked like some kind of musician's electronic metronome or a hand-held prospector. Then again, a Starfleet-issue hand phaser without the pistol grip didn't look like much either. Keep up the hope.

There weren't many shadows to hide in. This ship, unlike *Zingara,* had plenty of light. Which way was forward on this weapon thing? All I needed was to fire it and find myself minus an artery. Alien weapons—the ultimate crash course.

It was really warm here! How did Sasaquon's warranters have so much energy to spare? How could that be, when the others were running on threads and recycled parts?

Since the crew on board didn't know what they were looking for, they certainly weren't expecting a fairly light-weight woman who could duck into all the cubbies and hide in half the place needed to hide one of these lugs running past me. They hurried past me as I crunched into any possible nook, some of them involved in carrying equipment, and I got the idea that they weren't looking for me yet—at least, *these* crewmen weren't. Maybe somebody else was, but the word hadn't spread to the power decks. These men who rushed around were involved in the immediate business of crippling Quen's crew and taking *Zingara* in hostile tow.

And that was my immediate business too. I had to stop that neuralizer and bust the tow. Could this box in my hand do the job? Seemed awfully small for that kind of power, and I hadn't yet seen anything that packed the energy of a phaser into something this small. I could as well be rushing onto the engine deck to stick them up with a hand warmer, for all I knew.

I cut down through the processing deck, figuring that there wouldn't be many crewmen there during a battle situation, and found not only reduced production activity, but absolutely none at all. The whole deck was like a library. There was nobody here. Why was the processing deck quiet? Why was it clean? Where were the tried-out remains of the wrecks they were getting? The ship looked like hell from the outside, just like *Zingara* and Oran's ship, but inside, it was healthy, warm, well-provisioned.

The controls here were similar to Quen's ship, and I'd been learning about those. Certain things had to operate certain ways, and somebody like me, trained to Starfleet ships and general spacefaring technology, could translate what I already knew. Physics worked the same way here as in the Alpha Quadrant. Certain means had to be used to channel energy. Mechanics had to follow a certain logic. Propellants, fusion, atoms, controls had a few basic ways to work, and I knew the basics. Forward was forward, reverse was reverse, no matter how far we flew.

Thus, simple—find out where the energy was flowing and what it was flowing through, and disrupt it.

The neuralizer first, then the tow. If there was time for more, great.

Like *Zingara,* this ship had a coating of tile capacitors encrusting the inner decks. I ran my fingers along them, lightly brushing as I hurried down the very narrow corridor on what I thought was the power deck. Some of the tiles lit up, and I paused to look at what they were displaying. Not what I want . . . this wasn't either . . . nope . . . ah! A display of current heat flow through the ship!

Now, *this* I could use. The little schematic of the *Aragore* clearly showed where energy was flowing on this ship right now, and there was a convenient blinking blue dot that obviously was my current location. Smart. Somebody knew how to program a user-friendly system. *Zingara* had no such blue dot to show the crew where they were at any given time.

I was just aft of amidships, on the engine deck. Blue dot, yellow flashers . . . power emanations . . . computer banks . . . computer banks would do the job. There they were: my target.

And the tiles provided me with a map. As footsteps pounded toward me, I found the off-tile and ducked behind a laundry bin, just in time to avoid a thudding six-pack of Sasaquon's crewmen—and those sure weren't engineers. They all carried rifle-type weapons that looked, at the brief glance I got, clean and ready to fire. That was a security team, and they were looking for me.

After they raced unobservantly past me, which was the only reason they didn't notice my knee sticking out at the edge of the bin, I evil-eyed the little box I'd taken off the guard at the pod. If those rifles were their weapon of choice, what was this thing?

Hand warmer? I'll die comfortable.

It had fingertip pressure pads, color-coded, no dials, no numbers . . . This would be interesting. No instructions or hints about how to use it. Of course, a 1920s revolver didn't have instructions printed on the grip, either. Trial by error, and the error could take out the side of the ship if I was misjudging this baby box.

Once the six-pack had passed and the drum of their footsteps faded, I ducked back the way they'd come. Already minutes had been eaten up, long minutes of agony and damage for Quen and the boys. Move faster, Janeway, people are hurting.

The blue dot had showed me where I was, and the schematic had given me a goal. Aft, along another corridor farther to my right, possibly down this way—yes! Past the storage rooms and the bunking area . . . nobody asleep, of course, because they were in a battle situation. Nobody here to notice me, either.

Before long, I didn't have to rely on the dot map I'd bothered to quickly memorize. The pulsing sound of hot energy led me to what I hoped was the power center, or at least the center of something where great damage could be done. I wanted to do some damage. I could taste it.

My shoulders turned and I had to inhale to squeeze

through two horizontal support stanchions. Crouching behind some crates, I surveyed the area quickly. Two crewmen tending that cylindrical thing over there with the clear housing through which the yellow energy flowed . . . Physically I couldn't take them both. Time to test the hand warmer.

There was a red button, and although ocular powers varied across the galaxy—and even between humans and dogs—I'd learned from Quen's ship that red was still red, a universal signal for heat among those who saw the same thing. This hand warmer had a red pad, several levels of gray, a gold one . . . no really good hints. If red meant what I thought it did, I'd better try out some grays first.

The lightest one. My thumb pressed the pad.

There was an actual *click*. Then, nothing.

Just when I was about to push another button, the box started to vibrate in my hand. Now it was humming— louder! I knew an overload when I saw one!

As if shedding a hot rock, I put it on top of the thing I was hiding behind and dived for cover, closed my eyes, plugged my ears, and made sure I wasn't leaning against anything.

The little box built up and built up, humming not really louder but certainly with more intensity—

Pop-*pieuw!*

My ears! The force of the pop knocked me over onto my side. If I hadn't been crouched already, I'd have been wrapped up in that batch of cables hanging over there. All that built-up power had been released at once!

It *was* a weapon! That or it was one heck of a welder.

Slowly I peeked out.

Before me, the whole cylindrical assembly, all its computer bank consoles, and half of the wall behind it were engaged in a complete meltdown! The whole bank was sinking into mush like a dessert mold being suddenly heated.

I felt no residual heat at all, but I sure saw the effect of something like it. "Please," I uttered, "let that have been the neuralizer . . ."

Stepping out onto the open deck area, I glanced around to make sure no one was coming immediately, and peered around the soggy mess I'd made of some very nice machinery. There on the deck, dead and partially *dissolved,* were the two crewmen who had been tending this area.

So I'd crossed that line. That ugly line. Now Quen, his ship, his crew, were embedded in my life for the rest of it. I'd killed for them.

Alarms started going off. If this had been a secret, if no one had been watching the monitors up there until now, the grace period was over. This machine had stopped working and would never be repaired.

I swung around, scooped up the hand warmer, and said, "Baby, you got moxie! Okay, Quen, I bought you time . . . think of something. Counterattack. There's got to be something you can do.

As I slipped back into the corridor, ran about twenty feet, and angled up a ladder hatch onto another level, I found a set of tiles and fingered them until they showed me the nearest intraship diagram. Wonderful! The yellow pulse of active energy had gone dark, and instead was flashing with red and purple emergency lights. The blue locator dot now showed me on the middle deck, aft, port side. It blinked dutifully, as if all else were well and I should be calmed.

Yet, there was a haunting whisper. Something I was missing.

Push, push on. The tow cable, before time ran out.

Nagging the tiles, I got them to show me where the controls were for the cable. Computers are the most wonderful pets, aren't they?

The activity on board was heating up. Footsteps and shouting voices rang all around me, but I had the advantage of knowing something about covert raiding. I knew how to lurk.

I crannied, nooked, niched, and cornered my way to the very lowest deck, the processing deck, figuring that since Sasaquon wasn't involved in salvage at this moment, preoccupied instead with a conquest, there wouldn't be very many crewmen down here. If I could avoid killing anyone else, I would, though not out of any misplaced humanity. These situations were hardly the kind where passivity played a part. I wanted restraint for one very clinical military reason: There was no way to predict what I'd need in my favor later on. Free-flung brutality might serve the immediate battle but might strangle deals later on. Nobody with a brain played the hands before they were dealt.

Therefore, when I get to the towing area, how could I clear it before using Moxie?

Sure was quiet down here . . . no machinery working or even warmed up. I paused and looked at the recyclers and processors. Not even lubricated. How could that be?

"Haven't been used in weeks," I muttered, touching one of the shredders.

And there were no crewmen down here at all. Nobody. Didn't they man this deck, even in trouble? I would've.

I didn't like abandoned decks, even when they did me a favor. While rushing almost the whole length of the ship down here, my suspicions grew and grew.

That blue locator dot was still blinking in my mind. Quen's ship didn't have anything like that. Oh, it had intraship diagrams, but no locator dots. Why would one ship need a blue dot for the crew, and another ship not need it? This wasn't exactly a vacation vessel that had lots of tourists on board who needed to find their way around with YOU ARE HERE signs. It had done me some good, but I was a saboteur. Pretty obvious they hadn't provided the blue dot for evil intruders like me.

I had a chance—a few seconds to myself—and I'd take them to figure out how Moxie worked. That meant pushing another color and firing it again. Working completely in ignorance of what these settings meant, I took a horrid chance and pushed the yellow pad.

Moxie vibrated to overload again, this time almost instantly, sizzling in my hand. I put it down and ducked for cover, but peeked out at it to see what the feisty box would do on yellow.

Charging up in just a second or two, this time Moxie gave no sudden plasma crack. Instead, a pinpoint beam speared from the box and drilled into the casing of a processor. In seconds, the processor was violated all the way through and the yellow beam, without diffusing at all, speared out the other side.

After ten seconds, the beam shut down, leaving a sizzling hole in the processor and a notable mark in a stanchion beyond.

I jumped up and reclaimed my new toy, blurting, "Oh, I've *got* to take this apart! Some kind of short-range plasma scalpel! Bet I could make you work on a large scale, baby."

If only I could find its stun setting. I'd have to remember that the plasma crack took several seconds to power up, but the scalpel almost no time at all. There'd be no way to test a stunner because I had no one to test it on. Sure couldn't stun a machine. I had a wide-range melter-killer and a pinpoint scalpel. Those would have to suffice.

Scalpel . . . Why was I bothering to look for a ladder or a conduit through to the tow cable tier?

I dropped to the deck, hit the yellow button, aimed, and let Moxie overload itself. The pinpoint beam spat onto the deck. The mini-torch spindle started boring through the deck. Top layer . . . structural beam . . . insulation . . . another beam . . . the ceiling of the deck below. As if peeling back layers of archaeology, I stripped my way through to the next deck, managing to keep any large pieces from falling through and giving away my position. Just to make sure nobody saw the beam, I scored only the last layer, then punched through and pried it back.

Slowly I poked my head down and looked around. I almost got a mouthful of some burly thug's blue hair as a team of crewmen dashed by. Armed. More guards. Why would a warranter ship need so much security?

They passed by, and an unlikely elf dropped from the ceiling. Moxie had done it again—I was minutes closer to the tow mechanism.

Break it, break it, break it. Concentrate.

As I made my way farther aft and down one more half-deck toward the cable tier, I did all the damage I could. I took Moxie's scalpel to every computer access point, every conduit, every bundle of wires, cords, cables, and circuits that I could expose quickly. I also threw every switch and reversed every control on every panel. Those would be easy to turn back on or off but might contribute to the general chaos I was conjuring. Quickness was the key. I had to break the tow and get the ships away from each other.

If only Quen were moving over there, doing something, crafting, conniving, cooperating with me. There must be some trick to use in their own defense. I hoped they were working on whatever that was. Ten bits of havoc popped into my mind right off, but so what? I was over here.

On the other hand, I could be all wet about everything. Maybe that yellow beam wasn't even the neuralizer. It could as easily have been the waste control plant. Maybe all I'd done was shut down the ship's heads.

Oh, well, keep a good hope. And keep moving, madam.

Footsteps! On this level! They resounded clearly as the corridor funneled the noise right to me. They were coming!

Of course they were! Where was my head! Was I slipping? What a fool! I'd been causing damage along my route, and that would be dead giveaway about where I was heading. I should've restrained myself until the tow was broken!

I broke into a run—not what a clandestine saboteur would prefer—and raced dangerously around corners and through hatches without checking to see whether the coast was clear. Once I ran through a small area between two bulkheads where at least a crewman was working on something, facing away from me, and I don't think he even saw me at all.

The whole dash to the cable tier had a surreal craziness about it, and a swiftness that made me dizzy, but in seconds I was there, cracking out into a giant industrial garage the whole ship wide and several decks tall. Before me lay a flank of twenty-foot-tall winches and housings, and spools of extra cables. Here, across the deck from me, the next-to-last winch was squawking and working furiously. An automatic spray mechanism was dousing the whole drum and its cable in cold water every few seconds, keeping it from heating up as the winch furiously reeled and reeled. From the winch to a hawsehole in the aft bulkhead, a huge parceled and served cable ached its way back into the ship.

At the end of it, out there in space, was Quen's ship. This was it—the umbilical causing most of our troubles.

Behind me as I turned to glance was a huge computer bank, which I instantly recognized as primary drive controls. The engineering mainframe! What luck!

With footsteps drumming toward me, seconds eating away, I pushed the right pad on Moxie and placed my toy on the nearest winch brace, a housing that was taller than I was, and all it did was hold the winch. Moxie was now aimed at the winch that was working.

I dove for cover. Moxie vibrated, rattled, then hummed wildly as energy built up to overload. That was beginning to make sense to me: Somehow this culture had taken a turn that mine had skipped, concentrating on power storage, buildup, and sudden release. Moxie worked on the same principle as the capacitor tiles on these ships. Build up energy to a dangerous point, then suddenly—

Pop-*pieuw!*

The whole deck roared as the winch suddenly melted down. Around me the *Aragore* heaved up in spasm, and everything grated to a factory-level halt.

I ended up sprawled sidelong on the deck, my head ringing and my hair in my face. Scratching to my feet, I grabbed Moxie, fitted the grip-formed casing into my hand, ran to the far side of the deck, and swung around.

And I started to shout.

"Hold it! Hold it! Stop!"

CHAPTER
9

My shout broke even before any of the men chasing me tumbled into the cable tier. Five . . . six . . . eight of them, all in red vests. With Moxie aimed at them, they all ground to a halt and stared at me, aiming their rifle weapons but not firing. They knew better because in my hand Moxie wasn't aimed at them. It was aimed at their engineering mainframe. I could take out their whole bank even as they killed me, and they knew it.

Instantly one man plowed forward from the rear, and all the others let him come through.

And I recognized him.

Sasaquon.

And what a striking fellow he was, I must mention. He looked like the sort who might be an ambassador or a judge or one of the steam-pressed admirals back at Starfleet. His shoulders were straight, his complexion ruddy, his hair gunmetal gray with touches of white at the temples, and his eyes might have been friendly had I not known the underlying purposes and unforgivable methods of this attack dog.

He wasn't lean or pale like Quen's crew, nor were any of his men. This crew was well fed, well provisioned, healthy.

Their clothing had no patches, their hands needed no gloves in the warmth of this vessel, and, strangely, they had no healing injuries. Oh, I saw a bruise or two, and one bandaged hand, but the bandage was clean and the bruises were all fresh.

It was as if these people hadn't been through a battle before today. Were they really that good?

He motioned to his men to restrain themselves, though no one raised his weapon. Neither did I.

"Who are you?" Sasaquon asked.

"Let Quen's ship go," I sternly warned. I aimed Moxie at the engineering computer bank. "Let it go right now. If you take any action, I'll melt this whole bank. It's not my first choice to leave anybody stranded in space, but I'll do it to you, be assured."

Sasaquon surveyed me cannily, trying to figure me out. I knew the look. I knew the pause. I'd used them myself.

After a moment of tense silence, he took a measured step toward me. "If she doesn't surrender in the next ten seconds, turn all the turrets onto Quen's ship and slice it to pieces."

Uh-oh . . . he'd figured out what I cared about. I'd given him a tool to use against me. My nearest chance for a win was to call his—no, he probably wasn't bluffing. Maybe I could call my own bluff somehow.

"I'm not putting the weapon down," I said. "This isn't a waltz, Captain. If you want to destroy that ship, then get to it. You're killing them in daily increments anyway. Make the commitment to murdering those men, or take a stand and tell them what you really want, but don't keep stringing them along this way."

"Stringing them? What's that mean?"

He actually had a nice voice. Rather mellow. He could read poetry.

"It means you're playing the part of just another warranter, but you're not playing it well enough for me. I've been deceived before and I know the signs. You're not in honest competition with these other men, are you? You wait for Quen or Oran or somebody to get a grip on a wreck, then you move in and take it from them. You're a barracuda, Mr. Sasaquon, you're raiding somebody else's catch before they get it out of the water. And where's the parceled salvage? This is your processing deck, isn't it?"

"What's any of this to you?" He moved toward me slowly, though not so close as to induce me to open fire because we both knew I'd do it. "Why do you come on board my ship and make all this destruction? Who are you? *What* are you?"

With far more satisfaction than I can describe or explain, I squared my shoulders and lowered my chin just enough to make an impression.

"I'm Kay Janeway, deckhand aboard the *Warranter Zingara.*"

Awww—that felt so good! The sheer humility of it was invigorating! Could I say it again?

Sasaquon squinted his doubts. "That's some kind of funny lie. Quen doesn't have any women over there. Why are you there? You're not Omian or anything we recognize. What are you?"

"That doesn't matter."

"Where did Quen get you?" he persisted.

"Doesn't matter."

"Did he hire you?"

"Doesn't matter. Where's your salvage?"

"Are you somebody's mother?"

"No. Why isn't your processing deck in operation?"

"Why would he bring a woman to space?"

"Doesn't matter."

He paced before me, then concluded, "I know why. He thinks I won't fire on a ship if I know there's a woman on board. Is that why he brought you?"

Stretching my arm to full length, I kept Moxie aimed at the center of that computer bank, letting him know that I wasn't about to ease the threat or hand him any answers.

"If you're not having any luck finding wrecks," I said instead, "or if somebody else is taking them away from you, then why aren't you starving? You got hit pretty hard at the Sands by two ships, Quen's and Oran's. How is it you're ready to attack again so soon? Why aren't these men bandaged? Why isn't anybody limping? I don't see any swellings. How did you get out of a battle with hardly any injuries? And just tell me this, Mr. Sasaquon, how is it you all have good haircuts?"

"Sasaquon."

A comm unit from somewhere spoke up with a mechanical buzz behind it.

"Go ahead," I told him. "Answer it, Captain. I want to hear the status report."

Sasaquon measured my demeanor carefully. He held his men back with a gesture, then pointed to the wall unit. One of the men clicked it for him.

"Go ahead," he responded.

"Clear to talk?"

"I said, go ahead and talk."

"Quen just severed the cable grapnel. He's moving off. Our cable's just flying out there. You want us to rig a retrieval or open fire?"

"Nothing yet. Is he getting away?"

"No, but he's drifting away. I don't think he's got control yet."

"Can we get repaired faster than he can?"

"Probably."

"Get working on it." He motioned for his crewman to click off the comm, then looked at the others. "You two go see what else she did and tell me how long to repair."

One of the men asked, "Me? Or—"

"No, Tor—Torma."

"Tirga," another man corrected.

"All right, Tirga and . . . you." He pointed at those he wanted to go.

They turned and ducked out the hatch. I probably should've opened fire on the bank. Still, I wanted to find out some things before I destroyed everything in sight.

Sasaquon turned to me again, narrowing his eyes. He took a few steps away from the bank.

"That won't do you any good, Captain." I kept my aim on the computers.

He stopped. "What won't?"

"Moving away and hoping my attention will follow you."

He gave up that tactic.

"Why didn't you know that man's name?" I asked.

Something about that stung him just right. Just wrong for me. Sasaquon grabbed one of his own crewmen, yanked the man off balance, and threw him across the deck toward me.

I had no choice but to fire. Moxie's scalpel beam cut across the deck and burned into the crewman's face, then down his neck and into his chest.

The poor man fell against me, knocking me backward. The diligent weapon in my hand went flying.

Sasaquon took that moment of distraction, balled one fist, slammed it into a two-switch panel on the stanchion he'd paused beside, and I heard the *snap* over my head. I tried to dodge—too late!

A crushing force slammed down on top of me, a smothering weight of fabric and lines, cargo netting and straps. How foolish not to have looked up just once! He'd hit a release!

Something cut into my lip. Another solid weight cracked the back of my head, and some kind of metal weight hit my right shoulder. A frazzle of pain left me numb for a few seconds, and then I started kicking.

At least two hundred pounds—probably more, because I could scarcely move. One leg hung in the open, and with it I lashed out and felt a connection with somebody who had plunged in to capture me.

The man tripped and with a hard grunt landed on the deck beside me.

The muffling weight lifted. I was hauled to my feet. One leg was still numb. Blood trickled down my chin from the side of my mouth. My shoulder burned, tingling all the way down to my fingers. My face burned too, but with pure indignation.

As Sasaquon picked Moxie up off the deck and squared off in his victory, I wrenched against the two men holding me so hard that one of them had to get a better grip on my arm. I watched the dying man on the deck, whose wounds now bubbled around the man's clawing fingers. As we watched, his body convulsed twice, rather horridly, and he reached out for Sasaquon to help him.

A moment passed, and the man's beseeching hand tumbled to the pile of straps and gear that had crushed me down.

I glared at Sasaquon.

"So tell me . . . why would a captain sacrifice a member of his own crew just to catch one scrawny woman?" I let the question ring and watched his men for a moment before looking at him again. "You could've hit that button without throwing him at me if you'd tried a little harder. Do your shipmates mean that little to you? Or is it that you just don't know them very well?"

My voice had an ominous rasp. As Sasaquon's men held me firmly before their captain, I licked my bleeding lip and stared at the man who had nearly killed Quen, the *Zingara* crew, and me.

"This isn't a pledged crew, is it?" I prosecuted. "You're getting fresh crew from somewhere."

"How can you guess something like that?" Sasaquon responded fiercely. "What do you know about our planet or our people? Who *are* you?"

"You're getting new clothing and stocks from someplace. Who are your suppliers? Why don't the other warranters have the same favors? You have a code of behavior, don't you? The Assembly has declared you outlaws, hasn't it? You're all on an even plane, aren't you? Aren't you, Mr. Sasaquon!"

His face flushed. His deeply exotic eyes speared me. I got the idea he wasn't quite as elegant and in control on the inside as the first impression he delivered.

"Did Quen send you here to do sabotage? He's never done that before. Why is he changing his tactics?"

"Maybe he's wising up, finally," I whipped back with unveiled sarcasm. "Why were you towing Quen's ship? You're taking us to a place where it's illegal for warranters to go, aren't you? Why would you do that except to prove to somebody the warranters are bad people? Who are you trying to impress? Are you under orders from somebody to turn public opinion against the warranters?"

Sasaquon's men shifted uneasily, their body language hardly needing a translator, so obvious that he scooped up a cargo strap and whipped it viciously at them, catching two of them across their faces. They instantly stopped giving things away, but it was really too late.

I smiled nastily at him. "I'll bet public opinion favors the warranters in the hemisphere, doesn't it? It's hard to hate Robin Hood, Captain."

Sasaquon scoured me with a disturbed glare. "Put her below with the other one."

We'd been passing a small star when Sasaquon jumped us. As cluttered as this area of space was, there were plenty of them. All I could hope was that Quen had been taking the time to maneuver closer to the star nearby and suck the solar energy into the capacitors. One light kick would put them far enough away from Sasaquon to have some time to put themselves back together, even if they went no farther than the next power pocket, any nebula or star where energy could be bled off.

Anywhere at all, just away from here.

Now Sasaquon's men were dragging me below to lock me up somewhere because Sasaquon was such a sweet guy that he didn't want to kill a woman. Quen's ship was now adrift out there. I'd apparently done enough damage to *Aragore* that Sasaquon couldn't reestablish his hold on Quen quite yet. The two ships were drifting within spitting distance of each other. A race of cleverness, resourcefulness, against time had begun.

How long Sasaquon's repairs would take, I had no way to know. Whether they could establish another tow with one of those other big winches, I also didn't know.

I hoped Quen and his crew were using this chance to get away if they could. Did they have motive power or was everything crippled?

Could they do anything at all, or were they helpless? Were they even conscious?

The questions, the doubts and dark unknowables ate at me as Sasaquon's men hauled me to a two-man lift, crammed in there with me, and delivered me to a lower deck.

This was some kind of bunking deck, with a dozen doors to small cabins. That made sense, their bringing me here. They probably didn't have anything like a brig.

All the doors had magnetic locks—I noticed that right away. They were going to cram me into one of these bunking quarters and bolt me in. I could be Houdini, and there was nothing I could do with a magnetic lock that had a central control.

Pretty regimental for a warrant ship, wasn't it? Lock and unlock all the crew cabins at the same time? Did they blow reveille too?

Another clue.

Halfway down this corridor of bunk doors, the men drew me to a stop. One of them punched a signal into a comm unit on the wall like the one Sasaquon had used back in the garage.

"Release the locks," this one said.

A few seconds passed before the order could be followed, but then the locks—all of them—up and down the corridor suddenly clacked and all the doors popped open like a row of cells.

With my last suspicious glance, the two men unceremoniously shoved me into the quarters and slammed the door behind me.

Momentum bumped me up against the opposite wall, where there were a sink and some drawers. On either side of me were four bunks with basic blankets and pillows dumped on them, unfolded and in heaps.

As I turned and looked around, one of the heaps moved. They did have somebody else prisoner! Why was Sasaquon taking prisoners? What authority could he possibly carry?

This wasn't the time to be polite. I pushed off the sink, grabbed the blanket that was moving, and yanked it clear of whoever was underneath.

Another woman! She lay with her back to me, and there was no mistaking the feminine form, unless I'd forgotten how to read the general formations of male and female humanoids in the galaxy. The shadow of the upper bunk muted what I was seeing, and the lights were indirect anyway, so I couldn't see much until she turned over.

"Come out of there," I ordered. "Who are you? Why are you being held here?"

Groggily, the woman turned over and moved her legs out of the bunk. Her head dipped under the top bunk, where a blanket hung halfway over, obscuring us from seeing each other.

She reached out to brush aside the hanging blanket, and

the first thing I saw was her hand—a long-boned violet creation with a thumb and three fingers, not four. Instantly I knew she wasn't one of these Omian people, who all had five digits the same as I did.

She dipped her head to come out, and the second thing I saw was her hair . . . soft spools of vanilla silk lying flush against her scalp, thick skin the color of quartz.

She turned her face up now and looked at me. Large brown eyes, like chestnuts set in molded clay, blinking like a doe's eyes.

I dropped the blanket and stumbled back. Bumping my head against the opposite upper bunk, I pointed at her as a witch-hunter might point at a black cat.

My heart was ice. My voice was scarcely human.

"Menace!"

CHAPTER 10

"MENACE!"

The alien woman flinched and stayed in her bunk, gazing at me in deep-riding suspicion and silence.

She was wearing a heavy and warm slipper-pink chemise, knotted at the shoulders, spreading out over her thick waist and hips, down past her knees. Her boots were simple brown mukluks. She wore no jewelry of any kind.

"Who are you!" I demanded.

She winced. "My name is . . . Totobet. Why are you shouting at me?"

"You killed my crew!"

Her quartz skin flushed almost purple at the intensity of my accusation. She paused, pondered what I had said, then tilted her head slightly.

"Were you . . . part of the big docked ship?"

I jabbed a finger at her. "It *was* you! You can't deny it!"

She blinked her chestnut eyes and seemed confused. "I haven't denied it."

"Then tell me why!"

"Because . . . it's what we do to survive."

"That's a lousy excuse."

We fell into bitter, doomful silence. I kept staring at her, no matter how she looked away from me or huddled or pulled blankets over herself. I looked at her hair spools. I looked at her skin. Her hands. I memorized everything about her for future despise.

These Menace people were humanoid, generally speaking, and had rather humanlike faces, except for the hair and the eyes, and of course the fingers were missing one. In my more lucid moments, when I could briefly banish the hatred eating at me, I tried to regain control of myself by analyzing what kind of evolution this was. Totobet had a slight bump of flesh and bone on each hand, in the place where I had a little finger. So the Menace had once been five-digited.

Like the human tailbone, the support for the little finger still existed even though the finger had evolved away. That might mean the Menace was farther along the evolutionary track than humans or Omians. Or Cardassians and Klingons. Perhaps maybe by as much as a million years. I thought of the comparisons with cats, dogs, even some reptiles and amphibians. All over the known galaxy, animals had five digits. There was something about that mechanism that nature liked. Some paleobiologists and anthropologists back home had explanations, but I'd never bothered to read them. Now I wished I had.

A million years' difference, but not technologically. The Menace was beatable—I knew that. It was a clear indication that technological and physical evolution didn't necessarily sail abeam.

As if I were some kind of scarecrow in a gutter, lost of mind and confused of spirit, I began to prick the air with ugly mutterings, scarcely even realized the simmerings were bubbling all the way out.

"Sitting there . . . looking so innocent . . . big brown eyes . . . Shirley Temple hair . . . trying to look so peaceable . . . You don't even know what you've done, do you?"

The Menace turned her head only enough to catch me in her considerable peripheral vision. She hugged her knees and tucked her chin.

I kept muttering.

"You and your kind . . . just fly in and start cutting into

any civilization in your path . . . any ship in your way . . . don't know who's there or what they've been striving for. You don't pay attention. Don't even think about how much you're destroying beyond the lives and the buildings . . . how many aspirations and goals you've shot out of existence . . . I really *don't* like you."

Her narrow shoulders squeezed tight. She seemed afraid of me, and I liked it. I wanted her to feel in her bones the terror her people had caused and the misery in their wake. I narrowed my eyes and lowered my head as if I were a wolf on the hunt.

"Do you know what you destroyed that day? Do you really comprehend what you did?"

She turned to look at me now and quietly said, "Why are you treating me this way? Some things have to happen. Birth must come. Death must come. Why are you angry?"

A mirthless, vicious smile gnarled my lips. I spoke through the grating of my teeth.

"The *U.S.S. Voyager* was on its way back to the United Federation of Planets. We had a crew made up of Starfleet personnel, combined with Maquis rebels. You don't know what those are, but let's just say we didn't like each other at first. The Maquis captain became my first officer. His name is Chakotay and I miss him . . . I need him. Our first-watch helmsman was the son of an admiral and had a lot to overcome. Tom Paris, he was a brave young man who fought his own flaws and drove our ship through some of the worst conditions I've ever seen. Then there's Tuvok, who left a wife and five children behind. Even for a Vulcan, that's got to hurt in the middle of the night. Neelix, who tried so hard to make everybody happy . . . Harry and B'Elanna and our Doctor . . . He was so funny sometimes, even when he didn't mean to be . . ."

My chest was aching now, tight, muscles in spasm. Eyes hurt. Hands trembling. I didn't want her to see me cry. I wanted her to stay afraid of me.

I hadn't wept yet at all. Relentlessly I'd beaten off the grieving process, protected and distracted and tile-scrubbed myself past that. Now, suddenly, it wanted out.

No, no, not here! Not until everything I have to do is completely done.

In desperate defense I let the anger surge back over the misery, let hatred take over and raw contempt for Totobet and all her people be my guiding light.

Like a cobra I glared at her.

"We learned to work together," I said through gritted teeth. "We became a family. We absorbed expatriates from races we'd never met. We became a *bigger* family. We helped each other and supported each other. That's the kind of people you murdered. We even accepted a member of our most hated enemy into our ship, our lives . . . Her name was Seven. Yes, that's right, she was just a number to them. A lost child in a dangerous body. But to me and my crew she was becoming much more than that. She was just beginning to adjust. Then you came along. You didn't even give us warning. Didn't even give anybody a decent fighting chance. You just blew in and opened fire and burned all of those fine young people out of your way."

She did a good job of being pathetic. I wasn't buying it.

"Why do you do that?" I grilled. "Why do you fly in and start killing, just like that? Without even a word? Not even an explanation? Not even fair warning to get the children or the sick or old out of there? Why do you *do* that?"

"We have to," Totobet responded. Her voice was meek, but her words had no shame or regret. "We don't hate you . . . or your sevens or your toms . . . There is one survival device in the ocean, and I know you're going to fight me for it. When that time comes, we have to fight. I wouldn't hate you because of that. Why do you hate me because of it? Nobody's ever hated me. I don't understand you."

For the first time I hesitated. What was she talking about? Was that a metaphor for the Menace's murderous ways?

I offered only a nasty sarcastic huff. "You don't? Why not? Because the farmer's not supposed to hate the wolf for killing his sheep? Fine, but I can tell you this: I don't intend to *let* the wolf kill my sheep."

"No," she agreed quietly. "We understand when there's a fight. But we have to get room. There are too many of us all the time. We need more place. We have too many babies. There's never enough room."

"Wait a minute. Are you telling me . . . your slaughter of

the Iscoy and my ship was part of some big overpopulation problem your people have?"

She blinked, paused, then shrugged. "Yes . . ."

My stomach twisted. I hoped this was a lie or a tall tale. "Are you out of your collective mind? That's one of the oldest problems of civilization and one of the easiest to solve! Why don't you use some kind of conception control?"

Totobet nodded in such a way as to tell me she'd heard all that before, and something about her manner made me believe her. "We have to conceive, or we die. Our men have to mate through their prime, or they die. Our women have to give birth and nurse, or we die. We have lots of babies. We need lots of place."

"Oh, swell," I droned. "A race of talking tribbles. Stay away from me. I'm busy."

Keeping as far from her as the cramped quarters afforded, I went back to the sink and pawed through the drawers. Nothing. Totally empty.

I turned to the bunks and investigated them. Just blankets, pillows, mattress—then, a bit of hope. On the underside of the top bunk were support slats for the mattress. Good enough.

A solid pull on a slat did nothing; they were riveted on. Casting a bitter glance at Totobet, who was watching my every move with a perplexed expression, I climbed onto the upper bunk, got my legs under me, braced my spine on the ceiling, and applied pressure.

"Why are you doing that?" Totobet asked.

"Shut up."

The bed started to squawk. The rivets were holding. I pounded with one foot, then the other. When that failed to work, I clawed the blankets away, then dumped the whole mattress overboard, until I was standing on the bare slats. Spreading my feet all the way to the sides, where the rivets were affixed, I slammed again and again, alternating feet.

This was dangerous. Any second now, one of the—

Snap. My left leg speared through the place where a moment ago there had been support. The rest of me followed, not very gracefully, except for my right elbow, which caught on another slat, and my chin, which hit the edge of the bunk. Dazed, I slithered through to the bottom bunk and fought off the blur of having socked myself in the jaw, but in one hand I had my prize. The metal bunk slat.

Well, part of it, anyway. A couple of good yanks demolished the second rivet and cut my palms pretty well too, but now I had a tool.

Totobet watched me. "Are you trying to build something?"

"None of your business." I stumbled off the bunk and went directly to the part of the wall where there must be some kind of internal circuitry. There were controls for temperature, lighting, air, and a comm unit. The comm had been deactivated, but maybe I could activate it again.

With the slat I pried off the wall panel and got to the bare circuitry. The circuits and mechanisms inside the cramped space behind the wall shivered and jumped in my fingers as I worked to find the live bits and connect them. Then the tiny speaker . . . there it was . . .

Behind me, a weak voice rose. "Are you trying to hear what they're saying?"

"Be quiet."

She was.

"ZZZZZZ . . . dzeeet . . . dssmuzzzbez . . ."

"Getting something!" I blurted. "Come on, come on . . ."

The sound was vibrating directly through the composites. If I could just hook it up to this speaker, I'd be able to eavesdrop on the ship's doings.

". . . levels frrraaapa . . ."

"Trajec—ards . . . erkk . . . ridor . . . before the prad on the rackers frrrasdisses . . ."

"Almost," I grumbled. "Almost!"

". . . grooves check on the curry cards bef—halo. Otherwise we'll have to make a strike before the fleet's ready."

"Got it! That's Sasaquon's voice! Fleet," I repeated. "Who's got a fleet?"

Must've looked weird, both hands pressed against the wall, talking into a hole. What if I'd made a mistake and also hooked up the send? They might be able to hear me!

I clammed up briefly and listened.

"—footway's blocked."

". . . *cable befouled . . .*"

So far so good—they hadn't heard me. I was effectively eavesdropping on a conversation between the command area and the engineering decks.

"*What's that? What's he doing?*"

"*. . . limping around, stern to—*"

"*They've launched something . . .*"

"*. . . is it?*"

"*I don't recognize it.*"

Behind me, Totobet asked, "What are they talking about? Is there another ship out there?"

The blood boiled under my skin. "Yes, there's another ship. My ship."

"And they've launched a weapon?"

"Or something," I said. "Be quiet. I want to listen."

"*It's got a clamp!*"

Victoriously I slammed the heel of my hand into the wall. "Good boy, Quen! That's command thinking. Now, if only—"

"*It's a drill clamp! Drill clamp!*"

"*Where'd they get that!*"

"*I think they built it.*"

"*It's on! It's on the hull!*"

"What's on the hull?" Totobet asked, a tremor in her voice.

She seemed to know nothing, but I could tell from that tremor that she was a spacefaring creature who at least lived aboard a ship, even if she didn't help run the ship. She knew we were in danger, knew that our lives depended exclusively upon the structure around us. As seafarers and spacefarers had for thousands of years before the two of us, we both knew the ship we were on meant our very lives. If it died, we died.

We were both aware of that, and of my lack of answer, when a fierce clacking noise hit the hull and rang through the metal bones of the ship. The clamping mechanism was above us somewhere, on *Aragore*'s upper external skin.

Even here in the lowest caves of the ship, we heard it reverberating, droning through the ship: *rowrowrowrowrow-rowrowrow.*

And from the wall, the buzzing communication:

"What's it over?"

"The racker section! We've got no way to seal off that much area!"

"He knew that . . ."

"Who knew?" Totobet persisted. "Do they know something?"

At first I wasn't going to answer. Then I found myself talking, perhaps to sound out the logic for myself.

"My captain knew where to put a clamp on this ship, in a place where they can't seal off the chamber. If it drills through, this ship is hulled instantly."

The fear rose again in her voice. "Would he kill this ship? Knowing you're here on it?"

"I certainly hope so."

Fear widened Totobet's yellow eyes. "What would a hole do?"

"It'll punch through the skin of the ship and unequalize us. The whole ship is finished if it gets through."

"We'll be killed?"

"If we're still here."

Rowrowrowrowrowrowrowrow . . .

She turned away from me, curled up against a wall, and apparently decided there was no more to speak of since we were both dead.

"Are those your people in that other ship?" she asked. "But your ship was in the spacedock—"

"No, that's not the ship you're talking about. These are the people from here. They picked me up. I was in a survival pod. Just like Sasaquon picked you up."

"You escaped from the big ship?"

"I wasn't on board when you attacked."

"But how—"

"Shut up, I told you already."

Once she was silenced, I ignored her completely and listened carefully to the buzzing comm connection.

"That'll short out all the systems! We'll be down for days!"

"We'll be dead in ten minutes! Do it!"

The excitement vibrating through the comm drove Totobet to the enormity of touching me on the back of my arm and asked, "What does that mean?"

I cast her a smoldering glance and squelched the temptation to spit a suggestion that she live with the mystery. "They're probably going to send a surge of energy through the ship, trying to short out the mechanism on the—"

Suddenly I stopped, fitting together a dozen thoughts. Was it possible . . .

"Yes!" I bolted. Totobet flinched, but I didn't care. "That's it! Quen knew Sasaquon would have to flush the ship in order to turn off the drill! This door has a magnetic lock! He probably knows that too!"

She shook her head, confused. "What . . . what does . . ."

"Never mind," I snapped. "My captain's giving me a chance. I'm taking it."

I reached inside the wall until my fingers found the basic mechanism that powered this whole panel of lights, heat, and comm. With a single yank I pulled out the whole power coupling and wrenched it around to the hatch knob. Whatever went through this ship, I had to make sure it also went through that lock.

"Somebody's got a fleet," I muttered. "I think I know who that is. And it's ready to launch. Sasaquon's a traitor. Even worse, he's a cheater. I hate a cheater. I've got to warn Quen and the other warranters. They're up against something much bigger than they think."

"Why would you warn them?" Totobet asked. "They're not your people. They don't have your skin . . . they don't share your past—"

Fiercely I cut her off, yanking hard on the power cords as if these were the tendons of her throat. "They're my people if we believe the same things. I should've died in space anyway. Quen rescued me and gave me a few extra weeks. If they want to die out here, I'm ready to die with them. And I'm taking you with me."

"Me . . ."

"That's right. I'm going to keep my eye on you. You're not pulling any tricks while I'm around to stop you. No more."

I'd scarcely got the power cords secured on the hatch handle when the shout of a voice on the crackling comm got me by the instincts and I let go just in time. Well, almost in time—a surge of energy zapped my fingers in that last instant while my hands were still too close to the hatch.

Conducted through the exostructure of the ship, the hull, the inner capacitor tiles, the bulkheads, and interior electrical system, Sasaquon's desperate attempt to shut down Quen's drill gave me a jolt that threw me backward.

My shoulder hit Totobet and knocked her into her bunk, and I fell against the sink, ramming my left hip hard on the edge. The sharp pain dazed me for an instant, and when I gained control I looked at the hatch.

A pencil line of smoke trailed up from the hatch handle, the only sign—other than my aching hip—that Sasaquon had tried his surge.

No . . . not the only sign! The *rowrowrow* sound had stopped! The drill clamp was out of commission!

My window was now closing.

Limping back to the door, I grabbed the handle, careless of whether or not the energy surge on the magnetic lock had caused a heat buildup. It hadn't. The handle turned in my grip. The hatch door clicked and opened as neatly as if I'd used a key.

Without pausing to enjoy my win, I reached back and grabbed Totobet unkindly and dragged her out of the bunk quarters, hauling her down the corridor at a quickstep.

"You do everything I say, or I'll kill you. Don't make any noise, or I'll also kill you. You understand killing, right? Sure you do. Get in my way, and it's all over. There are a lot of lives at stake. You're right on the top of the list right now."

I dragged her aft, running the diagrams of *Aragore* through my mind, trying to remember where I'd seen what I needed—a hangar area for several small craft. Probably the little workbees were meant for outside maintenance operations or salvage assistance. Didn't matter. Today they were going to be used to get me the hell out of here.

And with only a minor detour, why, here we were back in the winch garage, and right there was the sweet bank of computer systems I'd threatened before. Just how critical this bank was, I really couldn't guess, but I was here and so was a solid iron winch hammer.

In all the years of technology since the Middle Ages, my civilization had struggled to find some way to process metal to make it stronger, more pliant, less pliant, and always to make it lighter. For sheer weight—and even in deep space there were sometimes uses for the just plain heavy—there wasn't much of an improvement on good old iron. And these people had some, to be used, I guessed, to bludgeon a stuck winch into turning again or slam a twisted cable back into place.

"When in doubt," I uttered, heaving up the biggest iron I could lift, "use a sledgehammer."

Totobet hovered in the hatchway. "What are you doing?"

"Damage."

Wham!

One good swing of my hammer did the job. Luckily, I knew something about computer banks and was able to put that one swing where it counted—right where a blow resulted in a chain reaction that boiled through the whole bank. Totobet flinched and stared at what I had done, and for a brief moment I let myself watch the bank fry itself to a melted mass.

"I hope that's part of the main drive controls," I commented. "Let's go."

We were off again, before anybody could come down here and find us. There'd be no second chance. We had to get out right now and clear the *Aragore* while the chaos I hoped I'd caused still had a grip on Sasaquon's ship and crew.

The workbee craft, scarcely more than oblong bathtubs not much different from my rescue pod, were waiting for us, all lined up in a cute little row on the starboard side of the lowest deck, each sitting in its launch cradle, ready to go. Each had a little Plexi-viewport where the pilot could look out and see what was going on outside.

"Get inside!" I shoved Totobet to the nearest workbee and motioned for her to climb up to the open hatch. She had trouble, so I got under her and shoved. "You're heavier than you look. Come on, hoist. Get in there."

"What is this cubicle?"

"It's not a cubicle. It's some kind of free-flying maintenance scooter."

"It flies?"

"Yes! Inside. We're leaving."

With one leg inside the workbee, she tried to look back at me. "We're going out in space? In this little thing?"

"It'll be enough."

"Do you know how to fly it?"

"I do."

"Where are we going?"

"We're going back to *Zingara,* and I'm going to show you to Quen."

"Won't Sasaquon stop us?"

"He will if you keep stalling and they have enough time to get their cable system back up! *Move!*"

CHAPTER
11

I FELL OUT OF THE WORKBEE LIKE A FROG INTO POND. A TERRIBLE screaming whistle on either side of my head—what was that awful noise?!

The airlock wasn't completely sealed! The hull must've taken so much damage that the cuff wasn't making a tight fit. The atmosphere from the *Zingara* spewed out with a ghastly shriek. I pushed to my knees, looking for some way to lock down the system, but before I could even stand up, several crewmen plunged in around me and went to work with the flanges and gaskets and valves.

"Don't jettison the workbee!" I called over the noise. "There's somebody in it! How soon can you make a light kick?"

It had been a rough ride. Sasaquon had fired on the workbee as I piloted away from his ship, and I was forced to go into a very uncomfortable series of evasive maneuvers that doubled the time it took to get back to *Zingara*.

The workbee was burning from Sasaquon's relentless open-fire, but I was heartened by the fact that Sasaquon hadn't managed to turn his ship to follow me. That meant I'd done some good sabotage.

Now Massus was standing over me and gave me a concerned glance, then snapped orders at the other crewmen, whose faces I couldn't see clearly through my watering eyes in the smoke. Within seconds—long seconds—the shriek diminished to a whine, then to a light hiss.

If that little remaining leak couldn't be securely patched, *Zingara* would be in trouble within days, but for now we could function.

"Kay!" Lucas exclaimed—at least one friendly voice. He appeared beside me out of a cloud of lingering electrical smoke, his bright hair so coated with dirt that it now looked gray. "I told them it was you over there! Zell thought you ran off!"

"No, I didn't run off. Where's Quen?"

As I crawled to my feet and looked up, Quen came limping toward me, with Zell helping him across the debris-strewn deck. The young captain looked ten years older, his pantleg torn at the knee, his left arm bandaged from the elbow to the fingertips with a stained rag, his hair crusted with lubricant and dirt. His limp was so pronounced as to indicate a possible hip or back injury, not just the leg.

"Did you do that, Kay?" he rasped. "Did you break us free from Sasaquon's tow?"

"Of course it was me!" After a pause to cough, I added, "You think they oversurged their own compensators and backflushed their own fusion?"

"It's a good thing," Zell admitted. "We were almost finished."

"How soon can you make a light kick and get out of here?"

"We're almost ready," Quen said, and that was a great relief to me.

At least we were thinking alike. I'd cut off the tow, he'd provided a distraction, forced Sasaquon to surge his own ship, and I'd taken advantage, done more damage, and gotten out of there. Now he was doing what I'd hoped, building up for an escape light kick. Not bad teamwork for one afternoon.

"We've almost bled enough solar energy into the tiles," Quen said. "Pretty soon, we'll kick."

"Sasaquon won't be able to follow you," I said with a

gasp of relief, "if you move fast enough. We'll have time to make repairs and organize ourselves. Why didn't you fire on him when you had the chance?"

Quen blinked at the sudden accusation, but recovered quickly and said, "I couldn't fire on him as long as he had us in a tight tow. After you broke the tow, we were still drifting too close. The detonation would've done too much damage to *Zingara*."

Begrudgingly, I muttered, "Well, that's a point, I guess." I turned to the workbee and called inside, "Come here."

Reaching in, I grabbed Totobet by one arm and yanked her forward, all the way out, and made her stand in front of Quen, Zell, Lucas, Massus, and everyone else who was looking.

Shocked by the appearance of Totobet, Lucas flinched in amazement—and bumped Massus, who also was staring.

Quen and Zell, the more experienced as command officers, managed to control their reaction, but I could see that they also were stunned that I'd shown up with this completely unexpected prize.

"Do you see this woman?" I demanded. "This is an alien woman. You haven't seen this race before, but I have. This is the race of people who attacked the Iscoy and slaughtered them mercilessly. This is what you're going to be fighting. Have you ever seen anyone like her before? Her eyes? Her skin? The little spooly hair things? Do you see her hands? Four fingers instead of five? That's alternative evolution! Look at her! Can you finally see what I'm warning your about? Can you see she's nothing like you?"

Quen and the others uneasily surveyed Totobet, her bleach-white hair, her silvery skin, her eyes, her hands. They seemed very uncomfortable, which I didn't know how to read, so I let the moments of silence speak.

Totobet held her breath and for a moment I almost felt sorry for her, though that didn't last long. I kept a firm grip on her arm, as if she were some kind of prize over which I had sole jurisdiction.

Drawing his own breath roughly in the acrid, dirty air, Quen shifted his weight from whatever hurt.

Carefully, he said, "You're . . . nothing like us either."

"I'm a lot more like you than this Menace!" Angry, I

pulled Totobet a step closer to him. "But look at her and at least get it through your heads that I'm telling the truth about an alien race coming closer! These are the people who came out of nowhere and attacked the Iscoy and destroyed my ship! Here's living proof of the existence of the aliens I told you about! Here she is!"

"How did you get her?" Quen asked. "What's she doing here?"

Zell angrily pushed forward. "And what was she doing on Sasaquon's ship?"

"Sasaquon picked up another escape pod, just like you picked me up. She was in it. I found her in their brig."

"Their what?"

"Held prisoner on their processing deck. Which is another subject I have to discuss with you. But right now, do you at least see that there really are aliens you don't know about? Do you see that they're close enough that one of their escape pods got over here at roughly the same time mine did?"

I was kicking myself in the backside with this line of effort. From their faces I could tell they didn't know what to think or whatever to conclude. They saw was two little alien women in front of them, that's all, and Totobet certainly didn't look like much of a threat.

My next hand had better be well played.

"I'll go back to scraping tiles," I began carefully, "but first, I want to have my say."

They looked at each other like a panel of lawyers each waiting for the other to answer. Of course, the only one who could answer was Quen.

Eventually all eyes went where mine already lingered— Quen, our captain.

Soon it came down to him and me, gazing at each other on a much more level plane than ever before.

"You broke Sasaquon's grip," he began slowly. "You got him off us . . . risked your life and saved our ship. You deserve to have a say."

I nodded. "Good." I was about to turn my back on the one law every Starfleet official must uphold. That meant that for better or worse, I was in this for the long haul.

But at last, they were going to listen to me. After a moment to gather my wits, I decided where to start and took a header.

"I've been inside Sasaquon's ship. It's not like *Zingara* in there. It's warm, for one thing. They don't even have a working production facility. They're not processing the wrecks at all, Captain."

"But they fight for them," Massus said. "They tow them away—"

"I don't know what they're doing with the salvage," I responded instantly. "Mostly I suspect they're just keeping you from processing them. It's a good bet they've been driving down the worth of the wrecks you do manage to process."

"Why would Sasaquon do that? He has to live on the same deals we do—"

"No, he doesn't," I told him forcefully, with all the convictions of my belief and experience. "Sasaquon's being supported by the TCA."

"Do you have any kind of proof for this?" Quen justifiably asked.

"Not a shred. Just adding up what I saw over there. He's got food, good shoes, new tools, a full complement of supplies and fuel, and decent clothing that looks like it's on its way to being a uniform. Nobody living on the edge has all that. I can tell you with absolute assurance that the *Aragore* is not the ship of people who don't know what to do beyond survival."

More of the crew gathered behind Quen, Zell, Massus, and Lucas. They approached with both contempt and curiosity, taking the leads of their officers. None made a single sound as I went on. In fact, I raised my voice to make sure all could hear me. There might not be another chance.

"You warranters think you have a general mutual agreement going on, but Sasaquon's not living up to the code you've set for yourselves. His ship is all banged up on the outside, but inside it's warm and comfortable and his crew is well fed and well supplied. Sasaquon's sold his soul."

"What do you mean by that?" Zell challenged. "The TCA's only—"

"The Temporary Civilian Authority has no intention of being temporary," I said. "I've seen this kind of thing before. They don't intend to reestablish free elections or free speech. They're using the threat of the other hemisphere's rising again as a stall, so they have time to build power. They declare a crisis, then declare themselves the only solution. They're building a military for themselves, with captains like Sasaquon in collaboration. I'd bet they've promised Sasaquon a high position if he distracts the other warranters and keeps you from being healthy and strong and banding together. It won't be long before they're strong enough to just come out here and clean up. And the warranters will be too weak to resist."

To be honest, I couldn't tell from their expressions whether any of them had ever thought of this or not, or had tampered with it in the privacy of their own thoughts without ever admitting these possibilities to each other. They were troubled, obviously, by the ring of plausibility in my words. It seemed I was striking paydirt underneath their hopes that such ideas were just bad moods or loneliness.

Sympathy ran through me suddenly. Who would want to admit that their families might be at the mercy of tyrants? And admit to each other that they had no power to do anything about it?

"You *won*," I offered, angling to keep some echo of their hopes alive. "What did you fight to protect? The TCA is having you compete with each other so they can debilitate you and solidify their power. Is that why you fought and won your war? For Napoleon's crown?"

They didn't know what that meant—I didn't expect them to—but I saw in Quen's face, in Zell's and those of the other crewmen, that they got the idea.

"All right, you fought a war," I went on. "Thought you won. You turned your back to lick your wounds, and while you weren't looking, the old tyrants slipped in and took over. The tyrants run the planet now and you can't bring yourself to rise against your own people. Are you harboring some delusion of someday being allowed to become merchant traders again? You're fooling yourselves. The TCA will always consider any free ship too dangerous. Your war isn't over, gentlemen. You just stopped fighting it."

Massus frowned and interrupted, "Are you suggesting we band together and attack our planet?"

"Will things be better tomorrow?" I asked. "Will you be weaker or stronger tomorrow? Maybe you've been too close to this situation. I'm a completely objective arrival here and I'm seeing things you're missing, boys. You've got to get over this idea that there's a bond between the warranters. There isn't! You're bound up by your Pledge and this weird code of chivalry between yourselves, but Sasaquon's not playing by the code. That means you're not bound to it either in dealing with him. He's turned this from a standoff into a siege, and you don't even realize it. Did you see that coming? If you can't expect him to play by the rules, why are you playing by them? One of the principles of conflict is that you must be willing to meet your enemy on his own level of behavior. Whether down or up, you've got to be willing to go there."

Around us the ship hummed and throbbed with its damage and efforts to live. The clank of repairs going on belowdecks rose through the metal and plastic of the bulkheads and put an eerie percussion on these new thoughts. The struggling, aching, tired old ship was putting in her two cents, saying she had almost reached her limits, that her time had come to make that last surge of effort or linger into ineffectiveness.

Somehow these thoughts were almost telepathic now.

"You'd better start reorganizing to fight again, before it's too late," I said. "Evolution sticks intelligent beings with a thing called stubbornness. Where's yours? There are principles here. You and the TCA want completely different futures. The governing system you fought for has been suspended and that's a bad thing. The TCA is suspending the laws you fought to live by, and you people just slog along from day to day, saying, 'This is how things are, it can't be stopped, and this is how we have to live.' You won your war, but you're still losing."

As I paused for a breath, I was heartened by the expressions on these young men's faces. They'd clearly never heard such things in their lives, never been spoken to this way by anyone, much less a women old enough to be their ... aunt ... their young aunt. As I had often found on board my own ship, being a little older than most of my crewmen could be a distinct advantage, if manipulated with the right panache and reserve.

Taking advantage of my sudden hitch upward in respect, or at least the shock factor, I paced a step to my left and put my hand against *Zingara*'s tired hull.

Beside me, still fast in my pointy little grip, Totobet looked at me and said, "You don't understand everything like you pretend to. You don't understand my people or what we're doing—"

"You be quiet! I don't trust you." I swung back to Quen. "You can't put me off the ship now, not now that she's here. You need me. There are things I know—"

Quen held up a volume-lowering hand. "I can't put you off anyway," he admitted. "Not until we find a fuel source. We don't have enough to get anywhere that I would want to leave you."

"Good, because I don't want to leave."

"That really doesn't matter. You're here and we have to let you stay—"

"Quen, she's still just a stranger!" Zell waved a hand at me fiercely. "We don't know her! How do we know she didn't sabotage *Zingara* so we couldn't fight? She was at the tiles everywhere on board. She could've done things. We don't really know her."

Quen turned to him, weary and troubled. "She's done good work for the ship. She went over there when we were all going to die and smashed Sasaquon. She could've gotten away, but she went over there instead. If we had even one turret working, we could destroy him. Then she got herself back here. We're in better shape because of her, not worse." He motioned at Totobet, but looked at Zell. "She's been telling some version of the truth, Zell. I want to keep listening. I won't make any decisions right now, but I want to listen."

Without getting too full of myself, I understood that he was making absolutely no commitments to whatever I said. He was a better captain that I had first thought, and being more judicious than I expected, wise enough to at least listen to all the perceptions around him. I perfectly well understood that he might decide completely against me.

Again, this might be my last chance to speak up. Take it, take it, take it.

"Thank you," I offered. "The first thing we should do is to stop thinking of Sasaquon as just another warranter. He's not competing with us—he's starving us out on purpose. I inflicted enough damage on Sasaquon's ship that he'll need weeks to repair. I also botched his communications so he can't call the TCA for help—at least not right away. That buys us time too. We should repair our own damage as fast as we can, forget about wasting time and energy on the processing deck, and concentrate on battle readiness. We should make a plan for action. Start organizing a plan of some kind. Start communicating with the other privateer captains. Start planning how to handle Sasaquon when he appears again. Start with your brother. Start!"

The crew who were gathered here stood as if under a kiln-hot pall. No one even twitched. They were absolutely stunned by the whole concept of aggression.

A distressed shudder, perhaps pure caution or an internal red alert, ran down my back. I had overloaded them, given them too much, too fast, just told them that their existence had a diabolical splinter, and now they were afraid.

Without turning, Quen eyed his crew sidelong as if to read these twitchy and taut undercurrents. There was great pressure on him now if even half of my words turned out to be true. Even a quarter. If only for the fact that Sasaquon was stronger and better supplied, there was danger and failure for the other warranters in the foreseeable future.

Quen sank back against whatever was behind him and leaned there, folded his arms, and consulted the deck. He closed his eyes for a brief moment as if fighting a headache, then pressed his lips tight and blinked with fatigue. Anxiety showed in his face.

Was I helping him or hurting him? Had I overstepped? Would I want anyone to do this to me? I'd been in his position so long, and after just a few weeks I'd forgotten what it was like to be in the hurricane's eye.

Caught up in my fresh adventure on Sasaquon's ship and what I'd discovered there, I had let myself get carried away and climbed a podium as if it were mine to pound.

Briefly suspending the press coverage of the crewmates

standing nearby, watching and listening, I paused, genuinely regretted my grandstanding, and spoke intimately with Quen. "I'm sorry, Captain. I don't mean to outshine you."

He blinked at me, sighed, and made a limp gesture with his bandaged hand.

"Please," he uttered, smiling weakly, "outshine me."

With that simple gesture and those little words, my respect for him ratcheted up by half. Rare was the captain whose pride played so minimal a part in his command method.

Zell winced and wouldn't look at me. He turned away. Lucas seemed like a frightened child. His arms shook visibly. Massus touched Quen's arm in feeble reassurance, and Resi watched Zell for a cue of how to act.

Maybe there was a way I could've done this better, more diplomatically, less cruelly. I wished I'd paused to think, to realize how young they were, how desperate and tired they were, and how inexperienced.

I had to let them off the hook somehow, to cut through the sick fear just for a few hours, till they had time to think.

"We all have work to do," I began, searching, "and I'll do mine willingly, every tile. I'm asking only that you think about all this and . . . just let it settle until the captains can talk. Where's Vince? I should report to him now that I'm back on board."

A tremor of discomfort rolled visibly through the crew, as if I'd pinched them. Now they did twitch and shift, and looked to Quen suddenly.

"Vince, uh—" the captain said tightly. "He got a full dose of jeklight radiation. It was . . . over in seconds."

The announcement caught me by surprise. As close as I had been to death and dying the past few days, somehow the sudden death of such a strong, forceful crewman took me unawares.

I hesitated, perhaps too long, before saying, "I'm so sorry. He was an asset to the ship."

"He was." Quen's voice was rough, tired, and the touch of grief was unshielded. His words came with difficulty, as if he were forcing himself. To his credit, despite the struggle inside, he went on. "We don't judge by guesses and suspicions here. We judge action. Merit means something to us here. You worked hard on the tiles, and when your chance came to flee a dangerous situation, you risked your life for the ship instead and it helped us. We have to keep you for a while, at least. It's my duty as captain to make the best use of any resource I have here."

He paused, limped a pace or two away under the cloying eyes of his own crew, then turned to me again, as if making the final commitment in a lingering decision.

"If you agree to take the Ship's Pledge," he said, "you'll be the new deck boss."

CHAPTER 12

"I, KATHRYN JANEWAY, PLEDGE MY SERVICE AND ALLEGIANCE to this ship and this crew. I pledge to abide by the rules of engagement, to obey the order of any senior unless it violates the Ship's Pledge, and to put the ship and crew above my own life. I will not falsely accuse any crewmate. I will be honest in all pursuits. I accept the right of senior officers to punish me up to and including death if I violate the Ship's Pledge. If at any time I cannot keep to the Pledge, I will inform a senior officer and refrain from any activity until I can be put off the ship. I understand that all around me at this moment have also taken this Pledge, and to them I promise my devotion. From this moment forward I will use all my knowledge, experience, and talents to help and support my ship and my crewmates. I swear solemnly that this oath will . . . that this will supersede any previous oaths or obligations. On this day I, Kathryn Janeway, so pledge."

"Now turn, and face your ship and your shipmates."

Shivering like a midshipman, I turned. Before me, the main deck sprawled like a small stadium. Crowded before me was *Zingara*'s crew of one hundred nine, missing only the seven who were in the infirmary, still unconscious. They all looked at me, seeing weakness in my manner for the first time since I'd come on board, and I wondered if they held in full comprehension the reason for my little pauses.

My heart was splitting. That was the reason.

Beside me, having cleaned his hair to a soft pine shroud and changed into a fresh shoulder cape, Quen appeared more captainlike than I had seen him yet. He was quiet and circumspect, probably wondering whether or not he were making a mistake, pledging a woman, and someone whom they had met only a few short weeks ago.

We'd made our light kick. Now we passively drifted near a completely different star from the one we had used to power up the tiles. Hyperlight-speed had brought us to a place of relative safety, and we were slowly making repairs. Things were still very hard. There were almost no resources in this miserable solar system and scarcely any connections with which to get supplies. We were quite on our own, moving between distant settlements and deposits, trying to bribe, buy, trade, or collect what we needed to get along. And that was down to food and water, not just fancy composite for the ship's systems.

Somewhere on this ship, Totobet was locked in a bunk, just as she had been on Sasaquon's ship. Our nervous medic Ruvan was having a look at her, and I could only imagine his face at trying to figure out what she was. In the back of my mind, a thousand questions for her rose as logic set in over my raw disgust for her. I needed answers. Sooner or later, I'd get them from her. For now, there was only crushing emotion filling this rite of passage.

Sadness lay upon my chest. Tears pushed at the backs of my eyes. My own words, my new oath, galvanized the deep emotions that I could no longer banish. A profound weight had been lifted, and another came to rest on me. The universe had turned without me, and I was in a whole new place, never to see any other.

This was my life now. This was my place, my ship. I had a living duty, crewmates, and I had a captain to serve. There was nothing left between *Voyager* and me but misplaced fidelity. For me there was no more Prime Directive, for there was no more Federation, zero chance of ever returning, ever again fulfilling my oath as a Starfleet captain. Even the wind must someday accept that the storm has changed course.

Starfleet didn't expect us to sacrifice all that we knew and could offer to other life-forms; the Federation wasn't that stingy. If we were trapped, as I now was, in some distant place, they'd rather we live and survive, but not live like hermits. I'd want my crew to join a culture if they could, to assimilate and use what they knew to the betterment of any and all, wouldn't I? Even when *Voyager* was displaced, we were still all Starfleet officers. We always had that to cling to. But I couldn't cling all by myself.

Now, as I jumped up a step in rank on my new ship, I had obligations that no previous oath could smother. I needn't let go of my identity, hide my abilities, or forget my Earth heritage. The Federation had something to offer to this culture . . . and that something was me.

"I, Quen, pledged captain of the *Zingara*, promise to stand behind Kay Janeway, to consider her suggestions, to believe her words, and to act in her defense. Kay, your crew accepts your Pledge, and we pledge ourselves to you."

A miserable thank-you rattled in my throat, but my voice utterly failed. Not exactly graduation at the Academy, yet . . . a blessed moment in its way. A glance back, a step forward. Today, with my heart aching and my mind clear, I made a new oath, devoting myself to this ship, these young people, and this culture in upheaval. The real had to take precedence over the hypothetical. I was here now. I was *here* now.

That was all there was to it. Another major change in my life. No champagne reception, no shaking hands with admirals, no wondering whether my father would be proud of me. Deep sorrow for the crew engulfed me as they murmured their congratulations and shielded their doubts. This was all the ceremony these poor boys had. They didn't have much, but they were betting it all on me. This was much more poignant than momentous accolades and fanfare and pageant.

Those who were off duty wandered back to their bunks. Those assigned to other decks wandered to their posts. Those assigned here, on the main deck, assigned to me, stayed and waited and watched me, and watched Quen. There were about twenty of them. including Lucas, the helmsman Resi, and the strong and reserved engineer, Massus.

On quivering legs I turned to watch Quen make his way back toward his quarters. Had he promoted me out of some kind of strange chivalry that I didn't understand yet? Because I had freed the ship from Sasaquon? Or was there more to it—was he perhaps giving tacit approval to changes I might make? Had my words to him not fallen on barren ground, as I'd first suspected?

Until I knew, my plans would have to be careful and reserved. On the other hand, I was in charge of a deck watch now.

I was in the command line, one of very few officers on *Zingara*—the captain, the first mate, six deck engineers, and six deck bosses, of which I was now one. I would have to coordinate, somehow, with the two other deck bosses on my watch—a diplomatic tightrope to say the least. This was different from Starfleet, this sudden promotion business, and I didn't know how to handle it without churning up huge resentment among the crew.

Yes, there'd been a vote of confidence from the captain— or perhaps it was less than that, just a quick thank-you— but I could easily abuse that goodwill with the crew who had served him a long time already. In Starfleet, promotions came through many means, from time served to extraordinary action, but they didn't usually come suddenly and unexpected. Generally speaking, very few servicemen flew high and fast over the heads of those before them, rarely without great tragedy in that wake. For me to have launched myself over the heads of all these men wasn't necessarily a good thing.

On top of everything else, I was a woman and they were distressed with my presence.

On this ship there were four watches in a day, seven and a half hours each. The crew complement was immediately cut in half and shared the day, standing alternate watches into eternity, interrupted every other watch by the team that was now trying to get some sleep. That made for three deck bosses and three deck engineers awake and handling the ship, and either Zell or Quen in command. Zell had been in command when I came on board, which was why Quen had been in his cabin. In times of emergency, all hands came on deck, but the on-watch bosses and engineers called the shots. It was simple, redundant, workable, and generally familiar. I could live with it.

All this raced though my mind in those first few seconds as my watch crew looked at me and fretted over what the woman would do first. I had some authority, limited and tenuous, a captain to serve who felt obliged to give me some say, a first officer who doubted and suspected me, a crew who didn't know what to make of me but were now as pledged to me as I was to them.

A powder keg, if I wasn't very careful. The gloss of promotion came with a rusty edge.

As the crew dispersed, Quen faced me passively. He kept his voice quiet. "Do you feel all right?"

Blinking downward, I nodded, unable to keep a small hesitation out of it, speaking to myself as much as him. "I'm here now. I'm a member of *Zingara*'s crew. It'd be immoral to hold back my abilities. It's my obligation to be the best shipmate I can be . . . and give all my talents to you."

With the last phrase I raised my eyes to him. The pallor of his soft mushroom complexion had worsened with the stress of these past few days. His eyes were soft and deeply sympathetic. God, he looked so young to me.

"Choice is the blood of life," I finished. "No choice . . . no life."

Some things didn't need discussing.

He continued to gaze at me. If he did not somehow perceive what I had once possessed, he seemed to fully comprehend what I was giving up, and that even if it was a lunatic's wild fantasy, I at least very deeply believed it.

"When you're ready," he began, "we'll need a course of zero-nine-eight degrees. It'll take us to the Peliorine Belt, where we can pick up some ice chunks for water. We might starve, but at least we won't shrivel up."

"Zero-nine-eight degrees," I repeated. "Understood."

"Good luck." He caught my fingers in a light brush as he stepped away, just as he and his crewmen so often did to each other.

The cold creeps ran down my arms. He darned well knew he hadn't done me any favors.

Even colder was Zell's final glance as he disappeared down the deck well. Zell was the commanding officer for me now. Neither of us liked it much.

Lucas, Massus, Resi, and twenty-odd other young men on my watch lingered on the main deck before me, demoralized, curious, and waiting.

Would I turn their world upside down?

"I know you're all worried," I began. "This is a big change for me too. If we cooperate and take one thing at a time, we'll do very well together. I'm new to the ship. I'm a woman and that's unusual for you, but I have lots of experience in space. I'm asking you to trust me until you have reason not to. Is that fair?"

Lucas nodded right away. Massus and Resi glowered their doubt, but made no protest. The rest of the crew took their cue from Massus, who refused to make visible commitment. His wait-and-see attitude was nerve-wracking.

All right, I'd do without his approval.

I drew a deep breath, steadied myself, and tried to ignore the nagging facts about me that the crew was having such a hard time pretending weren't there.

"Okay, here are the immediate changes. I'm the deck boss. To me, that means if you have any problems or concerns, even about me, you'll come to me first. I'm bound to have lots of problems, and I want you to speak up and help me do better. The command structure under me will be Massus, then Levan, then Jedd. I know you've never done that before, but we're going to be prepared in case anything happens to me. We're going to one-hour watches on the wheel, sensors, power train, and ship check."

"What's a ship check?" Resi asked with a slight edge of challenge in his voice. "We checked. We know it's a ship."

I offered a smile, though he didn't return it. "It's a log of data we're going to check every hour. Rod levels, capacitor flow, compensators, thruster controls, rackers, pressure gauges, and the jeklight radiation charge."

"You want us to keep a log?" somebody asked. "Every hour?"

"That's right. That way we can monitor power usage and

figure out how to be more efficient. Generally, it'll make us more familiar with our ship and how she works and how to help her work better. It sounds like extra work, and it is, but you'll get used to it."

They muttered and shifted, probably figuring I was crazy to watch things that didn't need watching. First step taken. Next?

I held up a printout, written by the computer in the symbols of their language, and didn't bother to mention how many testy hours it had taken me to learn enough of their language to put this together. That was my problem.

"I've made up a station bill. It'll be posted right over there on the lateral support stanchion. It has all your names on it in rotation. It assigns helm watch, sensor watch, computer duty, spectroscopy and cartography, ship check, life support, tile duty, engineer's assistants, and standby, in those one-hour watches I told you about."

"Why an hour?" Resi asked. "Why can't we just get a post and stay there, like always?"

"Because, with the new rotation system, everybody gets a break and nobody numbs into a job for too long. And also, you get experience standing other posts, which is good in times of trouble. You'll learn to like it. You won't be as tired at the end of a watch. Oh, and if you're on standby, you've essentially got an hour off. Take it to rest or finish up something, change socks, or whatever you want, but stay available on the deck. Understood so far?"

They glanced at each other, wondering—oh, who knew what they were wondering—except for Massus and Resi, who were both glaring at me as if I'd grown pointed ears. They seemed to be two of the most experienced here, and the rest of the crew might take their leads. I'd have to win them over, or at least get them to keep any apprehension and skepticism to themselves for now.

"Mostly this work is for me over the next few days," I went on, "but I want you to know what I'm planning. I pledged to be honest with you, and to me that means letting you in on what I'm thinking about. I'll be making up an emergency station bill, and if you've got anything like this that I don't know about, please tell me and I'll try to keep close to whatever's familiar to you. Do you have a plan for abandon ship?"

They gawked at me, then Massus said, "Yes. Get out."

A nervous ripple of laughter ran through the crew, and in fact helped a little.

I smiled and shrugged.

"Good plan, but I'd like to refine it just a wee bit. Each of you will have an assignment for fire, rescue, abandon ship, and battlestations. Memorize your positions and get familiar with whatever equipment falls under your control in those positions. It sounds complicated, but it's not really. You have to memorize only three posts and get it into your head to go there. Each of the subbosses—Massus, Levan, and Jedd—will have an emergency leadership position. For instance, in the case of abandon ship, Massus will be in charge of one life craft. Those of you under his name on the bill will muster at that pod. As long as there are patients in the infirmary, some of you will have the assignment of getting the wounded to a pod—"

"What about the rest of the crew?" Levan interrupted. "We'll just leave them behind?"

Another roll of laughter, not quite so uneasy as before.

"That's right, we won't need them anyway," I said. "They'll just take up food."

Even Massus gave a grudging chuckle and tried to smother it behind a knuckle.

"I'll try to work something out with the other deck bosses," I assured. "They're sensible. They can be convinced to organize their crews too. We should all cooperate. We all have to abandon the same ship if it comes to that, right? Abandoning a ship means there's big trouble, so you've got to organize your thoughts and know where you're going long before that actually happens. A wild scramble is no good on a ship. Panic kills. No point letting it get a grip. Understand all that too, so far?"

A classroom nod bumbled across the deck. They didn't really understand all these unfamiliar and unexpected changes, but they were willing to give it a shot. I had to give them credit for not protesting right away. That was the sign of a good crew.

At first the station bills would be confusing, but then each man would get used to the fact that his name appeared only in select places, and he would memorize those places. For a while I'd float around every hour, making sure everybody was in place and knew what to do.

A few days from now, I'd start running emergency drills.

Oops—information overload. Better not mention drills just yet . . .

"What do you want us to do right now?" Resi asked, scratching his shoulder as if he were already tired.

"Oh . . ." I glanced around the cluttered deck. "Almost forgot about right now, didn't I? And I almost had you fooled that I knew what I was doing. Darn."

I cashed in on another ripple of smiles, which seemed to help everybody, including me.

"Well, let's start by squaring away."

"Squaring?" Jedd asked. "The tiles, you mean?"

"No. Everything. 'Squaring away' means to clear the deck. Coil the cords that aren't being used. Stow the work lights that we don't need right now. Sweep up the bits of junk all over and swab the spilled lubricant. Make this deck safe to walk around on. If we do have an crisis, there's no sense having a deck cluttered with shrapnel, is there?"

"Pick all this up?" Othien asked. "All the tools and everything?"

I looked at him. "Yes . . . Is there a problem?"

They glanced at each other, and then Levan said, "There's no place to stow all this. We usually just leave it out or push it aside. We always need things, so we don't put much below."

"Time to start. There's no organized storage for most of these tools and parts?"

They offered me only a collective shrug, but that wasn't because they didn't know the answer.

"Well," I said with a quick sigh, "we have to be ingenious, then. Take that skein of thin cord over there—yes, that's the one—and I'll teach you how to make gear nets. We'll hang them from these knees right at the edge of the decks and put the tools in one, the parts in another, electrical cords, maintenance gear, and so on. You'll get used to it. You might even like it. All right, let's consider ourselves on duty,

158

shall we? When the watch is done, we'll gather amidships and go off watch together. Then we'll go belowdecks and eat together and discuss how it went. Levan, I believe you're up on the helm. If you'll take that position, please, and put us on a course of zero-nine-eight degrees, as Quen requested."

The crew began slowly to disperse, and I caught Levan's arm. "Repeat the order," I instructed.

Levan paused, and so did Massus, Lucas, and others who had heard. "What?"

"Repeat the order."

"You mean . . . tell you the order?"

"No, but acknowledge it by repeating what I tell you. Say, 'Zero-nine-eight.' "

He glanced uncomfortably at Massus, then frowned at me. "Zero-nine-eight . . ."

"Then say 'aye' so I know you heard me clearly and understood."

"Zero . . . nine-eight . . . 'aye'? Like that?"

"That's right."

"You want us to do that all the time?"

"All the time. You'll get used to it."

He sighed, shook his head, and picked his way toward the helm.

"Bet we won't," he muttered.

I watched them disperse, wondering whether I had given them too much to think about, attempted to change their ways too quickly. My self-doubts surged into my throat. It had been a long, long time since I'd run a deck.

When most of them were involved with coiling cords and swabbing lubricant, I moved across the deck, around the deck well, to Lucas, who was cleaning up the area around the lower port scanners amidships.

"Lucas," I began quietly, "you're assigned to the computer system right now, aren't you?"

He blinked at me, perfectly well knowing I'd assigned him here. "Yes . . ."

"I want you to do something for me but not discuss it with anyone else. Do you trust me?"

Offering a childlike shrug, he admitted, "I don't know. So far, I do."

"Thanks. I want you to start organizing lists of the other

warranter captains and their ships. Help me get familiar with them. Type of ships, size, crew complement, power, communication codes, last known location. Can you do all that? Help me catch up with what everybody else already knows?"

He thought about what I was requesting, seemed to decide it was all innocent enough, or at least justified in my new position, and nodded. "I can do that."

"Thank you. Jedd, can I bother you a moment?"

What an odd thing . . . When I was a captain, all I had to do was stride into a room, catch a few eyes, and everybody was ready to tend my whims.

This was very different. I felt obliged to tend their needs, be more polite, make absolutely sure that any hint of arrogance remained muted. They had their jobs, and I shouldn't interrupt them, even if I assigned those jobs.

Jedd shoved his ratty blue hair out of his eyes and gave me a look I'd rather not see very often. "You're bothering me."

"Sorry. You know the weapons systems very well on this ship, don't you?"

"I built half of 'em."

"That's what everybody says. I need your help."

"What kind of help?"

"Would you teach me about the weapons? Show me the guts of the missiles, describe how the cables and clamps work, and make me understand the propellants?"

"Why? We know how they work."

Jedd was a rough sort of man, somewhat older than most of his shipmates, and I didn't know him except in passing, but I forced myself to stick to the promise of honesty until forced otherwise.

"Because you're not trained for this," I told him bluntly. "You fight to keep alive, but you don't know how to think ahead. Everything you've done so far has been weak and defensive. Only the most delusional minds think that a good quality of life can be had with weak defense. Now that I've got some authority, I'm going to help this ship grow antlers. For that, I need you."

His expression changed a little with the compliment and the confidence I showed in him—I'd have to remember that. For the first time, I saw a glint of anticipation in one of the crew.

"I'll show you everything," he said. "They're good systems. I like 'em. In no time, you'll know everything."

He stalked off.

I paused and took a deep breath before following.

"Bet I won't," I grumbled.

While the crew worked to adjust to the station bill and the new watch schedule, I worked also to familiarize myself with systems that any other deck boss would already know by heart. I'd always thought *Voyager* was a big ship, but I was finding out how little I really knew and that "big" was relative. *Zingara,* for an industrial tractor-processor, was a strong muscle in space that deserved much more respect from me than I had seen while gazing down my nose at her.

The other deck bosses, five of them, were variously indifferent or disdainful of my new methods, but how I ran my watch really didn't affect theirs, so any disdain soon wandered into curiosity. None suggested that it wasn't perfectly my business to run my crew in any way I saw fit, and even Zell, as commander on my watch, made no attempts to disparage the station bills. That was a relief, but I should've expected it. Running a ship had a certain intership, international, interstellar sense that just had to happen. Shipfaring from long ago had found its stride, and all over the galaxy we'd found similarities in management that just made common sense. For the commander to micromanage the crew was plain foolish and faulty to a point of danger. Zell had his job, I had mine, and the main deck crew was mine.

By the same token, I did not interfere in command, navigation, salvage decisions, or the running of the other decks, and I did not speak for the ship when we came up against other warranters or anybody else. The only other deck boss with whom I had interaction of necessity was a subdued fellow named Gashan who ran the other watch on the main deck. We had a few things to coordinate, such as which jobs still needed tending at the end of a given watch. I also arranged for both him and me to get our crews up and at their posts about five minutes earlier than the actual change of watch, then take over about two minutes early. This was something I'd learned on my very first ship. It didn't really change the duration of a watch, but just the illusion of getting off a couple minutes' early had a phenomenally encouraging effect on the crew. Everyone *thought* he was getting more rest and relief than he actually was, and the tiny attitude change worked miracles.

During the day's two meals, directly before and after each watch, we sat together on the processing deck—unless there was processing going on—and discussed problems and ways to improve things. Little things, not huge things. The huge things had been worked out long ago on ships like this. But incrementally, there was room for improvement. Gradually over the next few weeks, we improved.

The other deck bosses couldn't ignore the positive effects of my station posting tricks. My crew and Gashan's were better rested and in generally higher spirits than anyone else, and were more alert. Sworn, as I was, to do their best for the ship, the other deck bosses soon started trying similar methods. Some worked for them, others didn't, but they were experimenting with new ways, and from the general mutterings, that hadn't happened in a while.

After a time, with things running smoothly, I started using those quiet moments and off-watch times to get to know the technology. I discovered, for instance, that their energy storage methods weren't really different from what I was familiar with. I got the idea that the tile method, rather than being greatly divergent from the science of my culture, was just something my culture had skipped, and that this *Zingara* culture wasn't all that far from matter-antimatter propulsion. Already antimatter had been isolated and successfully maintained in a few of their facilities, so it was only a matter of time before they would figure it out.

As I figured out their technology, I started slowly to experiment with it. The tiles, my little square children, attracted me the most and I started to fiddle with their capabilities.

I kept my attempts to myself. What good would it do to stride around the ship prattling about microduotronics, reactant injectors, plasma distribution manifolds, and micron junction links? My job here wasn't to prance around showing off how superior I was. My job was to help these young men become superior too.

Besides, I wasn't superior. They knew a lot more about metallurgy and industrial recycling than I did. And much more about getting along day to day and surviving in a life-or-death situation than I did, right down to using real fur blankets because nature was sometimes hard to improve upon. Give or take the odd and rather limited adventure into stress I might've had while on board *Voyager,* no hardship had lasted as long as this for me, and certainly not as long as these men's working lives had been. I'd had a few hours, perhaps a few days at a time of trouble and strife. For this crew, trouble and strife were their whole existence. I came to laud less and less my own Starfleet-provided genius and appreciate much more the suffering-toughened resolve of *Zingara*'s crew. I even got used to the chill and dimness.

This had a bit of negative fallout. When I started fiddling, naturally I caught the eyes of the men on board. They wondered what I was doing and why. Loathe to sound pompous, I found myself explaining the general idea, but keeping the talk to a minimum. These fellows weren't stupid—they knew I was holding back. They started to wonder why. Funny little balancing act I found myself playing.

After a while, most of the crew left me alone to do my experiments unless they needed me, and I always made sure the watch was running smoothly before I got involved with anything of my own.

And those tiles kept attracting me. They seemed so simple, just capacitors, and yet they could do so many things—broadcast pictures, conduct communication, trigger mechanical response, and of course jump start the fusion engines—and yet all this was simply through adjustments in the type, frequency, and modulation of their basic storage abilities. Fascinating little acorns on a very prolific tree.

While I was busy with my favorite tile experiment and getting some mind-boggling numbers, Quen happened to stroll by with a bowl of the oatmealy former livestock we too often called dinner. As he saw what I was doing, he ducked under the low-slung diagonal beam and peered at the single lonely tile I'd suspended on a coil wand. It stuck out of the bulkhead like a perverse flower on a stalk, glowing many times brighter than he was used to.

"Life from beyond the pyre?" he asked.

I looked up. "It's my grandmother, come for a visit."

"Is that . . . just one tile?"

"Just one sweet little slab. And it's holding two hundred twelve percent more energy than we're putting into any tile on board."

"Two hundred and twelve!" He put his bowl down on top of the jeklight meter and dipped under the beam, having to bend in order to join me under there.

He was prevented from crouching beside me by all the meters, sequencers, monitors, and transfer coils I had littered in a crude campfire circle around me, all working in combination to juice up that one tile and measure the changes. Quen couldn't even kneel with all this stuff on the deck, so he remained awkwardly bent and cupped a hand over the diagonal beam above his head to keep himself from falling forward.

The glow of my single tile emboldened his fine features and cast a Christmas sheen on his dark green hair.

"How did you do that?"

"I've been trying to figure out just how much energy could be packed into a tile if we didn't have to worry about burning up by getting too close to a sun. If it doesn't have to be radiant energy—well, watch this. The tile is completely isolated. There's no place for its energy to go, so it just has to keep absorbing, and I wanted to know how much cold power it could handle. Advance the coil valve . . . modify the rod level sequencers . . . Excuse me, but I can't see the network assembly—thanks. Direct feed off the fusion generator . . . Now watch the jeklight meter. Watch how much more one tile can hold."

On the end of its conduit wand, the tile began to whine with pumped-up energy and sizzled to a high green-white glow, so bright that Quen flinched, blinked, and put his free hand up to shield his eyes until they adjusted somewhat.

"Look at the rod levels," I told him.

"It's already red-lined."

"Keep watching it." As he adjusted his stance, almost

hanging by his hand on the beam up there to twist and look at the indicator, I ticked off the numbers. "There's three hundred percent . . . four-eighty . . ."

The tile whined furiously, but did not vibrate, and shined with a glaring light.

"Five-twenty . . . six . . . eight . . . eight-ten . . . eight-fifteen . . . looks like it's topping out at . . . eight hundred seventeen percent."

The single tile was now brightly illuminating the whole lower deck, as if there weren't even any work lights on at all. Quen shielded his eyes from the glare and watched the meters in astonishment. "I had no idea a tile could do that!"

"I really didn't either," I said, "but there were enough similarities between this alloy and the properties of some things where I come from that it was worth a try. I just kept filling it and filling it. If you don't need a sun, you don't have to worry about the same limits."

Quen got a better grip on the beam overhead and leaned a little closer. "What can we do with it?"

"Ah," I accepted. "Those hard questions always serve to let us brilliant best-of-the-bests rise above the rabble and show what brainy wizards we are."

"Then what's the answer?"

"I don't have the foggiest idea."

He smiled. "There's got to be something . . ." He tilted a little to look at the conduit wand that so effectively isolated the single gleaming tile, and with his free hand reached around behind the tile.

I was watching the jeklight meter. I didn't see him reaching for the wand. Only as my peripheral alarms went off did I realize what he was about to do. I gasped an inadequate "Don't touch—!"

But my warning was swallowed by a lightning snap of power transfer. The force of sheer release drove me backward against the ship's rib, and from that low vantage I got a full view of the sheets of raw energy discharging from Quen's hand to his shoulder, through his body, arching upward through his other arm and into the beam over his head. His back arched convulsively as the tile purged all its stored power into him in a millisecond. His hair flew, his head shot back, and all I could see of his expression was his mouth gaping in shocky reaction and the triangle of his chin reflecting the sudden snap of light.

Using Quen's body as a conduit, the raw energy instantly bolted to the diagonal beam, popped a chorus of rivets, and cracked the wood to which the metal beam was bolted. The low overhead structure burst to shreds, shuddered as if suspended, then slammed on top of Quen as if driven down by the hands of titans.

CHAPTER
13

THE BEAM AND ITS ATTENDANT STRUCTURE DROVE QUEN TO THE deck and landed across his lower back and thighs. In seconds, there was nothing but the sizzle of burned wood and a faint wheeze from our captain's tortured lungs.

"Oh, no!" I crawled through hot wreckage, slamming aside my meters and monitors to get to Quen.

By the time I reached him, several men were piling down the ladder into the processor deck.

"Get Zell!" I called. "And Ruvan! Lift this beam off him!"

One of the men angled quickly back up the ladder, and three others came forward to lift the heavy metal beam off Quen's back.

Then Othien stooped in and started to grasp Quen's arm, a movement meant to turn the captain over. I quickly knocked him back.

"Don't move him . . . Get the top of that locker and bring it here. We'll use it as a backboard."

"Backboard?"

"We have to keep his spine immobile . . . My God, is he breathing?"

Sweat drained from my temples to my neck—the first time I'd perspired since crawling out of the pod into this chilly ship. A faint green glow made Quen look dead. He wasn't dead, was he?

Suddenly furious, I realized where the glow was coming from and lashed out to one side, cutting off the trail of power to the single tile, which was dutifully trying to recharge itself after the sudden discharge. Damn thing.

When I turned again to the terrible sight before me, Zell was there. He knelt at his captain's shoulder, his face a matte of misery and fear. He pressed his large hand to Quen's back with heart-wrenching tenderness. For a moment he just didn't seem to know what to do.

Nobody did. Nobody did . . .

CHAPTER
14

"I WANT TO SEE HIM."

"He doesn't want to see you. Ruvan's still treating him."

"You mean *you* don't want him to see me. I'm one of the deck bosses. You can't just push me aside anymore, Zell."

"I'm your watch officer. You can report to me."

"Fine. I'm reporting that you know I have to be able to put my crew at ease in order for the ship to run smoothly. I can't do that if I don't know what's going on."

We were in dangerous territory. All around us, settlements teemed with contraband. Other warrant ships stole in and out over the past few hours. No matter how we tried to isolate ourselves, we had no choice but to barter for supplies. Word was spreading about Quen. That couldn't be good.

Unenthusiastic about much of anything, Zell shook his head and stepped into the pitifully inadequate infirmary. While I lingered back, he went straight to the treatment cot where Quen now lay. The first sound we heard was Quen's tight moan.

Quen's face was nearly white with pain, his eyes stricken.

The dim light of *Zingara*'s thrifty interior did him no favors. Every breath was a knotted gasp. His hands clutched at the worn fur blanket draped over his hips and chest. Zell caught one of those hands, gazed at Quen's anguished face with the sincerest emotion I'd ever seen from him.

Ruvan flustered over a makeshift splint contraption holding Quen's pelvis and legs in place on the cot. Both legs were raised on a cushion and his feet were supported by another cushion. Didn't look very comfortable.

"Are his hips broken?" I asked quietly as Ruvan passed close to me coming around the end of the cot.

"Cracked pelvis," he said. "Lots of torn ligaments . . . possible spinal damage, three broken ribs. Almost every internal organ has been burned. There could be bleeding inside. Quen . . ."

The medic bent over our young captain and waited until Quen's eyes focused on him.

"I gave you something for the pain, but I can't treat all this. Not well enough. You've got to let us go back to Om and put you in a hospital. You need bone surgery. Maybe spinal surgery. There's no place to do that but on the planet."

Quen struggled to answer, managing a tight smile. "You do it . . . Zell's got a rigger's knife."

"Don't make jokes," Ruvan miserated. "Don't make jokes . . . please listen. We can't put you on another transport because I don't want to move you around. We have to take you back ourselves. It could be months for you waiting to heal without treatment."

"Ruvan's right," Zell intruded. "We can't load this all on him. It's not fair."

Sorrowfully Quen rolled his head on the small pillow to look at Zell. "We can't give in . . . we can't give in . . . Don't let anybody talk you into giving—"

A grueling spasm cut him in half. He twisted, valiantly fighting it. Zell held his hand, grimacing in anguish and empathy, and tried to keep Quen from harming himself further by shifting that damaged pelvis.

I found myself pressed back against the wall, arms folded so tightly that my ribs hurt. The two of them reminded me of Tom Paris and Harry Kim, just young men caught in a big ugly situation in which they were losing what little control they ever had.

Quen clamped his lips shut to bury the gasps, instead giving way to a series of compressed groans, one riding on each breath he drew. He pressed his left hand to his hip, crushed his eyes closed, and turned away from Zell. We could see the internal results of electrocution working on him, and could do nothing about it. For the first time in my life, I wished I'd gone to medical school.

Without trying to hide his inner torture, Zell looked at Ruvan. "Rig a traction. Do whatever you can for him. We're not going in."

Pain as deep-laden as Quen's cramped Ruvan's face. His shoulders hunched and he hung his head, envisioning months of ghastly discomfort for his patient.

Pressing a pale hand to his ribs, Quen opened his eyes wearily, reached out with the other hand, and caught Ruvan's wrist. When Ruvan looked at him, the injured leader of a ragtag crew heavily said, "I'm sorry I brought you here . . ."

The furtive glimpse into these boys' unspoken past gave me little information but somehow affected me deeply. In many ways they were lost, even more lost than *Voyager*'s crew had been, for we had at least known the way home.

"I'll need a couple of assistants to help with him," Ruvan rasped. "Someone'll have to build a slant-board. And I need nylon straps."

"Kay," Zell said instantly, "put two of your crew on infirmary duty."

"Right away," I responded. "I've got two men on standby."

"Straps and a slant board."

I nodded. "Less than twenty minutes."

He looked down at Quen and gripped his captain's hand reassuringly. "You . . . rest."

Quen offered him a minimal grin. "Between dances."

Zell, for a burly type who otherwise should've been guarding an end zone somewhere, was surprisingly gentle. He had trouble pulling himself away, but with a final glance at Ruvan that offered scant support, he forced himself out of the infirmary.

I caught him in the corridor, halfway to the main deck.

"Zell," I called. "Wait."

Turning to me, he visibly fought to regain control over his expression. "What?"

"We have to make a plan."

"Plan for what?"

"For battle. We're heading for one. We have to get the homeworld to understand there's an enemy coming. We can put the warranters in a stronger bargaining position if we all band together. Everyone has to unify in order to beat the Men—"

"We can't band together. I explained that."

"I know, hostile coalition. All I want is one face-to-face meeting with the other warranter captains and—"

"No!" He grimaced. "Aren't you tired of talking this way? You're making everybody scared for no reason."

"There's plenty of reason. We've got to be ready."

"'Ready' how?"

"This sector doesn't stand a chance against Hell's Aliens if we don't organize. I can't teach you how to build a warp core—I can't even teach you how to build a pencil—but I can hike your fusion efficiency, enhance your long-range sensors, organize the warranter crews for battlestations. Your weapons can be made more efficient—"

"How?"

"Well, you've got turret guns supplemented by secondary guns on the casements. Instead of rotating the whole turret, why not mount the guns outside and just rotate the guns?"

"We tried that last year. The guns are unprotected and we have to go outside or retreat to make repairs."

"But we'd get better results. We should start targeting installations. We've got to start getting ready."

"Fine, get ready." Once again he tried to get back to the main deck and away from me.

With a hopeful lilt, I asked, "Is that a command?"

He stopped and glared at me. "What?"

"Is that permission to get the ship ready?"

Clapping a hand to his head, he rubbed his face harshly, then said, "What are you talking about?"

I held out a hand. "You're the captain now."

As he suddenly realized the scope of what I meant, he backed up so sharply that he bumped his head on a transverse beam. "I'm not the captain! Don't say that."

"Quen's incapacitated. He can't command from there—"

A big finger poked me in the shoulder. "Don't you say that to anybody on this ship or any other ship. Look, I have to deal with you, but I don't have to like it."

Though he tried to leave again, I plunged forward and caught him by the sleeve. "Zell, you have to take over!"

Yanking out of my grip, he snapped, "Stop saying that! I'm *not* the captain. Quen is *Zingara's* captain. If things get worse . . . we'll have an election."

"Election?"

"I'm not captain until the crew makes me captain."

His big hand pressed against my shoulder and pushed me back, not roughly but very firmly. He fell silent for a few seconds, enough to put a buffer between us.

"Mind your own business, Kay," he warned. "Mind your crew and your business. Leave me alone."

Something in his voice made me give up. For a moment I'd forgotten that he was worn-out too, hungry, tired, probably frightened. He had spent his visible past in simple salvage operations and defending those salvages, a piratical but relatively simple and limited-range life. He had never before faced anything like what I was describing, and to his mind he had no reason to face it at all.

He filled up the hatchway as he stepped through to the main deck, leaving me blessedly behind. His respite was short-lived. Across the deck, now cleared of all the maintenance gear and safe to stride, came a wall of young men I didn't recognize. Warranters—and leading them was Oran!

Oran, Quen's brother—still, a competing warranter captain and a boarding party, on our ship!

If they'd been just boarders, I'd have known perfectly well what to do. Slam the hatch shut, lock it, and keep them from reaching our injured captain while I found a way to gas the main deck with sedative and knock everybody out.

The plan died aborning. Oran had more right to see Quen than I did. Brothers, right? What should I do?

Take Zell's cue—that was my second instinct.

Zell met the entourage halfway up the main deck. He and Oran squared off with something less than affection, but not animosity either. There was caution in the way they paused, looked at each other, exchanged a few words. Zell must be explaining what happened to Quen—yes, he was pointing at the wreckage that had crushed our captain to the deck. Then he put his hand on his own pelvis bone and his lower back and ribs, demonstrating some of the injuries.

Oran frowned in empathy with his brother, whom he hadn't even seen yet.

Quickly I dove for an equipment locker and pulled out several nylon harnesses and loading straps. Slipping back past the hatchway, I rushed toward the infirmary door, then controlled my motions so as to appear casual as I stepped inside.

Hovering over Quen, Ruvan looked up.

"Here are the straps," I said. "How much of a degree of incline do you want on the slant-board? Why don't you make me a little diagram of what you need."

That bought me enough time. When Oran and Zell appeared at the infirmary door, I was already inside.

Zell seemed plenty annoyed that I was still there, although Oran had attention only for his brother. Instantly Oran's captainlike distance and professionalism dissolved when he saw Quen lying there in a girdle of suffering.

"Oh, no," Oran moaned. "Oh, no . . ." His shoulders sank, and he thumped his hands on his thighs in frustration.

Quen gazed back at him. "You shouldn't be here," he whispered through the glaze of medication.

Ruvan's treatment had taken some effect. Quen's eyes were clearer and his motions less tormented as Oran came to him, and somehow they managed to get their arms around each other without causing any more damage. For a long time the brothers were nothing but a bundle of rugged clothing and forest-shadow hair. Ruvan and I stood aside, and Zell hovered near the hatch, letting them have this bonding moment. Apparently such times were rare in the lives of a warranter family.

Without really letting go, Oran raised his head enough that they could look at each other and talk.

"What is this?" he began roughly. "A pathetic excuse to get some sleep?"

Quen smiled, soon ruined as he tightened through a spasm. The sight of him cramped up like that drove the attempt at mirth away from all of us. Oran held his brother, and they endured the torment together until Quen managed to regain some control.

"You're going to have to accept help now," Oran said. "You know that, don't you?"

"We're . . . fine. We made two good . . . trades . . . and an ice catch . . . yesterday."

"Let me bring Murn over here. He knows something about internal injuries."

"No . . . no, Oran, don't."

"Ruvan can't handle this by himself. You're asking too much of him."

"He . . . likes it."

"Jokes," Ruvan mumbled disapprovingly.

Here were the captain, first mate, and chief medic of a working ship, yet they all seemed so very young to me as I watched them dealing with this tragic turn. I didn't want to be their mother, but maybe I had to be.

Keeping very careful control over my tone, I offered, "Quen, I agree with your brother. The warranters should start helping each other. This other way isn't working."

Had I lit a firecracker? You'd think so, the way they all looked at me. The whole idea of banding together was so foreign and dishonorable to them, given the promises they'd made to defend freedom on their planet and follow the rule of law, that even the mention of such a bond was some kind of transgression. They were all too decent for their own good. Now or never.

With my arms folded, trying not to appear overbearing, I took one measured step forward. "Captain Oran, may I speak to you about something very important?"

Suddenly enraged, Zell stepped in. "No, Kay!"

Oran looked at him, then back at me. "What's the matter? Who are you?"

"Nothing, nobody," Zell insisted. "Kay, get out."

I looked at Quen. "Captain . . . please?"

Still clinging to his brother, Quen studied my face for

signs of honesty or insanity, trying to decide whether he knew me well enough to judge my character quite this deeply.

They were all watching me, though the only one I was interested in was Quen. I wouldn't speak again until he did.

Through a long gasping breath, he finally said, "Go ahead."

"Keep it short," Zell bruskly warned.

From the pocket of my trousers, I pulled a single curry card. "I planned on keeping it short. Here's an explanation of what I think is going on and why. I come from another ship, Captain Oran, a ship that was destroyed along with the outpost we were visiting and most of the people on it. There was a slaughter by an incoming force. It's all described there. I believe that force is a conquering body and it's on its way here. This whole sector will be obliterated if we don't organize ourselves. The warranters have to band together to fight the TCA fleet, or we all have to band together to fight the incoming Menace. And it's the second part that had better happen."

"TCA fleet?" Oran repeated. "The TCA doesn't have a fleet. *We* were the planetary fleet."

"I was on board Sasaquon's ship and overheard them talking about a fleet that'll be ready to launch soon. I believe the TCA has been using Sasaquon to keep the warranters from consolidating, long enough for the TCA to build up its own fleet to come here and wipe you out."

Zell snapped his fingers at me and said, "Get back on the deck where you belong."

But Oran looked at his brother. "You believe this, Quen?"

Quen's face took on the trouble of decision under the tightness of pain. "Some things she says . . . make sense . . . We believe she came from a . . . from a better science than ours . . . She knows some things . . . but there's no—"

A surge of new pain cut him off, and as Oran gripped him in helpless support, Zell stepped in to finish the sentence.

"No proof," the first mate charged. "No proof at all for this crazy talk."

"There's proof," I challenged. "We've got one of their women locked up in our forward section!"

"I want to see her," Oran said.

"You can see her," Zell agreed, "but she's not proof of anything. It's a big galaxy. Even if Kay's right, even if that woman's part of some force, this Menace she talks about could be headed in any hundred other directions. There are millions of stars. It could be centuries before they get to us."

"Or it could be tomorrow," I shoved in.

"Wait," Oran said, holding up a hand. "I saw things at Pelior Station and at Rymon Line. Things I didn't understand, but things that make sense if there's a fleet. That could explain why there's been so much activity at the Tuskan smelting facility."

"There's activity there?" Quen asked. "At this time of . . . year?"

"Lots of it."

For the first time there was a glimmer of suspicion in their eyes that didn't involve doubting me. Not Zell, of course, but the young captains. Like all captains, they were used to having to think more broadly than anyone else on any ship. They looked at each other, distilling almost psychically what they knew, and then both of them looked at me again.

This was hard—trying to convince other people of things that really mattered. On *Voyager* I had been the supreme authority, the person everybody else had to convince. All decisions were ultimately mine. I'd gotten spoiled. Now the shoe was on a whole other foot and I was scrambling for our lives without the voltage to make the action occur.

"Before we can fight the TCA fleet or the Menace," I went on, "first we have to be ready to fight, period. That's why I've been making new star charts, concentrating on coordinating depots, pockets of population, friendly bases, installations—"

"You are talking too much!" Zell shouted. "You're making it sound like we *have* to fight! If you build up to fight, it means you have to go out and look for a fight. If you put resources into getting strong and powerful, you have to go out and use that power! That's how people react to things!"

"Depends on the people," I said quietly. "We have to be so ready for a fight that everybody else knows we are. We have to make ourselves so scary that other people won't attack us. When the Menace shows up, I want to be out there already between them and our planets, with all the warranter ships and the TCA fleet, and I want to be too scary for anybody to attack us. That's how you *stop* a fight."

"This recording . . . it's just you talking?"

Oran looked at the curry card I'd provided him, and it seemed he was willing to pay attention, but only to a point.

"Not ships or aliens?" he asked. "It's not anything we can look at?"

"It's not proof," Zell clarified. "It's just her doing a lot of raving. She could be making it all up. She could be imagining all this Menace, slaughter, fleet."

"I don't think Kay's lying, Zell," Quen offered. At first I was heartened, but then to his brother he said, "It could be imagination. She was in very . . . bad . . ."

He winced hard. His eyes cramped shut, and he pressed against his brother's hands as pain dogged his crushed body.

Ruvan stepped to the cot, but there was nothing anyone could do except wait for the pain to pass. "That's enough," he said, and this doctorly order was the most authoritative thing I'd heard him say. Usually Ruvan was easy to push around, but clearly he'd had enough.

"Kay, you've had your moment," Zell ordered. "They've heard you, and it's time to get out and leave them alone. Let's go."

Neither of the captains countermanded his order. I was assigned to Zell's watch. He had command over me. My one chance, whatever it was worth, was over.

To his credit, Zell followed me out and motioned for Ruvan to come out too. He really did mean to let the brothers have a few moments of privacy.

What would the captains talk about to each other? How the woman was crazy? Or how there was some mysterious activity at the Tucker facility?

"Tuskan facility," I mumbled, correcting myself.

Zell and I stepped out onto the main deck and went our separate ways. He had his work to do, and I had mine. I had a crew to run.

There were tiles to be scrubbed. There was a slant-board to make. There was sabotage to plan. Time to get to work.

CHAPTER

15

"LIGHT KICK! ZELL! ZELL!"

"What happened!"

"We're kicked!"

"Who made the buildup!"

"We don't know!"

"Why didn't anybody notice!"

"The readouts were shut down!"

"Can we stop it?"

"No, no! We're hyperlight!"

"How fast?"

"Full speed!"

"All right, don't stop it! Nobody touch anything! Kay! Where are you! Where is she?"

It had taken me nearly a week and a half to work out my plan. Finally, the button had been pushed and *Zingara*'s swelled-up capacitors released all their power at once, shoving the ship into light-speed, heading where I told it to go. It was an act of sabotage, even mutiny, and I'd done it with my own two little hands.

The way this technology worked, we were utterly committed. The capacitor tiles had skimmed off all they could of the nearest sun's energy as it streamed through the skin of the ship. Then, through some careful subterfuge and tricky crew assignments on my part, they'd built up to top-off without anyone's noticing. That could have gone on only for a matter of minutes. Soon the point of now-or-never had come, and I'd hit the switch. The tiles had emptied of all their energy in an instant, funneling a massive surge into the fusion engines. *Zap*—we were at hyperlight speed. Now the fusion engines could keep up until we reached the destination I'd preprogrammed into the navigation system.

Most of the crew had been knocked to their knees by the sudden start. The rest had been dumped out of their bunks. With a little luck, Totobet would have landed on her head. I only hoped Quen was all right.

Yes, I felt awful about it. When *Voyager* needed me to be there and be a captain, I'd been somewhere else. I'd never make that mistake again.

When Zell and Massus appeared before me like a bulky wall, I wasn't surprised. When they grabbed my arms and hauled me across the deck, I didn't resist.

They dragged me past the astonished and confused faces of the current watch crew, a crew afraid to touch their own equipment. Their ship had come alive around them and gone off on its own. If anything changed, if they tampered, the light kick would shut down and they'd be stuck in the interstellar void with no way to power up for a return kick. They hovered around, monitoring things, afraid to do much. That was for the best. Now that I'd set things in motion, we had to go where we were headed.

Quen was still in the infirmary, tractioned up to a framework Ruvan had designed and my watch crew had built. His upper body was raised on the slant-board at about thirty degrees so he could breathe more easily with those broken ribs, and his legs were strapped to a pelvic splint that kept his knees slightly bent but prevented his shifting around.

Quen, Zell, Massus, Ruvan . . . a jury at a murder trial would've been more welcoming.

Their faces were gray and they looked old. And disaster-stricken. Quen was still in pain—that showed in his face—but the sharp spikes were under some control. He wasn't getting worse, and that was good luck. He could easily have had internal bleeding or some kind of damage that couldn't be handled with a slant board and splints. His broken ribs were bound, and obviously just breathing was still a trial for him.

Zell stepped in and yanked me after him. Massus came in, too, as the engineer on watch who had been completely taken by surprise. From Quen's expression, I could tell he already knew we were at hyperlight-speed.

"She initiated the light kick on her own," Zell bolted. "She didn't consult me or you or anybody."

Ruvan was here too, barely able to keep standing, he was so frightened.

They all fell silent for a few seconds and just stared at me with the most terrible expressions.

"This is unforgivable," Quen uttered. His voice had a slight wheeze from a stubborn lung infection that had damned Ruvan's efforts for a week and was finally starting to clear up.

With an agreeable nod, I said, "It sure is. I'm desperate. I know I'm blowing all the trust I've gained, but you have to understand what you're facing.

"You don't *know* any of this," Massus argued. Apparently he'd been talking to Zell, but I had absolutely no doubt that his thoughts were his own.

"We didn't log a jump with anyone," Zell ranted. "Even Oran doesn't know. If we get in trouble, nobody'll know what happened to us . . . We'll just be . . . we'll just . . ."

Looking like he was about to faint, he gripped a medicine shelf with both hands and shuddered fiercely.

In the void of brief silence, I said, "We're aimed for a star. We'll be able to get back."

"You can't possibly be that sure," Massus snapped. "We've never gone where you're sending us."

"I've navigated a lot of space. More than you."

Zell turned and found his voice. "How far did you come in your pod? Even you said you had no way to know!"

"I checked the pod. I calculated its top hyperlight, its fuel consumption and—"

"You can't be that sure," Massus said. "We never, *never* make a kick unless we're absolutely sure."

From his bed, Quen wiped his face with a shaking hand. "How can you know how far, Kay? Or if there's a solar source at all where we'll end up?"

"She doesn't understand!" Zell pounded the shelf he had just been leaning on. "If we end up even six months away from a solar source, we starve to death! We starve!"

Quen reached out and grasped Zell's elbow to quiet him, but though it silenced Zell, the comradely gesture did nothing to ease the moment's tension.

He watched me for a few long seconds, as if trying to read my eyes. "How could you do this to us?" he murmured. "You took the Ship's Pledge."

My chest constricted. The idea that they thought I'd broken their most cherished bond was hard to take. My stomach turned as their eyes worked on me.

"Oh, yes," I said, "and I meant every word. I promised to do what was best for the ship and crew, and this is it. If it takes proof to get action out of your people, I'll get proof. I need you to believe me."

They stared and doubted what they heard.

Getting nowhere plenty fast.

"Look, this won't hurt the ship, it won't hurt the crew, we're going to fly over to Iscoy space and have a look at the remains, and then we're going to power up the tiles and fly right back. We don't even have to stay. We just have to look."

"What if there's no solar source?" Massus insisted.

"There is. Prettiest little yellow lantern you ever saw, give or take my—"

"What if it's not where you think it is?" Zell challenged. "What if you've made mistakes? Our navigation isn't that precise. Our sensors are completely blind through the whole jump. What if your calculations are wrong and we end up in the void?"

"I've fine-tuned some of the sensors. When we get there, we should be able to analyze some things long-range. We won't even have to get close to the Menace ships to see them."

"*When* we get there—" Zell paced out some of his initial rage and now stalked the small infirmary in less anger and more genuine worry. "*If* we get there. *If* we're headed where you think we are, and *if* there's anything at the other end of this jump where we can power up—"

"How far are we going?" Massus asked. "Do you know even that?"

"It should be a nine-day jump, if all my calculations are correct."

"Nine days? We can't get anywhere in nine days," Zell said. "We'll be out in the middle of nothing!"

"No, listen," I said sternly. "I told you I'm an engineer. I've multiplied your warping effect by a significant factor. In nine days we'll be covering the same distance as you would normally cover in twenty-eight days."

"Twenty-eight!" Ruvan came to life suddenly. "Quen!"

Quen held up a steadying hand. "Shhh . . ."

Zell made a sharp gesture at me. "What if her calculations are no good? That's farther than we've ever gone before! We've never made a jump longer than fifteen days!"

Quen looked at Massus, the engineer, who tightly confirmed, "All this is guesswork. We could be headed in a completely wrong direction, not toward where she thinks she came from."

"I looked at your star charts," I told them. "And I remember mine. Mine were better—"

"Was your memory any better?" Zell demanded. "In that pod, in that condition?"

"It must be there." I tried to sound confident. "Unless I'm completely crazy, and it's a similar system over that way. I did computer simulations to see which stars are—"

"We've never gone this far," Quen said. "Nobody has. We've mapped a few key systems and routes to them, and that's where we go. We're not an explorer ship with stock on board to survive for months—"

A twitch in a muscle choked off his words. He clamped his hand to his ribs and gasped. Overcome, Zell stepped to the cot and lifted Quen up from the cushion a little until his captain's pain released him. The interfering cramp reminded us all just how very mortal we were.

Ruvan shivered and sank down to sit on his bunk. "We'll starve . . ."

Despite my conviction about what I'd done, I felt suddenly like a black banshee flying over their heads. No matter how the pie was cut, I was giving them the scare of their young lives.

And even worse, when it came down to bare porcelain, Zell had a point—I *wasn't* really sure. There *were* a lot of stars in the galaxy. The Menace could be headed in another direction entirely. Was I obsessed? Had I forgotten how to be a captain and see all the possibilities?

And poor Quen, lying here . . . I'd made a fool of him. He'd trusted me, put me above his own crewmates because he was trying to be the best kind of captain. How much more was he suffering because of me?

"She's insane," Zell mourned. Some of anger's heat had boiled out of him as he eased his captain back against the cushions. He pressed a hand to Quen's shoulder. "You take her out of power."

That wrenched me out of those thoughts.

"Now, wait a minute," I interrupted. "My watch methods have been helping. Trying to be the commanding officer on both watches hasn't done you any good, Zell. At least admit that things have been running well enough that you've been able to get some sleep while I'm on watch. If you tell the other deck bosses to organize their watches like mine, *Zingara* will be ready to defend against the Menace. This is bigger than just this ship or just the warranters. The TCA will have to be convinced too, so their fleet can—"

"You haven't seen this fleet," Quen pointed out.

"I don't need to see the wind blow either."

He shifted carefully, one hand pressed to his bound ribs, and looked at Zell. "What if her conclusions are right about the TCA? Zell, our own people . . ."

Rather than snapping a disagreement, Zell paused and contemplated. "We could go somewhere . . . get our families and go."

"If we do that," Quen said, "and the big attack comes that she's talking about, we'll have abandoned our own planet."

"What if she's just delusional?"

"Where did that other woman come from, then? With the—" Quen pointed at his hair and made a circular motion.

With a shrug, I told them again, "Either we're going to

have a conflict with the Menace, or we're going to have a conflict with our planet, or we're going to have both."

Zell scowled at me. *"Our* planet?"

I shrugged and looked him right in the eye. "If it's yours, it's mine."

"But Zell's right, Kay," Quen said. "You don't know this Menace is coming. You don't know they'll attack if they do show up. You *think* they might."

"When they come, they'll attack. I know a strategy when I see one. I never got a chance to deal with them before, but I'm going to deal with them now. They destroyed my ship, they slaughtered citizens of a peaceful, progressive civilization, and when they get to our space, I'm going to be in a position to do something about them."

"Take her out of power, Quen," Zell repeated.

A small moan escaped Quen's lips. He sighed and said, "She hasn't been proven wrong yet. What if she's telling some version of the truth? What if we should be ready? Then we'll need her as deck boss."

"Either we get ready," Zell grumbled, "or we starve in the void. Until we know, I don't want to have to work with her. What if she does more trouble before the kick shuts down?"

Massus squeezed his hands into tense fists and muttered, "Nine days . . ."

Quen let his head fall back on the cushion and blanched visibly with the weight of his new decision, along with the discomfort of his traction and the throb of his injuries.

"We'll lock her in a berth until the kick is over. Then we'll see where we end up."

Quen gazed at me now, and the fear in his eyes nearly crushed us all.

"You've committed us, Kay," he said. "We have to go wherever you've sent us. If things aren't exactly as you say when we get there . . . I'm putting you off my ship."

CHAPTER
16

NINE DAYS, CONFINED. NINE DAYS ALONE WITH MY THOUGHTS and a few scanty meals. Nine days to fine-tune my plans to improve the warranter ships' abilities. Nine days of wondering what the crew was thinking of me, saying, and wondering.

What if Zell was right and I was wrong? What if my calculations were wrong and they wouldn't have any reason to believe me after all this? And then the Menace came anyway?

What if I was obsessed? Had a head injury in the pod?

No . . . obsessives didn't sit around wondering if they were obsessed.

Besides, on the starboard side, also locked in another berth, was that Menace woman. I sure hadn't obsessed her out of thin air.

The light kick was dangerous. If the fusion engine couldn't keep up, it would shut down and we'd be stranded in the interstellar void. If I'd miscalculated the engines' ability to keep up, we were all dead. They'd never gone this far in a single kick before. Most of their light kicks were a matter of hours. They were right—I couldn't be certain the ship could maintain thrust long enough.

We were committed to risk and danger—and if I was right, a terrible revelation—but none of that caused me the most worry. Strange, what really haunted me during these long hours was the attitude the crew might have about me now. In their minds, I'd let them down.

The heartache was insurmountable. That was what bothered me most.

Four . . . five . . .

I had to do something, get some answers. Parts of Totobet's story didn't add up. No civilization used up localities that fast. It would take centuries for a normal population to need that much room.

So I asked to speak to her. Nothing fancy, just put me in her room for a few minutes and stand outside and listen, and I promise not to pull her little spools out.

Zell didn't like the idea, but after a while he sent a couple of men to take me to Totobet. Apparently Quen wanted the facts known too, and had overridden Zell's big no.

She was resting in a bunk, wrapped in a fur blanket against the *Zingara*'s day-to-day chill.

"Get up," I ordered. "I want to talk to you."

As she came to the edge of the bunk, she quietly said, "You already talked to me. You told me to shut up."

"Well, I don't want to you shut up now. I want to know why your civilization needs so much area and needs it so quickly."

She nodded, seeming to understand the shortcut to answers. "We evolved reproducing," she attempted timidly. "We can't help it. If we don't find enough place, we have too many people to survive."

"So you think you can just come and steal the homes of others so you have a place to live?" I smoldered. "What if you don't find anybody? What happens when there's nobody to kill and no more room to grow? Have you ever thought about that?"

Her glossy chestnut eyes widened a little. "Of course. When that happens, we have to kill our children."

I stumbled backward as if she'd slapped me. I landed with my back against the locked door. Had I heard—

"What?"

She hunched her shoulders a bit. "We kill our children."

My arms were locked at my sides, my legs numb. Like lightning my mind processed what she had said, why she had said it, and distilled from her large brown eyes that this was no tall tale. I stared so hard, my face hurt. My soul hurt.

"We kill our children," she said.

Well, there was the missing element. There it was, right there. Right there.

My voice was shattered glass. "My God, I thought I'd heard it all . . ."

"You don't understand us," she attempted.

"Don't understand? I understand that a decent culture says, 'women and children first, and children more first'! You . . . your people, you say, 'Us first and children last'? Run out of space, so kill the kids? You're not helping yourself with me!"

Nauseated, I turned my back on her, but in just seconds I whirled to face her again.

"You can just say it out like that?" I charged. "They're 'killed'?"

Spreading her narrow hands, Totobet asked, "What should I say? That's what it is. Don't you have to stop things sometimes? What do your people say?"

A spike of rather hideous similarity went through my chest. "There are . . . euphemisms . . . 'aborted' . . . 'terminated'—"

"Are they killed?"

"Well . . . yes—"

"Then why don't you say 'killed'?"

She knew she had shocked me to the bone. At the same time her bluntness was strangely noble. They did this thing, but they owned up to it. How much had my own people done and called it something mild just to make it easy on ourselves?

Totobet's culture had apparently not bothered to make the intolerable into something you could mention in public without flinching. Why did she want me to know? Why had she said this? Why did I have to hear it?

"If we don't have a place to expand," she explained, "we have to resort to killing the babies. It's done decently, but it must be done. It's a terrible blow nature has dealt us. We have to survive by numbers. For most to live, many must die."

"You can be that heartless about it?" God, was that my voice? "Either you kill another race and take their planet, or you kill your own children? That's it?"

"When it comes to killing our own or killing others, we kill the others and have a place. If we can't find a place . . . we have a lottery."

"Lottery." I sank against the door until my pelvis got cold on the metal. "Damned whimsical . . . to kill your babies out of convenience."

"We have no choice."

"You haven't looked around enough," I spat back. "There's sure a lot here to dislike."

"We're not animals," Totobet protested quietly. "We're fully intelligent beings. In good times, we're really very pleasant. It's a terrible thing . . . Overpopulation is devastating. It ruins everyone. Rich, poor, young, old . . . The only way we can keep from revolution is if everyone's child has an equal chance. We can't lottery our adults because they're the ones who know things. The children can't build or grow food or make ships or fly them. Until we conquer another planet, most of the young are killed. If we have a place to expand, that's a big number of our children who can live. Some things have to happen . . . It's just survival."

A core-deep disgust forced bile into my throat, but not only because of what she had told me. It came because a part of me understood.

"This is a hard quadrant," I said.

For untold minutes I leaned against the door, shuddering, cold, absorbing the whole monumental concept of what I had been told, then rejecting it, then absorbing more. She was a liar. She was delusional. There was some other reason. It made no sense. It made perfect sense. Culture . . . habit . . . religion . . . biology . . . No answer served me today.

Savage, savage.

My lips pressed tight, I breathed in sharp sucks through my nose and turned back to the circuitry. I had to get out of here. I had to get out!

I had to change things in this sector. I had to have an effect or go crazy trying, or die maybe. Too often I'd accepted the role of onlooker in the Delta Quadrant, working hard at noninterference, even when involvement was forced by proximity or mandated by circumstance. Or by honor. And I had some.

More than she did. More than her people did.

Suddenly I wanted very much to change something. Even if it was only the condition of these goddamned circuits, why wouldn't they cut?

Population control taken to an extreme. Sickening. Couldn't use birth control because reproduction was a life-or-death deal with evolution. Us, them.

I felt as humbled and ineffectual as any human being, I think, had ever discovered himself or herself to be. Big things were happening around me, and there was such meager power in my scope that I could no longer affect them. That hadn't been the way for me all these many years in the captain's chair. I'd had many choices, some very hard, but the courses were mine to take or discard. Not for years had I been in a position of such diminished authority, such sweeping ignorance, and such utterly yeoman needs. Even as I struggled to hear what was going on in the sector at large, I was thinking about which of my tiles still needed grouting.

What was there to say? I pounded on the door until the crew let me out and took me back to my own bunk where I could curl up under my own fur blanket and sink into the hauntings that followed me there.

Six, seven . . . the ninth day.

The last hours were the longest. The last minutes almost strangled me. The ship was so quiet . . . only the soft murmur of the fusion engines and their supporting systems, and the whisper of life-support, artificial gravity, and all the things that gave us the illusion of security in space.

Children, children.

Thoughts of *Voyager* crept back in on me in the silent

seclusion. Had we been fooling ourselves all along? Trying to travel tens of thousands of light-years—our lifetimes would've been eaten up by the trip. Our grandchildren, if we bothered to have any, would be the ones greeted by strangers in the Federation with whom they had no bonds. We had been the only human beings in the Delta Quadrant. There were only a hundred forty–some of us, not a big enough gene pool, but still the option had kept us going. If things got too bad, we could stop, join a culture like the Iscoy or, as I had, the Omians, and simply become part of another race, a new creed.

Yet, every time that chance came up, we rejected it. Our duty, our obligation, our Pledge was to keep paddling up that long river.

When the hatch to my small quarters cracked open, I jumped as if somebody had popped a balloon beside my ear. As I rolled off my bunk, my knees clicked furiously and I almost fell over.

Massus was at my door. So were Othien and Levan. They'd sent my own crew to bring me out.

"Are we there?" My voice, after nine days, was a croak. "Can you see anything?"

"Come on out," Massus said. He was tense and reserved.

"What's out there?"

"Go on."

He motioned for me to go in front of him out toward the main deck. Even before I got to the hatch I could see that almost the whole crew had crammed onto the main deck and were staring upward and out over the vid rail. The deck-wide video tiles above us had all been repaired and were working just fine. Just fine . . .

Standing in the middle of the deck, leaning on the rail that partly surrounded the deck well, Quen held himself in place with Ruvan's help. Beside him, Zell pivoted around, then around again, looking. Their faces, and those of the entire crew of the *Zingara,* were upturned toward the stunning full-wide view around us.

I had in my time seen plagues and I had seen battles. I'd seen the galaxy's ugliness and its breathtaking beauty. From life to death and back again I'd seen rather a lot. Until today, though, I had never seen an armada of so many ships that I couldn't count them, each bigger than my hometown.

That's what we were looking at through the great open window of the overhead vid tiles. From rail to rail, from transverse bulkhead to transverse bulkhead, there was nothing but a vast invasion fleet stretching off almost to infinity. The Menace.

Between us and the armada, only the slaggy haze of asteroids hid us from prying sensors. To our right was the pretty sun I'd remembered as being so welcoming and so much like Earth's sun when *Voyager* first accepted the Iscoy invitation to pull up and relax for a while. There was the largest asteroid, which the Iscoy had been using as a base, now peppered with new configurations of lights on its dark side, proving that the whole asteroid had been very quickly set up for full occupation.

And all around us, caught in the flow of the asteroid belt itself, were pieces of wrecked ships, torn violently to bits, along with the twisted and burned remains of the spacedock and several satellites.

The whole region, and its current occupants, spoke quite horridly for itself.

Good thing, because I couldn't speak at all.

Shuddering against the splints and bindings on his hips and legs, Quen shook like an old man. Staring out into the breadth of space, he scanned the massive armada, battleship after battleship, support vehicle after support vehicle, transport after transport.

I shuffled across the deck, looking around in such rapt attention that I tripped twice. Behind me, Massus and Levan bumped into each other as we stopped amidships, near where Zell was turning and turning.

Without really planning to, I ended up standing beside Quen. Together we gazed out at the two hundred battleships of the Menace armada.

Quen's breathing was labored. He did not look at me. "Did you expect this much?"

My head shook slowly, my lips moved, but there really wasn't much sound. "No . . ."

In spite of the minimal scratch of my words, the ship was

so silent that I think everybody heard me. That old saying—one picture is worth a thousand words . . . I'd given them the thousand words, and none of them had the impact of these last five minutes. In virtual seconds I'd been proven at least partially right. The Menace existed, in invasion proportions. There had been a sudden and devastating battle here. If what Totobet said was true, and these people moved from place to place to have room to expand, then this little asteroid was nothing more than a temporary stop or a base of some kind. Maybe an outpost. There wasn't enough room on that asteroid for the occupants of even two or three of those ships to live.

"Whatever you do," I murmured, "stay hidden."

My voice was scarcely more than a whisper. We were hidden well enough, adrift with the flow of the Iscoy Asteroid Belt, and unless we drew attention to ourselves in some overt way, we could masquerade as part of the dusty mass of rocks, some of which were big enough to be moons.

Beside me, Quen rasped, "All this time, you were right . . ."

Though I'd expected to be happier, the win was cold as dead meat. "To tell you the truth . . . I was hoping I was crazy."

Through a haze of asteroid dust and the obscuration of larger asteroids rolling along with us in the flow of the belt, *Zingara* huddled with only docking thrusters to keep her from drifting into sight of the enemy.

I had the upper hand now. They trusted me again. Damned sour victory it was, too.

From behind me, Massus quietly suggested, "Maybe they're staying here . . ."

"No, they're not staying here," I said. "There's not enough living space for all the people on all those ships. It's got to be just a way station."

"On the way to us?" Othien wondered.

Offering him a supportive glance, I said, "That's what I suspect. A civilization like this doesn't stab in the dark. They must've sent advanced scouts around the sector. They know where the pockets of population are. They'll be heading toward us sooner or later."

A movement beside me made me step sideways, but then

an unwelcome form caught my attention: Totobet. I slithered away from her, not wanting to be close.

She was moved past me by two crewmen and brought before Quen.

"Are these your people?" Quen asked her.

"Yes," she said. No reason to lie, apparently.

"Is Kay right about what your people do?"

Totobet gazed out at the ships of her civilization, and the remains of a battle from which she too had escaped. "About what we do, yes. Not why we do it."

"And are you on your way to our sector?"

She looked at him. "I have none of that information for you. I know only we go where people can live, and we take their place."

"All our troubles," Zell uttered suddenly, "the politics, the warranters . . . the TCA, Sasaquon, us . . . none of it matters anymore because we're about to be wiped out."

Quen started to say something else, but Massus burst forward in his torment and clawed at Totobet, stopped only by the rail around the deck well and two of his own shipmates, who drove him back a judicious step.

"No!" I shouted abruptly, stepping in front of Totobet. "It's not her fault. Not personally, anyway." With an extended hand, I held off the surge of angry crewmen for whom Massus's anger was contagious. "If what she told me is true, they can't even begin to make peace. They can't make friends or treaties with anyone. Within a couple generations, they're everywhere—eating resources, taking up room . . . Sooner or later there's got to be a fight. Nobody would even want them around."

"How do you know all this?" Zell asked.

"I've seen it before," I told them.

Zell rounded on Totobet, grasped her by the shoulder, and shouted, "Tell us how to stop you!"

"No, Zell!" Ruvan came to life beside Quen and pushed Zell back.

Ruvan actually getting physical? What was this?

"Don't hurt her," the medic said. "She's pregnant."

I shoved my way between them again. "She's what?"

"Pregnant."

"How pregnant!"

The medic gave me a very strange expression and said, "Extremely. She's going to have seven babies."

Oh, now, hadn't I heard enough for one lifetime? Didn't I have enough to deal with? Agony, agony. Seven?

Seven babies?

I grabbed Ruvan's arm. *"When* is she going to have them?"

"Oh, I don't know . . . months, yet. I've never seen anything like her before. But a few months, I think."

Stepping back, I looked at Totobet with this new information in mind and wondered where she was hiding this interesting turn of facts. True, she was thick at the waist and wide at the hips, and she wore that heavy smocklike tunic; if she had months to go, I guess it was possible.

"That won't save her," Massus growled. "If her people come after us and we can't do anything about it—"

Staying between him and Totobet, I put a hand on his shoulder and pushed him back a little. "Stop that," I said passively. "I think I know how to stop them. Quen, please—"

Quen motioned to the two crewmen who had brought Totobet to the main deck. "Take her back. Stand a guard. Ruvan . . . keep her comfortable."

"As soon as you're comfortable," Ruvan said, and refused to leave with the guards and Totobet. Instead he stayed, keeping a firm grip on Quen's arm.

"You were telling the truth this whole time," Quen said roughly, and it took a few seconds to realize he was speaking to me. "We're finished . . . I wish you hadn't told us."

"If I hadn't, they would still come." I flinched stupidly as an asteroid passed very close over our heads, forgetting for an instant that the view was only a tile screen vision and the body of the ship was still around us, protecting us from hits. "We *can* fight," I went on. "The trick is going to be convincing the TCA and their fleet and all the warranters to band together, fire up the boilers, and face the Menace when they show up."

Weakly he asked, "Lucas, is this recording?"

From somewhere in the crowd of crewmen, Lucas responded, "Yes . . . I've got it all."

"All—all these—" Quen started to speak, but then

grasped the well rail and endured a harrowing wrack of pain.

Zell stepped to his side and made sure he didn't hurt himself further by falling, but there was no help for him or any of us. The crew watched him in undisguised empathy and worry—worry for him, worry for all of us and our future.

When he regained some control, our young captain looked up again with tired eyes and scanned the doomful armada.

"All these ships . . . they can go in the void without a kick?"

"Oh, yes," I confirmed. "They're fully flight-independent intragalactic interstellar vessels. See those elongated pods on the undersides and on top? Those are warp nacelles. They can go wherever they want, stop where they want, and start up again. No solar source required."

"Incredible," Massus murmured.

The rest of the crew was stunned absolutely silent by the concept. Silent and very obviously afraid.

There was something ominously endearing about that— despite the fact that they were all men, and all young, they didn't have a problem displaying that they were just plain scared. I liked that. It was honest. They'd still do their work, they'd fight if necessary and even die, but they wouldn't bother with any false bravado.

"We can't stay," Quen decided, which was a great relief to us all. "We have to go home and warn everyone. Massus, get ready to charge the tiles for another light kick."

"It'll take days," Massus complained. "If we can't get any closer than the belt, we'll have to make three or four passes."

"We don't dare leave the belt," Zell said. "We'll be seen by those . . . those people."

"Just charge up," Quen told them. "We can't just float here forever. Zell, anybody without a specific duty should sit down and stay calm. Don't attract any attention. No hull lights . . . no emissions. We've got work to do. We have to go home."

Without a word, Massus cast him a frightened glance, yet I could tell he was already working out the bleed-off in his engineer's mind. Soon, I hoped, his work would consume him and overcome that fear. I hoped that for the whole crew.

Yet we had days of charge-up and then another nine-day light kick ahead of us, during which all this would distill.

As the numb crew began slowly to disperse, another wave of agony swept over Quen. He faltered against Zell, unable to stand up anymore, even with the splints. Ruvan and Zell together managed to keep him from falling and harming himself further, but clearly his time on deck had run out.

"Othien," I spoke up, "bring that bench over here."

It was the first order I'd given in days, and it felt great. The fact that Othien did what I told him and nobody countermanded me, not even Zell, proved that I was once again the deck boss of my watch.

"If you lie him down on this," I suggested, turning to Zell, "we can carry him back to the infirmary. He won't have to strain himself."

From his expression, I could tell that Quen didn't like the idea, but also that pure anguish was working his resistance out of him. He made no protest as Ruvan supervised the process of laying his captain down properly on the plank.

By the time Quen lay upon the bench, ready to be carried back to his slant-board, he was worn out.

Zell gave an order to carry him away, but Quen caught Zell's arm and pulled him down to one knee beside him.

"One thing's certain," Quen weakly said, "we need a captain who's not bedridden."

The first officer shook his head. "No, Quen—a leader is his brain, not his body."

"I know that . . . I can run a small-cuff salvage, maybe, but I can't command battles, not like this." He gripped Zell's sleeve and gave it a gentle shake. "I'm on medication for pain, for infection, for respiration . . . other things I don't even know about. I'm awake, but I'm not sharp. I can feel it. Ruvan can't take me off the drugs or I'll die. Or the pain would be too much. I'm foggy, I'm tired, weak . . . and part of the Captain's Pledge is to admit it. We've got to have a vote."

"I don't want to have a vote." Misery rolled across Zell's face.

Dogged by the internal gnawing of his injuries, Quen rasped, "It always comes eventually, you know that. Nobody's captain forever." Resisting broken spirits, which would've been worse than fatal, Quen kept his composure in front of his crew and smiled tightly. "You set it up. When you're ready, we'll vote. It's just a formality, then you can take over."

I knew what that last part meant. There was no competition, no other candidate to consider but Zell. Of course not, he was first mate. On a Starfleet ship, there would be instant succession, without the "formality" of a vote. Things were different here. This ship was run like the old-time pirate ships on Earth, where the captains were elected or deposed by the crew. Suddenly a completely unexpected thought rammed through my skull and took root.

"Captain," I interrupted.

The sound of my voice actually surprised even me. I hadn't intended to speak up.

Everyone looked at me. Zell in particular glared harshly. My revelations had ruined his universe.

Keeping my voice down, I eased my body language too. Shoulders sagging a little, chin down, hands clasped unthreateningly in front of me.

"Zell deserves the job," I said, "if all we have to do is continue as warranters or even face the TCA fleet. But the goal is much more complicated. We have to do a lot of convincing over the next few weeks. We have to take recordings of all this and distribute them to everyone who will look. We have to unify a whole culture and reorganize battle readiness. With all respect—and I do respect you and I respect Zell very much—I'm best qualified to do those things. I'll do them either way, of course . . . I'll stand by *Zingara,* no matter who's in command. But you don't get anything in life you don't ask for, and that includes challenges. I have experience no one in the Omian sector has, not even Sasaquon. When the crew decides to have the vote for commanding officer . . . I'd like to be considered."

CHAPTER

17

"APPROACH! ZELL, APPROACH! THEY SAW US! ZELL! THEY'RE coming over here!"

So much for a moment's excuse for peace.

Quen was barely back in the infirmary when Lucas shouted the terrible warning that the Menace had spotted us, even in the shroud of the asteroid stream.

The ship coming up on us was huge beyond description, easily two hundred times the size of *Zingara,* and we weren't primarily a combat ship. It wasn't as if we were a stinger-fighter or a destroyer or a high-endurance attack vessel that could take on a more powerful ship even if it were something big and cumbersome. In fact, we didn't have anything going for us, battle-wise.

And the Menace was turning to attack. On several tile panels, screens popped on, reading firing solutions and showing increased energy production on the big ship. Didn't need to be an expert to know what that meant.

Lucas stood up from his screen and stared up at the monster on approach. "We're dead."

Clearly he saw in his mind what everyone saw: another

wreck floating about in this space, cut to pieces relentlessly and with great experience.

Zell stared up, too. He didn't know what to do, either. I couldn't fault him for it. This ship was utterly outmatched, unable to fight, unable to run.

His voice was rough and shuddering. "Man the turret guns," he attempted, dry-mouthed. "Power up for maneuver . . . mark the rackers and . . . Levan, take the helm stanchion . . . thrusters on maximum . . . Somebody . . . somebody watch the rod levels."

He sounded less like a captain designing a red alert than a mortician designing an autopsy.

I couldn't let this happen. I'd promised to serve this ship, and that would be hard to do if there wasn't a ship here to serve, wouldn't it?

The Menace ship was almost on us. It was still miles, but the size of the vessel itself made that distance negligible.

Moving to the middle of the deck, I rather loudly claimed, "I got us into this. I can get us out."

Zell spun to face me, as fiercely as a man about to launch a barroom brawl. "Get us out how?"

"First we have to clear the asteroids," I said as the ship powered up around us, and the crew ran to their quaint version of battlestations.

"Leave the protection of the belt?"

"The belt'll be our grave if we don't get clear. We can't dodge asteroids *and* fire from that ship. We've got to power up for a jump—"

"We can't make a light jump," Massus challenged. "It would take hours to charge up the tiles! And we can't possibly outrun that thing!"

"We have to get out in order to charge up," I said, "and we have to be clear to shoot. We have to get out of the asteroid belt."

Shuddering with bitter resentment and who knows what else, Zell ground out his order. "She's right. We have to be able to shoot. Clear the belt."

As he and I stood in bald competition amidships, we were blanketed in the awful mutterings and desperate complaints of the crew . . .

"I knew I was going to die, but I at least thought I'd be home—"

"No one'll ever know what happened to us . . ."

"What good does this do us now?"

The Menace ship was getting closer. Zell turned and just stared at it. His attitude was one of misery as he gazed up there, like a man watching the guillotine being rolled out toward him.

"Are you giving up?" I asked.

He didn't look at me. "We're dead."

Clasping my hands behind my back as if I had all day, I stepped to him and looked up into his face. "If you've given yourselves up for dead anyway, then get out of my way. Am I going to make you deader?"

Lucas turned from his collection of screens again. "Zell, Quen wants to talk to you."

Zell stepped to Lucas's screens, one of which showed a schematic of ships' positions, and another which showed Quen's face against the cushion on his cot in the infirmary.

"They saw us?" Quen asked.

"We're in trouble," Zell gave by way of an answer. "No time to charge the tiles."

"Do whatever you have to," Quen told him. *"I'll stand behind any decision you make."*

That was clear. Quen was tersely communicating that he couldn't run a battle from a bed, just as he had said.

Tormented, Zell watched the Menace ship loom over us with its weapons ports glowing. "Kay—"

"Yes?"

"You know what to do?"

"I've got a couple of ideas."

"Take over."

"Thanks. Levan! Steer angle two-two-four under the prad! Wait, make it two-two-three."

Everyone in earshot turned and stared at me in horror, and at the helm poor Levan almost fainted. "That course doesn't make sense! It's a collision course!"

"What do you care? You're dead anyway. Steer the course."

Muttering something about his sisters and parents, Levan

shook like a winter holly and steered the course I'd given him.

We surged out from the asteroids, took a stomach-wrenching dip, and came up under and behind the Menace ship and damned near rammed it. As one of the aft fins of the enormous ship sailed across our foreheads, Levan started to veer off.

"Hold that course!" I shouted. "Massus, plot a corridor groove and open the jeklights on the rod intakes. We can power up the cells for a light kick and get out of here."

"Are you crazy?" Massus shouted. "There's not enough sun way out here! We have to run or shoot or something!"

My hand sliced an abortive gesture between us. "No time to explain. You want to live? Do what I say!"

Enormous above us, like an elephant maneuvering beside a breadbox, the Menace ship was very clearly trying to come about, to keep us from getting a clear shot at their engine exhaust—a predictable battle maneuver, but *Zingara,* simply because we were smaller, was quicker. The Menace ship opened fire again, demolishing three of the king posts on our external salvage gear, and then we slipped behind them, out of the range of that particular weapons port—blessedly, because it was about to cut our whole bow off.

The *Zingara's* automatic collision alarms went off, whooping at a fever pitch. Behind that noise, an overload bell from somewhere rang and rang, but that would have to be ignored.

Zell shouted, "Turret gunners, return fire!"

"I wouldn't bother," I muttered, but nobody heard me. Didn't matter. If they wanted to have the illusion of fighting back, no point stopping them.

Suddenly a bright sulfury wash blew over the whole vid screen, causing most of us to look away or shield our eyes.

"What is it?" Zell asked.

Massus fought with his controls. "We're in the wash from their main drive!"

"Massus!" I called. "Take the absorption safeties off!"

He looked at me, then at Zell, then back at me. "The tile safeties?"

"Yes! Take them completely off!"

"We'll be cooked!"

"No, we won't! We don't have to protect the ship because there isn't any sun. We can absorb energy almost instantly if there's a nonsolar source! I've been studying this! It's not all that different from the early-light technology where I come from. You've got the storage capacity, and the Menace has the source. Take the safeties off!"

Absolutely fuming, his fists balled and his legs locked, Zell glowered at me. "Take them off!"

A click, a surge, and suddenly all around us the interior tiles encrusting *Zingara* began to glow with anxious energy.

"What's happening!" Zell cried. "Why is this happening!"

Massus shouted his astonishment over the noise. "The tiles are swelling up with power directly off their drive wash! I've never seen the tiles swell so fast!"

"Don't overswell, whatever you do," Zell uttered, but he was watching the tiles for himself and didn't seem to think that was the big worry.

Ordinarily this powering process would take hours or even days, lurking as near a sun as was possible without being fried to a crisp, but here there was energy without the destructive solar violence. The tiles were sucking energy directly from the Menace's engines. What the hell—power was power.

"Levan," I called over the throb of power, "veer off and put us on a heading for home!"

"Veering off . . . heading locked in!"

"Next time listen to the old soldiers's stories," I said victoriously. "Never give up! Never give up until you're dead. Never give up and die. Don't go peacefully. Make them come and get you!"

Several men around me cheered in sudden awareness that we were instantly powered up for a light kick and we could get away. Even Zell grasped the well rail and pounded it in mute triumph.

I turned to Massus. "Are the fusion engines ready to take the start?"

"Ready!"

"Trigger the light kick! Let's go!"

The vid screen went dark, giving us a ceiling again, and almost immediately the tiles made their sudden drain, jump-starting the fusion engines to hyperlight speed.

From where we had been a moment ago, we were now gone.

As the tough old *Zingara* bolted to hyperlight speed and streaked away from an enemy against whom we could not possibly win, a crew who had thought themselves dead and decimated realized now that they could fight for their ship, for their lives.

"I want to talk to you."

In the dim confines of a bunk, starboard and forward on *Zingara,* away from the hum of the fusion engines that now carried us back toward our endangered sector.

Now that we were on the light kick, there was more to do, and the crew were using their hands to work out their shock. Part of that was shock that we'd lived through a confrontation with a Menace monstrosity. With everything running smoothly, if with a certain death-row resignation, I slipped forward to Totobet's bunk.

Without a word, the man guarding the door let me pass. Nobody stopped me from much of anything anymore.

Totobet raised herself on an elbow, saw me, then sat up on her bunk. "Thank you for defending me."

"I didn't defend you. I just kept my shipmates from turning into a mob. You're not worth that."

Sitting on the opposite bunk, I ticked away a few seconds, searching for a way to begin an impossible conversation.

"I just want to understand." I began finally. "Your people have a drastic overpopulation problem. Rather than try to control your number of conceptions, you go ahead and have the children, then expand to find room for them, and this is on a scale of hundreds of thousands. Right?"

She simply nodded.

"You've done this for a while, generations upon generations, using hyperlight ships. Has your technology advanced much since you started this interstellar assault?"

"Yes," she said. "We learn from those we must push aside, if we can. Sometimes there are ships left, buildings, businesses, laboratories . . . but we don't need much . . . We need only place."

"You need a scientific solution to conceiving so many babies. You haven't bothered looking for it, or you'd have found it already."

"We have looked."

"Not well enough. There are lots of ways for advanced beings to avoid conception."

"We can't avoid conception," she insisted mildly. Strange, I was arguing, but she wasn't. "That asteroid, the outpost there—"

"The Iscoy Asteroid," I snapped. "The people there were real living beings, not just targets with ground you needed. They were the Iscoy, and I liked them."

"The Iscoy Asteroid," she corrected willingly, "means a million of our young who don't have to die. My people will have that place now, and we make better use of area than anyone we've met."

"Anyone you've conquered."

"A million of us can live where two hundred thousand lived before. We're very thrifty. We can live a dozen where others live two."

"That's no justification. You're completely amoral and I despise you."

"I don't blame you."

"And I hate you for that too."

"I understand."

"Oh, shut up . . ." With a push to my feet, I started pacing, though there was scarcely room to take three whole steps.

Totobet watched me as I went back and forth, as if she knew I was trying to come up with some prosecution that she could not argue. Then I could declare her morally evil and somehow win.

"We've been driven back many times in our history," she said eventually. "When we're contained and can't expand, we are forced to revert—"

"—to devouring your own young," I blustered back at her. "The specter of your civilization gets uglier the longer I look at you."

She shifted her legs as if the stiffness of all these days were getting to her—no doubt it was—but she made no attempt to stand up because then she would be in my way.

"We're not stupid," she complained. "We know that someday we'll come up against a culture that can stop us. On that day, we'll probably all die. But until then, we expand."

Pausing to glare at her, I said, "I have trouble believing people like you will just go quietly into the night."

She shrugged one knobby shoulder under the soft tie of her tunic. "We won't like it . . . but this other culture who defeats us, they have to survive too. They can't just let us kill them. It's nature's way."

Something about her tone calmed me some. Her tone and her honesty about it all. Why couldn't she just be rapacious and without remorse? That would make things so much simpler.

"That makes rotten sense," I grumbled. "Your people aren't very creative. There's got to be some better way, some biological solution to this problem—"

"But we found a way to survive."

"You found a technological way. Have you kept up on your biological sciences? Have you kept trying to avoid conception?"

"We can't avoid conception. We must have mating. We must have birth. So I and my kind have to take place from others in order to have room. That's how things are."

I glowered fiercely at her, battling to keep from boiling over. "'You and your kind'? 'Us and them'? That's how it is for you? Group mentality? Group rights? That justifies everything for you people?"

"It does for everyone, everywhere. It's natural to go with your own kind. Nature makes all life-forms at ease with others who look like them. Isn't that so where you come from?"

What could I do, argue with her? From alligators to elephants, she was right. From bacteria to skin color to religion, she was right. All life-forms of any level of development tended to cluster. It was natural, designed to be an aid to survival.

I hated that she was right.

"We have it," I allowed, "but we resist as much as we can."

"But you have it," she confirmed. She might be a mild individual, but she had no trouble facing me down on this. "You can scowl at me and hate me, but you have never faced this. Never faced starvation, anarchy, pestilence. Your culture has never contemplated mass-suicide. We considered it. That was when we made the lottery. We all accept it. You tell us we're wrong and immoral and we should find another way. What other way? This is the card nature dealt us. With the lottery, at least there is some chance that one or two of our children might survive out of each litter. This is how harsh nature has been on us . . . No other beings in the galaxy carry this burden."

A touch of indignation in her voice made me pause, and rightfully so. I'd failed in my moral duty to at least try to see things from their point of view. Perhaps it was a flaw of conflict—in order to be willing to fight, to kill, to win, it was normal to convince yourself that the other guy had no basis for his behavior.

"So you just give birth and drown the babies," I said. "Just get it over with, I suppose."

She gazed at me in a perplexed way, as if she didn't understand what I meant. Then she shook her head and I got the idea that I was the one who didn't understand, and she'd just figured that out.

"Oh, no," she said. "We can't kill them at birth. We have to keep them for many weeks. If a female doesn't give birth *and* nurse the babies for many weeks, she will die."

The berth fell to utter quiet. Only the soft hum of the fusion engines deep in the endless night. The cool room, the cool ship, seemed abruptly chillier.

I slowly lowered to sit on the bunk again. Empathy clawed at my heart.

"You mean . . . on top of this curse, you're required by physiology to get . . . attached to your babies? You have to take time to love them? Then you . . . That's . . . that's the cruelest thing I've ever heard."

"Very cruel. And hard," she agreed. "We've had to accept many hard things. To be completely evenhanded, and to keep parents from having to pick which of their children live and die, we invented the lottery."

"How long has this lottery been going on?"

"Four hundred of our years. Before that . . . we had a very ugly culture."

"I'll bet you did. You . . . your men . . . How do they handle all this?"

"The same as our women," she said with a little shrug. "We mate for life. Our men get as attached to the babies as our women. My husband was on one of the ships you saw."

"Are you a member of another ship's crew?"

"No, I just live there. We have to live in space, with each other, because we have to reproduce and nurse our children."

"One culture that has no choice for men and women but to ship out together, and another culture that never does. One that survives by never taking what's not theirs, and another that must take what's not theirs. The fabric of civilization is certainly tightly woven . . ."

Somehow at peace with all this, Totobet nodded sympathetically. How bizarre to sit here and see her sympathizing with me instead of the other way around, given the burden she and her people must bear.

We sat together in the oddest mutuality.

How had that happened? How had we gotten mutual?

Totobet watched me unthreateningly. After a while, she dug around in the heavy material of her sprawling dress and found what was apparently a big pocket hidden in the blanketlike fabric. She pulled a kind of thick notebook out, about five inches by three.

"You're the only person I know on this ship," she began again. "Although you hate me and I understand why, I think you're a good person. Would you help me with something?"

Now what?

She unsnapped the notebook's cover. Inside was an accordion-folded stream of laminated squares that fell out across her knees and went all the way to the deck. I tilted my head to see what was inside the laminate—

Pictures. Photographs. Little portraits. Big puppylike eyes set in lilac-moon faces.

"These are my litters," Totobet said, turning the stream of photos toward me. "My babies."

Oh, no. Somebody shoot me.

I slipped my hand under the trail of portraits. The faces of babies gazed back at me, so real I expected them to blink and make little noises.

"All these are . . ."

Totobet nodded. "Dead."

"But there are . . . ten, twenty, twenty-three children here. Are you telling me that . . ."

She nodded again, slowly, and gazed at the pictures. "I haven't been lucky in the lottery."

Why had I come to this stupid sector? Why had I accepted captaincy? Why had I signed up for Starfleet Academy? Why couldn't I just go home and, and . . . and—shoot myself?

Totobet ran her middle finger over some of the tiny mouths on the pictures, a distinctive mother's touch that only a brick wall could mistake for anything less. "Will you take these pictures and help me with remembering?"

I could barely speak. "Remembering?"

"It's the only way we have to honor their little lives. We give away pictures and help each other remember."

"Yes . . . yes, I'll help you remember them. Believe me, I'll never forget."

Anguished, hoping to get this over with, I started to hand the pictures back, but she pressed my arm away. "Don't give them back. We think that's a terrible insult. I know you don't realize."

With a stone in my stomach, I sat on the bunk, holding twenty-three babies. Most cultures with a pattern of abortion or infanticide did everything to forget that the children ever existed and that their lives were somehow less than precious.

"My babies that I'm carrying now," Totobet said, "if I die, will you take them back to my husband?"

I looked up sharply. "If you die? Why would you die?"

"Sometimes women die."

"Oh . . . yes, of course."

"I'd like to teach you their names, so you can remember.

'Tulu, Tessalit, Tamchaket, Totobet, Tishikot, Tippi, To-barra."

Utterly wilted, I just stared at her. The babies weren't even born, but they were already named. My eyes hurt.

A nervous smile cracked my face. "Tippi?"

She blinked and smiled back at me. "It was my husband's mother's name. Now you say the names. Tulu . . ."

"Tulu . . ."

"Tessalit . . . Tamchaket . . ."

One by one we repeated the names of her unborn children. My voice was almost gone, my throat closed up so tightly that I could barely breathe.

Cursed with multiple births *and* a strong parental instinct, how could they keep from going insane? A culture that has to demolish its young would develop traditions like remembering if it didn't want to break down into anarchy. Or maybe it was even simpler than that. Maybe they just weren't the horrible race I'd thought they were. Stop the presses . . . maybe I was *wrong*.

As the names of her children rolled and rolled in my head, I forced up some very gravelly words. "I've misjudged your people."

"Do you have children?" she asked.

Uneasily, I glanced at her. "No . . . well . . . In a way, I guess I did . . ."

"What were their names? I can help you remember."

"Oh . . ." An unexpected smile trembled across my lips. "Well, all right . . . Chakotay . . . Paris . . ."

"Chakotay, Paris."

"Kim . . . Seven . . . Tuvok . . . Neelix . . . B'Elanna . . ."

She repeated the names, and before I knew it we were working our way down through crew members on *Voyager*—a dozen, another dozen—and then my voice trailed away. The weight of this ritual was too much for me.

"You have a big family," she told me, and she nodded in the strangest, most complete understanding I'd ever seen.

The most extraordinary thing occurred then. Totobet reached out for me, and I reached to respond. She gathered me into her arms and we met in the middle of the berth, sinking to the deck on our knees. Together we dissolved into a sobbing clutch.

Many long seconds trailed away as we crouched together, and the more we cried, the more we couldn't stop crying.

Into her ear I gulped, "Who are you? What do you call yourselves?"

So quietly that I could scarcely hear, Totobet squeaked, "Lumalit . . . Lumalit . . ."

The syllables spun from her lips like a strain of music from a harp. Such a beautiful, melodic word. They weren't the Kazon or the Klingons or the Cardassians, where the harshness of the word gave clues as to their ingrained disregard for others. They were a culture forced to kill their own beloved children in order to survive. They were the Lumalit . . . they loved their children. They understood their enemies. They were complex. They were sad. They were resigned.

My grip on Totobet tightened as sobs that should've come through me months ago came through me now. In my arms she shuddered and poured out her own misery. In her hand was one end of the laminate stream of photos of her babies, and in my hand was the other end. We held her children together and were utterly consumed with grief for her lost family, and for my lost family.

In the mild therapy of her desperate culture, Totobet began to murmur against my ear.

"Tulu . . . Tessalit . . . Tamchaket . . ."

CHAPTER
18

"ZELL? YOU WANTED TO SEE ME?"

For two days we had bolted along on our light kick, heading back to an endangered sector, knowing that the Menace—the Lumalit—now knew we had seen them. The nature of a light kick caused us to head off in the very direction of our civilization. There had been no way to hide that. The fatal flaw was that, now that they'd seen us and we'd pointed the way home, even if they hadn't known we were there, they sure knew it now.

I didn't like that part. I didn't like aiding the enemy, even unwillingly, and I didn't like forcing the confrontation early, but that's what might have just happened.

Hell, at top warp, they could probably still beat us home.

All I could hope for was that the Lumalit weren't quite ready for another conquest yet. There was no way to know or even guess.

Totobet and I had had a good old-fashioned cry, and because of that I felt much stronger and much better directed. I had a very clear goal now—to stage a war, then trump the inevitable.

The commanding officer on my watch had summoned

me, and here I was, meeting Zell in the quiet of the processing deck. The huge winches and cables around us were a strangely peaceful forest, even providing a trickling stream of spilled lubricant down the center of the deck.

Zell was sitting on a crank casement, his elbows on his knees, staring at the deck.

"It's not an easy job," he said, "being captain. You don't know much about salvaging. You don't even know the names of the other warranter ships or their captains . . . There are things about this ship you don't even know yet."

Without going into the overview of my past, I asked, "Are you trying to talk me out of running?"

He looked up. "Yes, of course I am. It's bad for the ship. You're not ready."

I'd have accused him of something else, of looking out for himself, but something about his expression stopped me.

"It's bad for the crew," he said. "You haven't been here very long. The rest of us, we've been together half our lives. We've been through everything together. We know each other better than our mothers know us. You've done good things around here, sometimes . . . Other things we don't like so well. Some people like you, and others think you're dangerous. But I'll tell you this . . ." He looked up now. "You don't have the votes. I know this crew. You can't win. By running for captain, you're dividing a crew that's never been divided on anything. Is there some way we can avoid this?"

Folding my arms, I paced away from him and back, then stood looking at the deck and playing with the lubricant puddle with my toe.

"I'd love to avoid it," I said. "But I took the Pledge. I promised to do what's best for the ship. This vote is not the worst thing for the ship. Not even close. Whatever you think, I'm not casually trying to depose you. I actually think you're a very good commanding officer. We haven't agreed on everything, but that's not required. But I know things you don't know. I have training you don't have. I even know things about your technology that you haven't figured out yet. A decision like this shouldn't be up to the crew, in my opinion, but if that's how this ship runs, I'll accept that. I don't think it's in the ship's best interest for me to withdraw, or I sure would. When the vote comes, we'll see what happens."

Zell rubbed a big hand over his face and sighed, then stood up. "We'll see now. Quen's called a crew meeting."

"Now?"

"Right now."

"Kay, you talk first."

Quen motioned weakly from the cot that had been moved out on the main deck for him. Apparently it was customary for all the crew to be present, excepting anyone who was unconscious or simply couldn't be moved. Quen almost fell into that latter category, but he insisted on being here, so here he was.

Here they all were, looking at me.

Over there, Zell stood between Massus and Lucas, leaning uneasily back on the transverse bulkhead with his arms folded and his ankles crossed. I got the feeling he'd have sat down if he'd thought it wouldn't look bad. It would.

Truly regretting what I thought was my duty, I stepped to a point amidships where most of the crew could see me. And I started talking.

"I've only been here a matter of months, I know that . . . I don't want to be your captain. When it comes down to time served, I don't deserve to be yet. Considering what we all saw two days ago, things are not normal. The fact is, you need me. This isn't salvage we're going into. It's either a confrontation with the TCA fleet for which the warranters haven't prepared, or it's a full-out war for your civilization's survival. Either way, I know how to do it and you don't."

Now I paused and raised my eyes, scanning the crew and trying to make contact with each of them in some small way.

"I'm a trained battle captain. I've been a commodore in two engagements. That means I've commanded more than just the ship I was on. I know how to coordinate several vessels. What we're facing is big, too big. I'm trained to face it and you're not. Believe me, right now I'd rather retreat to some quiet planet, put in earplugs, and start a garden. That's not . . . very good citizenship, though. The fact is, this is bigger than *Zingara* and bigger than everybody. The

Mena— the Lumalit people have a huge problem, and the worst part is that they can't be allowed to slaughter other people's children so theirs can survive. It just can't be allowed. This is the nastiest situation I've ever faced."

Some of the crew shifted nervously. I gave them a moment to compose themselves and took the time to draw a long steadying breath.

Then I forced myself to go on, aware of how very unwillingly my soul tagged after.

"Please . . . understand this," I told them. "If you decide to elect Zell—and I think he deserves it very much—and you decide to march into the cannon's maw, I will march there with you. I took the Pledge and I'll absolutely stand by him. Whichever of us you elect, you must understand what's coming."

Deliberately, I didn't look at Zell. That would be uncalled for, cruel, competitive. It might even be taken as theatrical or calculated. I didn't want to take the slightest chance of anyone's misinterpreting my motives.

Changing my posture a little, I rubbed my chilly hands, gazed briefly at the deck, then looked up again.

"There are times in every civilization's history when there's no way to survive playing by the rules you're used to. You have to step outside. We have to suspend the normal way of doing things and take the only chance we have. We've got to adapt our technology to fight a very powerful force. I've got a few ideas and they might work. Now, I'm not a politician making a speech and promising things I can't deliver. I don't know if we can win. This may be the death of the sector coming on. But if we play it right and don't squander the chance, we might not only survive but prevail. You might finally be free. This is a momentous time in history—a time when you, a handful of people, hold the fate of civilization in your grasp. You've taken incredible risks for so long . . . take one more."

Was there an echo in here? Why were my words rolling and rolling?

Some of the crew were staring at me, others refusing to look up. All were listening to my words again in their minds.

After a long pause, Quen gingerly turned his head to Zell.

"Your turn," he invited.

Zell scanned the crew, gave me a very brief glare, then gave a longer one to Quen that had some underlying communication in it. Quen offered a spontaneous grin without much cheer, but with a lot of support.

Slowly Zell pushed off the bulkhead but didn't unfold his arms. What would he say? And did it matter? These men had invested their whole lives in Quen and Zell, had trusted them for years and were still alive, still surviving, because of them. Whatever they had, it worked for them.

As the crew waited to hear what he had to say, Zell cleared his throat. Very resignedly, he let his arms fall to his sides. He never quite looked up.

"All of you who were going to vote for me," he said slowly, "vote for her."

CHAPTER
19

"I, KATHRYN JANEWAY, ACCEPT THE POST OF COMMANDING shipmate of the *Warranter Zingara*. I accept that this oath incorporates and assumes the Ship's Pledge. I accept the duty of judgment over any shipmate who violates the Pledge. I will administer justice according to the Pledge. I will remain captain until my crew releases me from my obligation. I swear that this obligation supersedes any previous oaths or obligations. I, Kathryn Janeway, so pledge."

With the exception of the pulselike murmur of the fusion engine carrying us in our light jump, the ship was eerily quiet.

I found Zell on the processing deck, sitting where he had been sitting the last time we talked, with his elbows on his knees again and his head in his hands. His eyes flicked a little when I came in, so he knew I was there, but he didn't change his position at all.

In a way that was nice—even he was comfortable enough around me not to put on any performances.

For a few moments we floated in comradely silence. Odd how much we seemed to understand each other now.

"I have a couple of ideas," I began finally. "We'll be back in two days. We should come out of the kick with a plan of action ready to implement. The first thing we should do is attract attention to ourselves as a signal to the TCA that things have changed."

"How?"

"Well, by creating a lot of sparkle and panic by bludgeoning automated outposts and maybe some TCA factories."

"Mock attacks?"

"Oh, hell no, real ones. Just very specifically targeted, with a bigger goal than just the destruction. It'll remind the TCA just who fought and won their war, and it'll focus public attention on the warranters. We'll need that."

"What do you want me to do?" he asked.

"We'll need a distribution network for our recordings of the Menace armada. As soon as we come out of the kick, we should fire off about a thousand copies of the recordings. You supervise making the distribution plan. Other warranter ships, media sources, TCA captains—"

"TCA captains?"

"Yes. Don't forget, there's a fleet."

"Oh . . ."

"You'll have to be ready to pin down the locations of any TCA ships in our range and broadcast that recording. I'll make a video introduction to what the problem is as I see it, a recording of Tobobet explaining very briefly the problem her culture faces and what they do about it, and then I'll narrate what we saw in Iscoy space, including a description of antimatter modes of power. Now, I need your advice . . . I think I'm overstepping propriety by narrating the recording myself. Do you think it'll be taken as grandstanding? I don't want to make the wrong impression. I'm not really out to make any impression of myself. I think Quen should do it."

Shifting his legs, he gazed at the deck.

"Quen should make the introduction," he suggested. "You should narrate the recording and explain the modes of power."

"All right, I can work with that. We have to be ready with

something to give our armed forces, so they will be ready to fight the Lumalit."

He glanced up. "If this Lumalit Menace managed to destroy a force superior to ours, what can we do about them?"

My arms tightened around my ribs. "I think I've got that figured out. It's an old trick. Shields have to cover a huge band, a wide range of frequencies in order to protect against a range of destructive power. If you know your enemy's frequency, you could calculate its maximum, then concentrate all your shields to that, and make your shields seem almost invincible. It would give you a hell of a surprise advantage."

Looking like a shrunken doll, Zell nervously asked, "How do we beat that?"

"Well, if you're using energy weapons and you know ahead of time, you phase the frequency shift, and suddenly it's as if they have *no* shields. The Iscoy didn't have the technology to recognize that. You don't, either. They've been stomping whole civilizations because their shield trick hasn't been figured out. I've figured it out because my civilization came up against a group of beings called the Borg who could figure out what we were firing at them, and adapt so they couldn't be hurt. It's basically the same kind of trick. The Lumalit shields must have huge gaps. I know that because of their power consumption—well, never mind about that. In the Federation, nobody would get away with that trick for long because we all communicate. In this quadrant, though, with so many unaligned cultures, word doesn't get around . . ."

My words fell away and I stopped for a moment. There wasn't any point in scolding him about how his science hadn't caught up to mine yet. Really, that was never in my mind, but suddenly I was aware about how such things sounded. Zell didn't deserve this. Nobody here did.

I forced myself to change tack.

"They must be sending scouts ahead and analyzing weapons capabilities, then presetting their shields to those frequencies. You see, they weren't generating enough power to do what it looked like they were doing. If their shields were preset to be frequency-specific, then it made them seem a lot more powerful than they were. It gave teeth to their surprise attack. They've probably done the same thing to this area. They probably already know about our missiles and anything else we've got. But there's one thing they don't know—"

"That you're here," he handed out.

"Right. We need to use something they're not expecting at all, and hardshells won't do the trick. We need a wide-spectrum quantum discharge."

"What's that mean?"

"Mostly, it means spending the next forty hours or so finishing my experiments on the tiles."

Zell sat upright. "You mean, like what hurt Quen? Like *that?*"

"We have to be creative, Zell. We've got to have a computer program already on curry cards and ready to interface with any compatible system, any ship, any armed station on any planet. There won't be time for people to do what I have in mind. We have to let the computers do it all. I'll need one full watch crew for that, so we'll have to call all hands on deck. The on-watch crew will handle the ship, a second crew will work with me on the quantum discharge, and I want Lucas to head a team that will extend the capabilities of our long-range sensors. When the Lumalit come in, I want to know ahead of time."

"Lucas doesn't know how to do that."

"I've already told him how."

"Oh . . ." He leaned forward again and gazed at the deck, soaking up all this. "You'll need to know how the external gantries work and how to get them out of the way quickly. Jedd can show you that. And you should have Levan or Othien explain the markers and signals we use on the grooves and corridors."

I tilted my head. "We're going into a battle situation. We won't need the usual signal and corridor rules."

He looked up briefly. "You'll need to know them so you'll know how to break them."

A trickle of embarrassment ran down my spine. "Mmmm . . . That's a pretty sad comment on how well you're getting to know me . . ."

"Didn't mean anything."

"I know you didn't."

Pacing off a few steps, half my brain working on all the things I suddenly had to learn in order to be captain of this ship, to deliver all the things I'd said were possible. Now that I had command, before me rose a mountain of sur-mountables.

I'd forgotten about that. Becoming captain didn't mean the height of knowledge or the pinnacle of accomplishment; it was in fact just the beginning of the learning process. Suddenly a restful sleep was a joke. There wasn't anywhere to shift any burden. Far from knowing everything, I now had to seek out those who knew and use their abilities to the best service of the ship and our purpose. Everybody here knew more than I did about *Zingara*, the warranters, and the culture I had adopted. This was not a time of lofty victory for me. It was a time of numbing humility.

Moving back to Zell, I paused, but not so close as to intimidate him in any way.

"I never wanted to be the captain," I told him honestly. "They'd have voted for you."

He scratched his head and sighed.

"They did what I told them," he muttered. "I got only two votes. Quen's . . . and yours." A mirthless chuckle jogged his shoulders. "Even I didn't vote for myself."

I offered a nominal smile. "What you did was uncommonly noble. You could've easily been captain."

Zell didn't look up. One shoulder moved in a small shrug.

"I took the Pledge," he said.

LIVE FREE OR DIE!

State slogan of New Hampshire

It was the forty-fathom slumber that clears the soul and eye and heart, and sends you to breakfast ravening.

—*Captains Courageous*

CHAPTER

20

"THE LUMALIT SHIELDS ARE FREQUENCY-SPECIFIC. THEY WON'T be able to block more than five percent of a total wash. That's how we take them by surprise. They won't expect us to be able to blow through their shields. This discharge'll go right through."

"What are you going to use as a housing for this? Missiles?"

"Missiles are pretty fragile. But a ship isn't."

"Not . . ."

"No, not *Zingara,* don't worry. We'll tow a wreck in and use it. As long as it has the tile technology—"

"All the ships around us have tiles."

"Right, of course."

Massus, working at his engineering post before the aft transverse bulkhead, turned and called, "Kay, the engines are about to shut down from the light kick. We're almost back."

"Is the boarding party ready?"

"They're ready."

I turned to the crew and raised my voice. "Boys, this is it.

Let's see how well we've learned our new tricks. Zell? Do your stuff."

With a dubious glance at me for last-second support, Zell cleared his throat, drew a tight breath, and tried his new trick.

"Orange alert!" he called.

With a quick laugh, I corrected, "Yellow!"

"*Yellow* alert! All hands to battlestations!"

"Engines are down. We're out of the kick!"

"Lucas, long-range sensors on."

"Long-range sensors . . . on."

"Massus, adjust engines for sublight."

"Adjusted."

"Say 'engines sublight, aye.'"

"Oh . . . engines sublight, aye."

Lucas suddenly turned. "Kay, there's a ship in our path!"

I leaned over his shoulder and looked at one of the tile screens that showed our ship approaching another. "Oh, well, there's a shock. The *Aragore*."

"You want the overhead vid on?"

"No, too distracting. We'll just use the small screens. I don't want anybody craning his neck when he should be doing his job."

Zell appeared about twenty feet down deck from me. "You won't be able to see as much."

"We'll see enough. Everybody clear on what to do if he won't get out of the way?"

Around the deck, the fully mustered crew made anxious but purposeful shifts and nods, moving to their positions, keying on their tiles, testing their systems, making sure they were ready.

"Don't be nervous, anybody," I told them. "He's not scary enough."

Lucas turned his pale face to me. "You're not worried?"

"About Sasaquon?" I huffed. "He's the smallest potato around. Go ahead and hail him. Why wait?"

Tensely, he flattened his lips and touched the right tiles. A new screen appeared on a set of dark tiles. Sasaquon's communications man was standing there looking back at us.

"This is *Zingara,*" Lucas announced. "We want to talk to Sasaquon right now."

Without waiting for the formalities, Sasaquon shoved his comm guy aside and appeared on the screen. I moved next to Lucas to make sure Sasaquon could see me. Damn, that was a good-looking man. Why did he have to be a rat?

Not bothering with greetings, I asked, "How did you find us?"

"This is where you were last seen," he responded. *"You're all under arrest."*

"Arrest? Then you've decided to drop the act and stop pretending you're just another warranter?"

That one annoyed him. He scowled and demanded, *"Why are you talking for the ship? Where's Quen? I want to talk to him."*

"He's here. You'll have to talk to me."

"Is he dead?"

"No, he's not dead."

"Then where's Zell? Have you taken over that ship like you tried to do Aragore?"

Zell stepped up next to me so he was in the screen's capture range. "We've given her command, Sasaquon."

"Why would you? Is Quen dead?"

"We're making the best use of our crew's abilities. And Quen's not dead."

"You're moving in on us, Sasaquon," I said, making it clear that there'd be no sneaking up. "This is fair warning— don't get too close."

"I'm coming in to cable you. Your engines will be shut down and you'll be towed in under my authority."

"You a gambling man, Sassie?"

"What?"

"You'd better get out of my path. This civilization's way of doing business is all done."

"Why are we done?"

"Because I'm here now and I'm not letting this go on."

Even over the brushed surface of the tiles, with the grid of adhesive etching his face, Sasaquon's anger virtually glowed across space.

"Who are you to say?" he demanded.

How gratifying it was that I remained a mystery to him,

that my presence in this sector and certainly my authority on this or any ship utterly confused him. The rules were changing and he didn't know what they were—what a grand advantage.

But that wasn't the answer. My answer was much better, far more satisfying to me.

"I'm the one that's here," I told him with firm and fiery conviction. "I'm the one who accepted command of a ship and said I'd use it to change things for the better. I'm the captain."

Around me the crew of *Zingara* bristled with underlying pride so crisp that I could feel it and was bolstered by their confidence.

"You're too late," Sasaquon said. *"Oran's gathered up all the warranters. They've formed an assault unit, and they're attacking our planet."*

With a single clap of my hands, I glanced around at my crew. "Hear that, everybody? The warranters are standing down the TCA's hired guns!"

A rallying cheer trumpeted through space over the comm lines.

Without waiting for the sound to fade, I said, "Sasaquon, you've got to move aside. We have critical information about an incoming armada. We've got to get to the planet. Whatever the political differences are, they've got to be stopped. If there are heavy casualties to the warranters or the TCA, there won't be enough—"

"It's called the CASF now. Civilian Authority Space Force."

"You can call yourselves the Starfleet Space Hockey Team, for all I care. What's important is that you get out of my way. Move and move now."

"There's no point in resisting," he countered. *"The battle at the planet is almost over. The warranters are negotiating a surrender. The Space Force has them surrounded. Since you and your crew fomented this revolt, you're under arrest. Accept defeat gracefully."*

"All right, that's it. Here's my idea of grace. Gentlemen, we have a little change of plans here. Red alert."

Zell's voice boomed across the long deck. "Red alert!"

"Turret gunners, fire! Massus, release *all* cables—proximity range!"

"Approaching home space, Kay."

"Understood. Maintain red alert. Have our engineering team ready to get off Sasaquon's ship if things go wrong. Is Sasaquon's crew locked down over there?"

"They're all tied hands and feet and locked in their bunks."

"Have somebody take an armed unit and go untie their feet, walk them through the airlock conduit, put them on our processing deck, and tie them up again."

"I'll do it myself."

"That's a good idea."

My conversation with Zell was far from private, and that was how I wanted it. Much better for the crew to hear my thought process and know what I had in mind. In order to fulfill my plan of attack, we needed a derelict ship. We'd been willing to go look for one, but since Sasaquon cooperated so nicely, we'd just use his ship.

The *Aragore* was under tow and we were making repairs from a remarkably quick assault. We'd made a good bet: Sasaquon had some authority, but he was a bad captain. He didn't have the loyalty of his crew. Sasaquon and his crew were soldiers pretending to be warranters. They hadn't expected to come up against warranters trained to fight, but that's what they got when they tried to stop us. Unlike any other warranters, we'd been ready for them and not on the defensive. We went instantly on the attack. The crew of *Zingara* were already at battlestations and ready to go on the offensive. Our turret gunners were already targeted, and Sasaquon was utterly overwhelmed by the quick unexpected firing off of not only guns, but cables. Twenty cables, all thicker around than I was, shooting at once and acting like a giant butterfly net.

Sasaquon tried shooting back, but by the time he figured out that he should be shooting at our cable releases instead of our turrets, the job was done. *Aragore* was netted and reeled in, instantly brought too close to continue firing without doing damage to themselves. While they tried to cut our cables, we plugged in an airlocked conduit and boarded an armed party, which they certainly hadn't expected.

None of that was the remarkable part . . . and I confess I hadn't counted on this. Sasaquon's crew, faced with armed guards who they knew were fighting for the freedom of their planet, had weak stomachs when it came to cold-blooded slaughter of warranters.

Of course! I hadn't expected that—the soldiers of the TCA perfectly well knew the warranters weren't dangerous. When it came right down to blood and bone, they wouldn't back up the corrupt government Sasaquon represented. Despite Sasaquon's posturing, *Aragore*'s crew surrendered.

Now they were on their way to the belly of *Zingara*, to await trial in a court of law if we could push this civilization to actually go back to a rule of law.

Time would tell—very soon. We were almost to the planet. Now we had only the TCA itself to deal with.

Even before the planet came into view around its nearest moon, we could see the flashes of battle casting a halo on the moon's perimeter. Ugly recognizable flashes of missile detonation spiderwebbed through open space, carrying sparkling debris and hot shrapnel.

"This is it," I said to my nervous crew. "That's the TCA fleet and the warranters. We avoided a big problem with Sasaquon. We might not be able to avoid one here. Massus, release the *Aragore*. We'll leave it orbiting the moon until we need it."

"Releasing the *Aragore*, aye."

"Lucas, get that broadcast ready. All right, boys, we're going to go in fighting! Everybody ready?"

They let me know with a rolling cheer that they were ready to back me up, and even though the decibel level on the cheer left something to be desired, I took whatever I could get. This was a crew that had been battle-trained to my strange methods for mere days, not years or even months. They didn't even know the history of the methods I was telling them to trust, but they were willing to give me all they possessed.

"One-half sublight speed," I ordered, and gripped the well rail while watching the largest of the tile screens on the starboard side. "Lucas, put the main action on the large screen like I showed you."

Lucas was juggling nearly a dozen screens, but we'd stationed two other screen guys there to help him. He had trouble delegating and was still trying to handle it all himself. I didn't interfere. After a few minutes, he had no choice but to concentrate and let the others help him.

The screens readjusted as he worked them, and right about amidships appeared a single wide-angle view of the action in space. Maybe I was just more comfortable with this arrangement because it looked more like Starfleet viewscreens than the huge overhead vid capabilities of the tiles. Right now I needed something familiar.

There were at least thirty ships visible on the large amidships screen, the gaggle of warranters, whose ships were all slightly different from each other, and a collection of brand-new ships, much more streamlined and obviously sliced by the same cookie cutter.

"Look!" I said. "There they are! Those are the TCA ships . . . there's Oran!"

"The warranters are almost surrounded!" Zell gasped. "Sasaquon was right!"

"They're not surrounded," I told him. "Look more closely—that's a wedge formation. They're still very much in the fight."

Blasts of missile fire and ensuing detonation rang across space, setting the hulls of the warranters ablaze.

"They're taking so many hits—" Lucas blurted, his hands shaking as he tended the screen, flinching with every new detonation.

"Yes," I said, "taking hits and fielding them. Those warrant ships are old and tough. Look at the damage on the TCA ships' hulls; they must be made of newer alloy, but they've been made on a budget, or too fast or something. They're being punctured."

"They must be double-hulled, though," Zell offered. "There's no atmosphere venting."

I squinted. "Oh, am I glad you noticed that! Good work! Jedd! Can you hear me?"

From down in the engineering well, Jedd called back, "I hear you!"

"Keep our strongest hull plates to the TCA."

"I can do that."

"Kay!" Lucas called. "They're turning on us!"

As we rushed through space toward the planet and the battle between here and there, a half-dozen TCA ships wheeled to meet us and opened fire.

Zingara rocked with missile impact but didn't crack.

"Hold your speed until we're closer," I called over the boom and rattle of detonation. "Turret gunners, target those missiles and detonate them in space."

"Don't you want them to fire on the ships?" Zell asked.

"Not yet." I gripped his arm. "Go below and supervise the gunners yourself. Don't waste ammunition!"

Without a response, he vaulted the deck rail and disappeared down the well.

"Lucas!" I came around the well. "Hail every ship in this area."

"H-hailing," he stammered.

To his left, a small screen popped out of nowhere on some dark tiles and showed a picture of me as the other ships would see me: head and shoulders, little cape, pale complexion, shaggy auburn mop, and notably more gaunt than I remembered myself.

"This is Kathryn Janeway, commanding the *Zingara*. I'm addressing all Space Force vessels. The warranters are not your enemy. Your true enemy is on its way from a distant solar system with an attacking armada of matter/anti-matter–powered hyperlight vessels. It's absolutely critical—"

A direct hit slammed the ship sideways under me, and I hit the deck on my side. The ship vibrated horridly for ten seconds, then steadied down. Othian hauled me to my feet and I tried to remember what I was saying. Even as I talked, the firing continued. The TCA ships shot at us and at the warranters. Oran's ship moved in to help defend us, but I had another mission in mind.

"It's imperative that the Space Force and the warranters join forces immediately before any more damage is done," I continued, nearly shouting over the bang and ring of impact. "I recommend that the TCA step down and call elections. This sector has got to organize right away. Where

I come from, there was once a state in a nation, and that state has a motto we would all do well to heed today. Those words are 'Live free or die.' I'm willing to do that. So are all the warranters. I challenge all of you today to look at what we are sending you now, and make a decision worthy of people who deserve to live free."

I paused briefly to let my words carry across space, and to watch the ships shooting at each other and at us.

"Lucas," I finally said, "broadcast the recording of what we saw in Iscoy space. Make sure they can pick it up on any frequency."

"What if they—"

"Doesn't matter. Broadcast."

Enduring a pounding that hearkened back to the most brutal I'd ever experienced, we steeled ourselves and took the hits as Lucas desperately sent and re-sent the message we'd so hastily created. Would the TCA think it was a hoax? Such things could easily be faked. Would they believe Quen on the recording? Would they believe me?

"Kay! Kay!"

Keeping a grip on the rail, I spun around. "What? Who is that?"

"It's me . . . it's—"

"Gashan, yes, what are you yelling about?"

"Look at this!"

Taking a step every second or so, between rockings of the ship around us, I pulled myself across the deck to where Gashan was crouched beside a tile screen we'd been generally ignoring. Luckily, despite the attraction of the battle being played out so near to us, he wasn't ignoring his station.

"Look at the readings . . ." He ran his finger along a sensory graph that made a strange series of dots on the tiles.

I didn't need Gashan to explain to me. Long-range sensors. I'd upgraded them myself.

"It's an incoming force," I murmured, suddenly hoarse. "Damn them . . . they're early."

My chest constricted as if some great flame had sucked the oxygen away. I pressed my lips tight and forced myself to breathe through my nose, just to keep from panting in front of my crewmates. The Menace was coming—the

Lumalit, coming to inflict the terrible necessities of their culture on these people.

With my hands trembling in fingerless gloves and my pulse tenor-drumming in my ears, I struggled back across the vaulting deck to Lucas's side.

Zell climbed halfway out of the well and said, "Rod levels are two over the prad, and we've got a halo on the chokes."

I motioned him to come up here. Perplexed, he climbed up quickly and joined me. With a significant glance, I motioned back across the deck to Gashan's long-range scanner. Zell looked at it briefly as if he didn't understand . . . and then he did.

His face dropped its ruddy color, and for a moment I thought he'd stopped breathing, but then he collected himself and stood beside me as we looked at the TCA ships and warranters moving on the main viewer.

There, as many of the crew gathered around us to observe the ships moving on the screen, we watched the action and fought a private battle, each in his own head, to keep from going mad from the noise and the tension. If the pounding kept up much longer, we would have to launch serious retaliation or we would be cracked like a stone on an anvil.

We took the pounding and watched more of the TCA ships maneuvering to attack us. The warranters turned, also. Oran's ship veered in to fire at the nearest TCA ship. He was defending us. In deference to Quen and the honorable actions of his brother, I would soon open fire.

Soon . . . a few more seconds . . . long enough for that broadcast to reach every ship . . . soon there would be no choice.

Oran's ship took a hard hit from the nearby TCA ship. A stream of liquid, possibly fuel or lubricant, sprayed from the port-side aft section.

That was it. I'd have to start cutting hulls. There was no time left.

"Zell," I began, "go below and tell the gunners to target the TCA point-blank, full missile power. Don't hold back . . . kill them."

Shuddering, he put his hand on the well rail and maneuvered to climb down again. I heard his breath rattle in his chest.

"Kay?" Lucas's voice barely sounded over the thrum of missile detonations.

I turned back. "Yes?"

"Look . . . on the other side of the warranters . . . those TCA ships aren't shooting anymore. What does that mean?"

Now it was my turn to stop breathing.

Zell reappeared at my side.

The crew gathered tighter around us. The bleeps and hums of the working ship seemed to echo like the inside of a living body as we watched the TCA ships—first one, then another, and another across inner space—began to cease fire.

CHAPTER
21

"IT'S AN OLD TRICK. IT'S CALLED THE 'FIRE SHIP MANEUVER.' In the oceanfaring navies on my planet in the past, they'd pack a ship with combustibles. Sometimes they'd even include incendiaries or explosives. Then they'd set the ship ablaze and send it sailing into a cluster of enemy ships. Everyone at sea is afraid of fire. In space, it's the same . . . everyone's afraid of energy."

"Are you sure it'll go through a vacuum? Shouldn't we put a timer on it?"

"If the potential is high enough, nothing'll buffer it. It'll discharge automatically when *Aragore* gets close enough to other ships. We've got to pack the fire ship with so much charge that it's unequal when it comes in proximity with another source, and the charge'll jump very much like lightning. It should even discharge through the vacuum of space."

"If the potential is high enough."

"*If* . . . it's high enough."

Beside me, Massus let out a doubtful sigh. "Well, the engines are adjusted to feed all their energy back into the tiles instead of thrust. I hope this works the way you say it will."

"I hope so too."

We weren't on board *Zingara*. We were on *Aragore*. Sasaquon and his crew were in custody back on the planet and were now somebody else's problem. Massus and I, with a team of five engineers from *Zingara*, were turning *Aragore* into a giant grenade when a call came from our ship.

"Kay!"

"Kay here, Zell."

"You better come back! They're almost to us!"

"All right, we'll come back."

"But we're not finished!" Massus protested.

"We're finished enough," I said. "He's the first officer. I should take his recommendation. He's right. If the battle starts and we get trapped over here, we're all dead. We'll try to finish by remote. Is the trigger in?"

"Yes."

"Let's go. Get the others."

Through the magnetic boarding cuff, into the airlock, and back onto *Zingara* we went, having left the *Aragore* rafted up to us and loaded with readjusted mechanics. We were on our way at top sublight to meet the incoming Menace armada. The farther away from the core of population, the better. That would give us room to confront them, and room to fall back if necessary.

Aragore was a virtually gutted ship. We'd scrambled to remove all the food supplies, water, blankets, mechanical portables, and anything else we might need if things went drastically wrong. No sense burning up stuff that could come in very handy in a survival situation, but of course all that took time and we had very little. We got what we could as the armada drew closer and closer.

The armada had reduced to sublight for their final approach, expected procedure for an assault that thought nobody was waiting for it.

"Are they changing formation at all?" I asked immediately as Massus and I joined Zell on the main deck of *Zingara*.

"No changes yet," Zell said.

"How many ships?"

"We've counted sixty-four."

"And we've got . . ."

"Nineteen Space Force ships and eleven warranters."

"Hmm . . . well, Nelson did it at Trafalgar."

"What?"

"I'll tell you later. Release all but the spring cable on *Aragore*. Massus, test the remote triggers. Make sure they'll start those engines. In fact, never mind testing them. Go ahead and start the engines. Charge it up."

Zell grasped my arm. "You want to start charging the tiles over there while *Aragore*'s still rafted to us? What if the charge jumps to us?"

"Then we'll be fried like fillets. Is the rest of the fleet ready?"

At his matte of screens, Lucas didn't turn to me. "Yes, they're in formation. We're in the lead . . . the warranters and Space Force ships are in formation behind us."

"Delta formation?"

"It looks like what you described."

"They should be able to handle that. It's almost the same as their wedge tactic. I hope so, anyway. Full overhead vid, please, Lucas."

"Oh . . . overhead, aye."

Lot of hoping going on here, I noticed, quite a nerve-wracking amount of it coming from me. My stomach quivered as the tile-encrusted ceiling and sides of the ship blurred and disappeared. Suddenly we were looking out into open space, able to see above and around us. I turned to check the formation of the Space Force and the warranters. To our right, Oran's ship flanked us just abaft our beam. It was good to see him there. I wished his brother could be here at his side, but Quen was under sedation as his broken bones and burned innards fought to recover. I felt deeply regretful about that; he deserved to be here. For a fleeting moment I thought of having Ruvan rouse him and station him here on his main deck for the big battle.

That would only be cruel, for I couldn't give back command. I was stuck with it.

"Zell," I began abruptly. When he looked at me I said, "Have Totobet brought to the main deck."

"That woman? Why?"

"I want her to see how we handle this. And I might have questions for her."

"She won't answer," he said. "I wouldn't."

"I wouldn't either, but bring her up anyway. I'd like her to watch this."

He stepped past me on his way to give that order, but quite unexpectedly he paused.

"You like this kind of thing, don't you?" he observed, keeping his voice low. "You seem . . . charged up."

I gazed back at him, a little embarrassed. What could I do? After all this, toe a pacifist line? Honesty was not only part of the Pledge, but generally a wise plan.

"Part of me likes it," I admitted. "I'd be lying to say otherwise. It's too easy to get away from."

"What's that mean?"

Pressing one hand on the well rail, I gave the old ship a warm rub of affection. "If you don't like heat and snakes, don't go to Tarkus II."

Zell was right. My whole body tingled with anticipation. My movements were darting, my orders inspired. I felt my eyes glow and my skin pulse with hot blood running just under the surface. Battle possessed undeniable intoxication for anyone trained to do it. Still, since I had met Totobet, spoken with her, understood her and the Lumalits' hideous natural burden, to have to fight them to the death became regrettable. The "us or them" rudiment of survival took on a rocky substance for me.

Of course, that wouldn't stop me either. I didn't hate the enemy. That wasn't required.

Totobet was here now, standing in the corner near the aft transverse bulkhead. She watched with her wide brown eyes as the armada of her people's advance flank streamed toward us out of the rhinestone-studded black fabric of space. She'd seen this before, of course, but not quite from this perspective.

"That's an advance team, isn't it?" I asked her. "There are only sixty-some ships there. We saw over two hundred in Iscoy space."

"All don't come at once," she said. Apparently she didn't see any reason to hide the obvious from me or try to tell me it wasn't true. "Others come later with the crew's families."

"Yes, transports," I responded. "That's how I'd do it. We can assume these ships are well armed, being the strike force, can't we?"

She watched the outflow of her people's armada. "Oh . . . yes."

I knew all this just from watching, but my crew needed to hear it. They needed to understand that they must do whatever the coming situation called upon them to do because there would be more of the enemy coming. And this enemy would not hesitate.

"Get ready to release the *Aragore*. Make sure we're at full sublight so she'll have the momentum we need."

Lucas craned to see me past the man crouching next to him. "Don't you want to hail them? Tell them who we are?"

"They know who we are," I said. "I've seen their tactics. They didn't give any warning to the Iscoy. I don't intend to give them any. Zell, hold back the *Aragore* until I give the order, no matter what happens. Is that understood?"

"It's clear . . . can't say I understand . . ."

"Kay, they're shooting! What is that!"

In the wide-open panorama around us, streaks of energy beams as white as the gleam off a knight's sword came bolting from the first flank of Lumalit ships. The first blasts sizzled across *Zingara*'s bow and the bows of Oran's ship and several others of our lines. They were directed hits, very effective, well targeted, and coordinated.

Very bright—we all shielded our eyes from the crackle of energy washing over our invisible hull.

And very noisy.

"Hold formation!" I called over the drumming hits.

Lucas would relay my choreography to the other ships. I hoped they would continue to take my suggestions, for certainly I hadn't been around enough for them to trust me as commodore and take actual orders from me.

"Oran wants to return fire!" Lucas called back.

"Not yet! Tell everybody to hold fire, batten down, and take the hits until we get closer!"

Massus stumbled to my side. "What kind of weapons are those white bolts?"

"Directed energy. Phased rectification using rapid nadions. It's got to do with high-speed reactions at the level of atomic nuclei. At least, that's what ours are. Theirs are some variation of that. The colors are different, sometimes the intensity, but the basic method . . . there are only so many ways to do it."

"Can you teach us?"

I glanced at him and raised an eyebrows. "If we ever get the time."

The Lumalit ships, once they had begun firing, continued to do so. Without shields in the sense I considered conventional, the warranters and the Space Force ships were cut horridly across the hulls, able to stand up to the pounding only because of their sheer toughness and overbuilt construction. They had nominal energy shields that were used only for protection from micrometeorites during the light kicks, and those managed to deflect enough of the Lumalit energy beams that the destructive power, by the time it reached the hull material itself, was depleted somewhat.

That might let us survive at this distance, but as we drew closer, as the angles on the beams became less glancing and more piercing, the slight advantage would disintegrate.

"Kay, they're getting close . . ." Zell paced back and forth behind me, his head swiveling as he watched the oncoming ships. "Are you sure we shouldn't fire back at them?"

"Not yet!" I snapped.

He didn't argue anymore. Everyone was tense, but to their credit they were not paralyzed. Crewmen stayed to their work, steadying the ship, plugging breaches, clearing damage, as *Zingara* rocked around us and we saw the other ships in our ragtag fleet also shimmy and suffer. Some fell from the formation, trailing great wedding trains of damage that painted space with lights.

"Keep forward motion, no matter what, Levan! Hold the course!"

"I'm holding it!"

"Massus, keep the speed up to one-half sublight."

"We're losing some speed—"

"Zell! Release the *Aragore!*"

"Releasing!"

"Levan, reduce speed and fall back. Lucas, tell everybody else to fall back, too. Massus, trigger the *Aragore*'s quantum buildup!"

"It's triggered! Hope it works—"

"How many ships have we lost?" I shouted. "Lucas! Can you hear me?"

"Yes . . . Oran's still with us, but thirteen ships are crippled!"

"Have the others close up formation!"

Part of the overhead screen went dark, and a second later that part of the hull exploded. Gutted mechanics, tiles, and structure crumbled on top of three men at the aft bulkhead, including Massus.

I pushed some of the hot junk aside and tried to see if they were alive. One wasn't. I couldn't be sure about Massus because I couldn't reach him.

Zell jumped to take over the controls. "Shouldn't we break up? Instead of making one big target?"

"Do you think so?" I asked.

"Seems it wouldn't let them concentrate their shots."

The rubble near me shifted—Massus! He crawled out from under the wreckage, shook his head, and let me help him to his feet.

I held his arm as he steadied himself, but I was still working on Zell's suggestion. "Or it might cause them to move apart and lessen our chances of taking out enough of them . . . All right, we'll try it your way. Lucas! Tell the other ships to break formation and draw fire. Othien, check the remotes on *Aragore.* Is there a buildup?"

Othian stumbled to Massus's screens and squinted at them. "I think . . ."

"Look!"

Zell stumbled to the middle of the main deck and pointed out, forward, at the *Aragore.*

As we fell back, still taking hits, *Aragore* surged forward like a good little robot, without a living soul on board, and the very body of the ship was beginning to gleam. All the tiles on board were mounting stocks of energy, building and building, without anywhere to release their stores. The skin of the warranter took on a brassy polish as energy built inside, sucking directly from the fusion engines that were turned inward upon themselves.

Predictably, the Lumalit ships began turning their attention to this single spearhead, assuming there were people on board and that *Aragore* was about to open fire on them.

How mystified they must be! *Aragore* took all their shots and returned none, sailing calmly into the mass of Lumalit ships as her hull was systematically seared by those energy bolts. The hull now glowed bright celery green against space, and a wide corona of radiant energy surrounded her as if she were painted with watercolors on a blotter.

"She's overloading!" Massus gasped.

"Not close enough," I muttered. "Closer . . . closer . . ."

Maybe I'd miscalculated. Maybe the Lumalit would destroy the *Aragore* before the ship could release its quantum discharge. Half the ship's tail section was flying like a kite behind her already. A few more shots—

A huge blue-white flash blinded us all. There was no sound, but inside my head was a single drum hit caused by the snap of bright light. When we looked again, there was another flash, and another!

Pure wide-spectrum energy branched again and again from *Aragore*'s overloaded tiles, conducting instantly through the vacuum of space, linking the former warrant ship with ten . . . fifteen . . . twenty-one Lumalit ships! Twenty-two!

Wave after wave of crackling blue lightning tied up the Lumalit ships near *Aragore*, setting them ablaze with raw deadly voltage. As we watched in a carnivalish combination of horror and delight, *Aragore* began to fall apart, chunk by chunk, destroying herself as energy blew from her tiles into the other ships.

Twenty-two enemy ships hit!

"Condition of those vessels, Lucas!" I called out. "What are you reading?"

"They're . . ." Lucas tapped his tiles and tried to keep a grasp on his panic. "They're . . . they're falling off! They're crippled!"

A cheer blasted from our crew in a single voice as nearly a dozen Lumalit ships rolled away from the center of the battle, obviously confused, damaged, and without the ability even to steer clear of other ships, which resulted in several collisions with the tight formation.

"Twenty-two ships crippled," I breathed. "Tell Oran and the others to move in while the Lumalit are confused. Open fire."

We all went in together, singling out a Lumalit ship and embarking on two dozen duels all happening at the same time. The Lumalit ships were faltering from radiant power that struck some of them when the fire ship released its quantum discharge, but they were slowly recovering and that worried me.

If the battle continued thus, this many ships against that many, we had a chance. Unfortunately, that wasn't how things were to go for us.

As we grappled in open space with our adversary, Lucas found me and tugged on the hem of my shoulder cape.

"Kay," he croaked. As I turned, he pointed across the deck at the long-range screen. "Uh . . . more . . ."

He didn't want anyone else to hear. In mere seconds, though, his gentlemanly forbearance wouldn't make a bit of difference.

On the screen were the jewel-clear blips that represented more ships coming in. Another wave of enemy vessels was about to fall out of hyperlight right on top of us.

Zell bent next to me to study the screen. "A second wave?"

"Looks like it," I grumbled.

"We can't beat them," he said. "We don't have any more fire ships to send in. They can take out our missiles too easily. Should we retreat?"

A brief silence crackled between us, and all around members of the crew listened to what we were saying. The silent moment had a damning voice: *What good would it do to retreat?*

"We're not retreating," I said. "We do have a ship to use against them. *Zingara* will be the next fire ship."

There were plenty of alternatives, but only one good alternative, only one that might give a message of example to the struggling fleet around us and show them all what we had to do, to what great lengths all people must go to live free.

I straightened up and paused for a second or two of deep consideration. When I spoke, my voice was strangely calm, almost melodic with purpose.

"Massus . . . adjust our engines to feed their energy back to the tiles. Levan, break off and set a course for the incoming armada."

Zell straightened and stared, but couldn't speak. His eyes worked furiously with all the emotions running past them. His fingers were splayed out pointlessly and trembling.

Massus stepped out from behind the helmsman. "You're sacrificing our lives? You get to decide? Just like that?"

I turned to face him. "That's right. Sometimes a decision just has to be made."

Stunned, he gawked at me. They all began to look at me. All over the deck young faces turned toward me, one after the other, as they realized I wasn't kidding. They had elected me as their captain, but that was where the concept of democracy ended. They knew me well enough by now to understand me. They'd have no choice but mutiny. Death or mutiny. Me or that danger out there. Which would they rather face? Two sailor's nightmares clashing up against each other. Orders or anarchy.

But there was more to it. Not just orders, not just death—the very depth of personal integrity was at stake. Everyone had to die eventually. A privileged few got to choose how and why they would die.

I had already chosen. I was willing to die for my adopted culture, and I hadn't even visited it in person yet. In the eyes of the crew, I was willing to die for *their* families, their nations, their planet.

Like the transfer of energy from the fire ship to our enemies, raw courage of conviction flowed from me to the crew. The change occurred before my eyes in utter silence, as skies clear from clouds to bright sunshine. Their shoulders straightened. Fear's pallor dropped from their faces. They crossed that line, to stand with me, to live free or die.

Without a further spoken word of our new bond, I gave them a sustaining nod.

"Zell," I said, "full sublight."

Our first officer slapped his hands on his thighs in that manner he had, then said, "Full speed, aye!"

He motioned to Othien and Levan, and we were on our way, heading into the nearest clutch of Menace ships to give up our lives and hope that others would follow. For this, sadly, would be the only way.

CHAPTER
22

"ZELL, HAVE RUVAN AND HIS ASSISTANTS BRING QUEN TO THE bridge. He should be here for this."

For our suicide mission, I avoided saying, he deserved to be here.

The interior tiles were beginning to glow with feedback, to pack themselves with potential energy.

"Everybody stay back from the tiles," Zell warned, then leaned down the well and repeated, "stay away from the tiles down there!"

When he straightened, I gave him a sustaining grin and said, "What difference does it make, really?"

He blushed, his hair taking on the cucumbery sheen of the glowing tiles, and his hands made a gesture of frustration and uselessness. Then he rubbed his face and couldn't help a miserable smile.

Out in space, the *Aragore* was still arching its last vestiges of blue snaggly energy to the nearest sources—whatever Lumalit ships hadn't been able to veer off in time.

"They're literally getting the shock of their lives," I muttered, then couldn't help a glance at Totobet, who was quietly watching the drama play out. Near her there was a movement, and my attention switched to Quen. He was being assisted through the hatch by Ruvan and Bren, one of the crew assigned to help in the infirmary. Quen was pale and groggy, but instantly looked up at the overhead vid to see what was happening, and as his expression changed I could see that he had figured it out already. He saw the tiles glowing with backfill around us, and he more than any here understood what that meant.

He was walking, though very stiffly, and there was still a canvas splinting device around his waist and hips. I could tell that most of his weight was being borne by Ruvan and Bren. Many of the crew reached for him and brushed his fingers in a sad and poignant gesture—they missed him. No level of experience offered by me could fill that void.

The bizarre part was that I missed him too. I wanted to have a captain again, to do hard hands-on work with the nuts and bolts of the ship and provide information to the command, then let somebody else broach the tricky decisions. Oh, I could *do* it . . . I'd just discovered something of great worth in myself that had been silent before this. A deckhand.

Like a long many-headed worm, the crew hovered in the middle of the deck now, unable to touch the tiles, and over our heads the vid screen tiles, even though we couldn't see most of them because they were busy projecting an illusion of open space, were washed in a sickly green haze.

The incoming armada still showed on the screen.

"They're close," I said aloud. "We'll see them in a minute."

These words were virtually our epitaph. As soon as we came within range of an unequal energy source, the power building up in our millions of capacitors would sizzle across space, frying us and everybody it could reach. The discharge, I hoped, would be abrupt and over quickly. With luck, we would not linger long to suffer the success of our mission.

Behind us, Oran's ship struggled to keep up, as did what was left of the warranters and Space Force vessels. They were regrouping, and I could only hope they had it within themselves to take our example if they had to, or the

Menace children would live and multimillions of others would be killed. A ghastly balance—and if there were nightmares beyond the grave, this would be mine.

Watching his tiles from a less than safe distance, Lucas interrupted my thoughts. "Kay? Somebody's hailing us. I thought you said they wouldn't hail us."

I moved to where I could see his comm screen, but there was no way to touch a tile and respond to the hail. "They didn't hail anybody the last time. They just came in and started cutting."

"How can we answer?"

Cupping my hand on his shoulder, I said, "We can't. Just ignore it."

He didn't like that. His devotion to purpose was heartening as we stared down the barrel of suicide.

The first ship in the new wave came surging toward us on the screen, our energy-stuffed tiles still fighting to give us a craggy picture that was blurred and flickering. The first ship was of a different configuration than the rest, which seemed to be roughly cone-shaped.

I squinted against the glare of hot tiles. "Those don't look like Lumalit ships . . . at least nothing I've seen . . ."

"What's that big one in front?" Quen asked from a few steps away. "An assault vanguard?"

"I don't know," I said, "but let's hope it veers in to hit us. It'll get a hell of a shocking response."

It was the ship that would kill us, and that we would kill with our overpacked capacitors. Energy would crackle from *Zingara* to that ship and pulse its deadly poison across the vacuum of space, using that ship's own power against it, sucking back the wash of energy and recycling it into new charges. We'd be gone by then, fried by the first surge. Streaking across space, crackling now with furious stored energy in all our tiles, *Zingara* actually looked as if she were ablaze around us.

"They're not coming toward us!" Zell called over the whine of collected energy. "Why are they angling away?"

I shielded my eyes and tried to see the screen. We still couldn't see the incoming ships on the overhead—they were behind our visible bulkheads—but on the screen . . . Zell was right. The big advance guard and the triangular attackers behind it were splitting up and going wide around us. What kind of maneuver was that?

"They'll reach their own ships with that maneuver and miss us completely," I complained. "Why would anybody do that? Levan, prepare to come about if we have to. They're not getting by us!"

With all this stored up energy, I sure didn't want to just sit here in space and fry. If we had to die, we'd do a better job of it than that!

"Here they come!" Zell backed up and turned his face upward through the green snapping haze of energy that wanted so much to jump. He looked up and forward of us.

Quen turned also, as did the crew, and as did I. We stood shoulder to shoulder and watched the darkness of space while haze-shrouded forms took shape in the nearing distance as icebergs might appear on an ocean horizon. They were angling away from us in a reverse pie-wedge, making room for us to go down the middle corridor and completely miss them if we kept to our course. Did they smell a rat? Were they avoiding *Zingara* on purpose, assuming we were the best foot stepping forward and the ships behind us damaged, or more easily smashed? Not a bad assumption, unfortunately.

"Levan, one-quarter about!" I called.

"One-third," Quen suggested.

"Make that one-third!"

"One-third about," Levan shakily responded. He was handling the only control on the ship that wasn't encrusted with tiles: the helm.

The *Zingara*, rippling with green banshees, began slowly to swing about. This turned the forward bulkhead away from the incoming armada and let us see clearly the ships coming toward us, ships that exploded in my mind with all the force of warp core detonations.

Gasping, choking, shocked, I plunged to the helm and pushed Levan aside so hard that he nearly fell against the deadly glowing transverse bulkhead behind him.

"Out of the way!" My shout confused everybody. Even me.

The helm tingled in my hands, hot with radiant energy from the packed capacitors all over the ship, but I ordered myself to ignore that and force the ship to slow down, to stop turning.

"What are you doing!" Zell demanded. "We'll miss them if we slow down!"

"We have to miss them," I gagged, but the words cracked in my mouth.

The big advance ship soared overhead like an albatross on the hunt, so close that I was afraid the tiles would release their charge—and now I didn't want them to. The long cetacean lines were like a song played on a harp and vibrating against my heart. Now I understood why they had tried to hail us.

Zell rushed to me and put his hands over mine. "We've got to get them! We'll waste the charge!"

"No," I said, strangely quiet, buffeted by a sudden peace in my whole soul. "I don't want to destroy my ship."

He gawked at me. "What? You mean *Zingara?*"

My lips parted as we watched the big advance cruiser sail by us and open fire on the Lumalit ships that had survived our trick with the *Aragore*. I saw with great satisfaction that the bolts of energy from the attacking ship changed every few seconds; they'd figured out the Lumalit's shield adaptation and programmed the weapons to make random alterations in frequency. The cuts went right through the Lumalit shields and sliced into the skin of the ships, several at once, in a blaze of successful hits.

Quen hobbled toward me, and together we watched the monumental show.

"She doesn't mean *Zingara,*" he told Zell quietly. "Do you, Kay?"

Slowly, as tears drained down my face and were instantly warmed by the energy pulsing around us, I shook my head.

"No," I told him. "I mean *Voyager.*"

On the faces of my shipmates around me, I saw with great joy the sudden understanding. They knew what I meant, they understood what we were seeing.

There, before us, with a flank of Iscoy fighters following and now swooping in to blast the Lumalit ships away from the warranters and the Space Force ships, the *Starship Voyager* was for me, for us, the grandest sight in the universe. I was—we were—no longer alone.

CHAPTER
23

"CHAKOTAY! . . . TOM . . . TUVOK . . . HARRY!"

I fought back tears and rushed toward them as the airlock opened on *Zingara*'s loading deck.

They were alive, they were *alive!* I was alive! And all my closest associates were here to greet me. Chakotay, Tom Paris, Harry Kim, B'Elanna . . . they were alive, alive, alive.

Funny how this was so much harder to accept than getting used to the idea that they'd all died. In my chest bloomed the strange delight that they had done all right without me. The lesson in humility was as great as any parent could hope for while watching her children fledge. As indispensable as a captain would like to be, if the crew were well trained enough, then they could do fine without . . . me.

What a bittersweet thing that was. What a moment of pride and intimidation, sadness and satisfaction.

Behind me, Quen, Zell, Lucas, and many more of *Zingara*'s crew watched the unlikely reunion, and I couldn't hazard a guess about what they were feeling. Shock, I supposed, and a little touch of contrition that they had doubted me, but who could blame them for that? I'd landed on their ship and declared myself superior. They'd done the smartest thing: They'd handed me a broom and said, "Sweep."

"Kathryn" was all Chakotay could manage to say, and he said it at least three times until I finally started laughing and crying at the same time.

Somehow holding hands with all of them at once, I choked out, "You got the random frequency thing figured out!"

Chakotay said, "Their energy usage wasn't deep enough for the shields to be that strong."

"B'Elanna figured it out," Tom Paris managed.

B'Elanna Torres cast her Klingon reserves overboard and absolutely shook with affection. I saw a thousand questions race across her mind, but the one that finally popped out was "What happened to your *hair?*"

Oh, what I must look like to them! Here I stood, my hair chopped and shaggy, my hands still scarred from the burns in the pod, my clothing more like a medieval forester than a modern spacefarer, and standing here as I was, with my shipmates behind me in very much the same clothing, with the same shag and the same gauntness and the same hopes, I felt prouder than I ever had before.

Summoning a whole new courage, I mustered up the operative point. "I saw *Voyager* blow up . . . I saw a warp reactor detonation . . ."

Chakotay nodded. "You did see that. But it was the spacedock's auxiliary test engine blowing up. It had an antimatter reactor."

I openly stared at him. The stupid spacedock. An auxiliary reactor core. The blinding flash of antimatter detonation.

Like an idiot I kept staring at him, ready to declare him a liar and insist that the ship had blown up and they were really all dead and so was I because *Zingara* had discharged her energy and this was all the dream of the last second of consciousness before I got electrocuted into vapor.

Then Chakotay reached out and gripped my arm as if he knew what I was thinking, touching me with such plain human warmth and reassurance that I shuddered with emotion.

"The spacedock clamps failed to release us," Tuvok

explained, buttering the moment with his Vulcan evenhandedness. "We had to let it disintegrate before we could break away. Mr. Chakotay was ready for it—"

"We hit emergency warp." Chakotay took over before he was forced to collect too much praise. "It knocked us all on our ears, but we were shielded by the blast of the auxiliary engine and ducked into the sun's corona. It's an old Maquis trick . . . from my 'better' days. You pretend you've been destroyed, and you get time to tend your damage. Once we'd made our major repairs, we met with the Iscoy survivors and just decided that these people weren't going to do this to anyone else if we could stop it. So when they warped out, we followed them."

Overwhelmed, I beat back a wave of new tears. "You deserve a commendation. If you ever do this to me again, I'll strangle you. Doctor . . ."

I reached out to him as he stepped through the airlock from the shuttlecraft linked up to *Zingara*.

"Captain," he said warmly, and with such emotion that I really believed for a moment that a computer-generated hologram could cry. I thought he was holding my hand, but then I realized he was examining my hand. "Look at these burns. You'll need skin grafts. Good thing I'm here."

"Yes, I'm very glad you're here," I told him. "We have one of the Lumalit people on board here. We need you to apply your medical analysis to her and try to figure out their reproductive systems. They've got a big problem—"

"Kay," Zell called from amidships, just below the deck well, "Lucas says the Lumalit flagship is hailing us. They want to talk to you."

"What's their condition?" I asked.

"All their ships are heavily damaged. Only two have motive power right now. They're all badly crippled . . . I think they want our terms for surrender."

His voice had a cautious lick of hope in it.

"Come on," I called, and waved everybody to follow me.

We dashed up the deck well onto the main deck, where Lucas had several of the now-calm tiles arranged in screens that showed many Lumalit faces, presumably those in command of various ships. They were harried and wounded. Defeated.

On the wide overhead video display, off to our starboard side, there hovered the enormous and beautiful *Voyager*, scarred from battle, many of her silvery hull plates scorched, lying in birdlike repose, having survived the unsurvivable.

How wonderful she was to my eyes. For the first time in my life, I loved two ships.

Nearby, Totobet stood in mute reflection as she watched me and both my crews come to the middle deck. I communed silently with her for a moment, then turned to the faces of anticipation.

"The jig is up," I told them boldly, without any greetings or formalities. "We know how to beat you. You're finished in this quadrant."

The Lumalit faces ran a gamut of reactions from misery to acceptance. Then one man about three screens away from me spoke up.

"We understand what you mean," he said. "What are your intentions? Will you destroy our transports? . . . How many of us will you allow to survive? . . . May we choose who dies? That is how we survive. Please allow it."

Again I glanced at Totobet. She returned my glance and quietly mentioned, "Please let me rejoin my people for this . . ."

"Don't be silly," I clipped. Stepping closer to the spokesman's screen, I pointed out, "You've got to be talking about millions of lives."

The Lumalit spokesman nodded. "Yes. If that is the best we can do, we will do it. It is the curse of our genetics."

Amazing.

Even after all this, the whole idea was still amazing to me. One more time I looked at Totobet, and in her eyes I saw the terrible burden of her people. She watched the scorched faces of those who piloted their attack fleet, and I knew she had seen such things before. These were people who had won many times, but also who had lost many times and been forced to enact their awful lottery. She looked upward and saw the ships crackling and breaking, and knew she was one of the vanquished.

In the pocket of my shirt under the shoulder cape, the small folded book of photographs ached against my chest.

In my victory, I saw the inevitable civilian victims. That was Totobet. She was standing there looking at her smashed fleet, and realizing once again that the children she was carrying would be the ones to die.

As I watched her, I came down out of the saddle of my victory and stood beside the price of it.

Turning away from her, I moved to Quen's side.

"Doctor," I began. "This is Quen. He was the captain of *Zingara* before his injuries, and he rescued me from the pod, brought me on board, and offered me a new life. If you don't mind, please admit him to *Voyager*'s sickbay and treat his injuries." Quen looked at me, seeming a little hesitant to hand himself over to strangers on a strange ship, but I gripped his hand and assured, "You'll be much better very soon. You'll be surprised."

Chakotay and Paris, more than the others, had caught something in my words and now stepped forward together, and Paris blurted, "Wait a minute—"

At the same time, Chakotay said, "What do you mean, 'If we don't mind,' take him to sickbay?"

"You're coming with us," Paris finished.

This was the moment I had dreaded from the first instant when my mind believed what it was seeing—that the *Voyager* had survived and my spaceborne family was alive.

Standing between Quen and Zell, with Lucas nearby and Massus behind me, I squared my shoulders beneath the little cape and looked at *Voyager*'s boarding party. Despite what I expected, my voice didn't crack, my hands didn't tremble.

"I've sworn a Pledge to this ship," I said. "I can't be citizen of two countries or captain of two ships. I'm not going back with you. I'm staying here."

CHAPTER
24

VOYAGER . . . THE SICKBAY. SUCH A BRIGHT AND BEAUTIFUL place, a locale of so much knowledge, the medical lexicons of a hundred cultures, a place of modern miracles wrought by the brains of the living. The brightness was shocking. The warmth alien and unfamiliar, seeming suddenly unnecessary, even wasteful.

Here in the light of these rooms, I stood beside the diagnostic cot, making sure not to crowd Oran as he stood at Quen's shoulder. Quen lay on the cot, and *Voyager*'s Doctor was finishing some of those modern miracles that suddenly dazzled me as if I'd never seen them before.

On the other side of the cot, behind the Doctor, Zell also waited to see what would happen. On another cot a few steps away, Totobet sat and waited patiently with her crossed legs hanging over the side, not sure what her fate would be. I knew she hoped I'd return her to her people. I would, but I hadn't told her that yet.

"Pelvic bones fused . . . internal burns, well, almost healed. And that spleen is rather improved now, I should say." The Doctor ran his diagnostics over his patient's body and somehow ignored Quen's winces and groans as medical science very quickly knitted tissues that otherwise would take months to heal. I'd been through some of that myself in the past—a rather stinging process at times.

"I'd like to avoid surgery," the Doctor went on, narrating his activities as he usually did. "So you'll have some internal discomfort for a week or so. Otherwise, you can return to normal duty, provided you avoid heavy lifting."

"He's going to avoid everything," Oran said, raising his brother to a sitting position on the edge of the cot. "I'm going to tie him down and feed him some good food."

"We'll all have good food now," I told them. "We just got word that the TCA has collapsed. Their own military wouldn't back them up. When the Space Force figured out that the warranters would rather die than go on without freedom, they stood up to their own government. No more forcing the warranters to keep from banding together. Everyone can go home and work on setting up a decent government of, for, and by the people. Not bad for three days' work, wouldn't you say?"

"I can't believe it," Quen murmured, but he smiled. He clasped Oran's hand, then Zell's. "We can go home."

"That's right, and it's about time." I looked around, beaming at my shipmates, and found myself looking also at Chakotay, Tuvok, and Tom Paris, who had invaded the sickbay when they found out I was on board.

Pretty obvious why they were here. I hadn't changed my clothes. I hadn't gotten my hair fixed up. The burns on the backs of my hands were treated with freshly grown skin, but that was the only change. I saw the disappointment in their eyes as they came in. They wanted me to stay.

As Quen sat on the bed, with Oran and Zell at his sides, and tested his mended body limb by limb, I strode to Totobet and invited, "Doctor? Do you have anything to say to this young lady and her people?"

Voyager's vaunty physician stepped forward to my side. "Yes, after examining her for these few days, and the male prisoners we took, I do have a few things to say. Madam, your problem is hormonal. In my medical laboratories I have synthesized the various hormones. With a tightly controlled series of treatments, we can make the male body believe it has already sired. We're still working on the female physiology, but I think we're close to solving that problem as well."

"What about the multiplicity?" I asked. "The multiple births?"

"Hormonal as well," he said flatly. "A mere subsection of the other solution."

Chakotay smiled. "Some of our prisoners confirmed that they'd never run into anyone with advanced medical capabilities. At least, not as advanced as ours."

Playing up the moment, I pressed, "Oh, really? Can you explain that, Doctor?"

Accommodatingly the Doctor said, "Certainly. They didn't have *me.*"

"No, they didn't." I turned to Totobet and put an arm around her—what an unexpected gesture. "You and your people threw all your technology into survival and conquest. You gave up on curbing reproduction because your people died trying. We understand that, but as your technology advanced, you forgot to try again and again until a solution was found. This physician and the Federation *Starship Voyager* are significantly more advanced in medical sciences than anything you're familiar with, and I'll bet Captain Chakotay will be willing to look into your problem. You've always been on a footing geared to survival rather than betterment. Here's a dose of betterment."

She tried to speak, but nothing came out. I think she was stunned. A solution to all this that didn't involve further struggle and slaughter? A biological solution? Her children would no longer have to die?

That was right, but only because *Voyager* had survived the attack of her desperate people. Without this ship and its crew, neither the Lumalit, nor the Om, nor the Iscoy had such a depth of medical indices to conjure up an answer. We would've had to keep fighting until one side or the other was utterly destroyed.

Sudden sympathy rose in me for the civilizations of the past who had been forced to fight over monumental things whose answers today seemed so available. I didn't prefer to understand, but all at once I did.

Before temptation took over and things turned sour, I moved back to the other cot and took Quen's arm. "Let's get back to the *Zingara.*"

"Captain," Chakotay began.

I stopped him with a look. "Please, don't."

He actually held his breath. Behind him, Tuvok's scowl was dark as space and Paris looked like a gutted jack-o'-lantern.

"Thank you all," I said. "It's been my privilege to serve with you. But now I serve another ship, and I'm going back to her."

After three days of postbattle cleanup and rushed summits of regions' leaders all over the home planet, and all the admirals or whatever they called themselves getting together and deciding things, not to mention the good scare they'd gotten from the Lumalit, the people of this sector were remarkably resilient and ready to make changes.

I'd been standing back in rather a lot of awe, watching how fast things happened, considering that they'd been stalled in this political limbo for . . . how many years was it?

But now the tide had turned and there was no pulling it back. The warranters wanted to see their families and live normal lives, the former TCA leaders were in exile somewhere and being hunted down for trial, local dartboards had Sasaquon's face for a target, and in between the chaotic events were soaring moments of real hope and reason.

Shipments of food, fuel, water, and fresh clothing were coming in by the hour for the warranters, who were finally getting the appreciation they deserved for their eight-year standoff on behalf of freedom. With some regret I turned over my tattered shoulder cape for one that had been freshly made by a little girl on a planet I'd never even visited. How wonderful to be appreciated by those for whom you had put down your very life. I'd forgotten that part. It was as if my heart had been polished and given a lube job.

On board *Zingara,* members of the crew were involved in a cocktail of damage control and giddy partying. Have a drink and pass me that wrench. When I returned with Quen, Zell, and Oran, and the crew could see for themselves that Quen and I were both much improved from our injuries, their young faces gleamed with mystification and delight. There really *was* hope!

Communiqués were coming in from all over, ranging from questions to interviews to congratulations, and most of them were fielded by Lucas or Zell, but ultimately one came in for me, and nobody else could answer the strange and heady request.

"This is Kay," I responded when the portrait of a rather small-boned elderly man appeared on one of the smaller tile screens.

"I am Samda, newly appointed chief justice of the Om Planetary Court, Captain Kay. This communication is being wide-broadcast to all localities and ships. We no longer wish to work in secret. No more closed doors. May I thank you personally and publicly for your valiant participation in the past weeks' events."

"You're most welcome, Judge," I said. "It was my pleasure to serve. I'm glad I could be here when I was needed, but I can't take all the credit. The warranters endured years of isolation and struggle before I ever came here. They are your sons and the true valiant among us."

"And we shall reward them for a lifetime," the old man promised. *"For now, though, for the immediate future . . . we have an unorthodox request. We all have taken a vote here, and on the colonies. We all know about you and your Federation, and where you came from. You are the only person who isn't a representative of some faction or other, some hemisphere, some loyalty, or some bias. You're the only person that everyone here trusts. Captain Kay, will you come to the planet and become the imperial leader and show us how to set up a government that will not collapse under the weight of corruption? Will you come here? Will you lead us?"*

What had he said?

I leaned toward Quen and out of the corner of my mouth I muttered, "Is he offering me a planet?"

Quen smiled. "Sounds that way. Why don't you take it? You could get that haircut."

"Do I have to take the Planet's Pledge?"

He laughed. I guess he knew I wasn't going to go be a dictator, no matter how many planets I was offered.

"Judge Samda," I began after a moment, "I don't want to run your planet. But on the *Voyager,* if you'll let me contact Captain Chakotay on your behalf, there is a library of documents that would serve you very well during this time. No one can do this for you. You have to decide your own direction. You've been running your planet the way you should run a ship, and your ships the way you should run a planet. The planet should be a democracy. The ships shouldn't be. You don't have the wrong rulers, you have the wrong rules. Just read what I send you . . . and make your world. Thank you again and best luck."

With a brief nod of salute, I motioned to Lucas to cut off the communication. No more of that.

"Lucas, contact the *Voyager* and tell them I have a list of publications they should duplicate and give to the planet's media and bodies of authority."

"Why don't you contact them yourself, Kay?" Quen asked.

My lips pressed tight for a moment and I shook my head. "Lucas can do it."

I hadn't noticed, but now did, that most of the crew had gathered around me on the main deck. What was this, another celebration of my wonderfulness? Couldn't we be done with that?

"You can tell them yourself," Zell said.

"Why?" I looked at him, then at Quen. "I don't want to go back there."

"Well, you'd better. We took another vote. You've been deposed."

Suddenly trembling, I swiveled around and looked at the beaming faces of *Zingara*'s crew. "You're releasing me from my Pledge? But I didn't ask—"

"We're not releasing you from it," Zell protested.

"Not at all," Quen said. "We're just reassigning you. We've just elected you captain of the *Voyager.*"

CHAPTER
25

"So I said, 'Go ahead and make your world.' And they did, gentlemen, they did."

"And tell us, Captain . . . which documents did you send to the new government of that planet?"

"Oh, I imagine you could guess many of them yourself, Captain Troop. And the other captains here could guess the rest. The Magna Carta, the Bill of Rights, the United States Constitution, the United Federation of Planets Articles of Confederation, the Fundamental Declarations of the Martian Colonies, the Vulcan Treatises on Logic and the Living Condition, *The Death of Andor* . . . and many others. They just needed a little guidance. The Berlin Wall always falls . . . it's just harder to find inside a free society."

"This episode seems to have changed you as much as those around you who were affected by your presence."

Across the table, the man with one arm chased his sentence with an aristocratic blue glare. He'd been making comments like that all the way through my tale, probing not for what happened, but for which changes came of the happenings. Even in this odd environment, he was trying to learn from what he heard.

Around me like a smoky cloak, the Captain's Table murmured its comforting noises. Tales being told at other tables, the *clop* of footsteps up and down the stairs, someone picking out a one-fingered tune on the piano, glasses clinking, laughter, sighs.

"Yes, Your Lordship," I agreed. "I had always doubted . . . wondered if I was captain because I had connections, or because of my father, or because I was lucky. What I found out was that you could burn my hair and clothes off, wrap me in foil, drop me on a ship, injured, alien, and raving, and I could still cope."

"That's right. You were captain again," the woman in the sweater said. "Whatever your plusses and minuses are, you could put that one away."

"Oh, but I was a captain greatly changed," I told her after a sip of my drink. "Silly as it seems, I kept wanting to go back to buffing the tiles. I found a deckhand in myself, and I like her. As a matter of fact . . . she'd better get back to her ship."

The table of interesting people raised their glasses to me but made no attempt to stop me from leaving.

"Fair weather," the woman said.

Her Vulcan companion echoed, "And best destiny, Captain."

The others, captains all, murmured their farewells. As I stepped away from the table and headed toward the arched entrance, another story had already begun. Something about a shipment of rice and the hold of a prize ship . . .

I was tempted to stay, but something else called to me. Somehow I knew this was time for me to leave, just as I had known before that it would be all right to stay awhile.

The warmth of the pub slipped down my back as if a cloak were being taken from my shoulders. I stepped out into the cobbled street, still moist from rain, and looked around.

"Captain!"

I swung about, and Tom Paris almost knocked me over.

"There you are!" he blustered. "Are you all right?"

"Yes, I'm really actually very well right now," I told him. "Where did you go?"

"I thought I was following you into that door, but I

must've taken a wrong turn," he said. "I've been walking around corners looking for you."

"How long?"

He paused and frowned. "Well, I don't really know . . ."

Putting my hand on his arm before he went any farther, I said, "Just a minute. I want to check something." I tapped my commbadge. "Janeway to *Voyager.*"

"Chakotay here, Captain. Is anything wrong?"

"What's wrong with the comm network? I tried to raise you about an hour ago, but I couldn't get through."

"An hour ago? Captain, you just beamed down."

"How long ago did we beam down?"

"It's been . . . eight minutes, thirty seconds."

"Mmm," I uttered. "You've been in command of a Maquis ship, haven't you, Chakotay? You've been a captain."

There was a pause. *"Of course. You know that . . ."*

"Yes. Put Tuvok in command and beam down, would you? I'd like to check out a theory. I'm going to shove you through a big oak doorway and see what happens."

"Uh . . . understood. I'll be right there."

"Janeway out." I turned to Paris again. "He doesn't understand."

Paris shrugged and gazed at the foggy street.

"That's all right," I said. "Some things are better with a little mystery clinging to them. Some romances, some tales, some adventures . . . but listen, Tom, do me a favor, will you? Some time in the future, when things look bad and I really need a boost . . ."

"Yes?"

"Call me 'Kay.'"

From Star Trek: New Frontier Book One:
House of Cards:

"You should never have resigned, Mac," Captain Picard said. "That's the simple fact of the matter. I know you blamed yourself for what happened on your last posting, on the *Grissom.*"

"Don't bring it up."

"But Starfleet cleared you . . ."

"I said don't bring it up!" Calhoun said furiously. The scar seemed to stand out against his face, and, bubbling with anger, he shoved Picard out of the way . . .

From Star Trek: New Frontier Book Six:
Fire On High:

"Then I want you to ask me for my help," the Promethean said. "No, better"—and he grinned wildly—"beg me, just like the captain of the *Grissom* begged you."

There was dead silence on the bridge.

Later in Star Trek: New Frontier Book Six:

Zak Kebron approached Commander Shelby, looking puzzled.

"What's on your mind?" she asked him.

"Commander," he began, "the Promethean mentioned the *Grissom,* and you could have heard a pin drop on the bridge."

"Spit it out," Shelby said.

"So I was wondering, what happened on the *Grissom?* To Captain Calhoun, I mean."

"I'm not at liberty to say," Shelby replied.

"And I take it you advise against asking the captain directly?"

"That's not a story the captain is ready to tell."

Coming in September
Star Trek: New Frontier
Captain's Table Book Five
Once Burned
The Story of Captain Calhoun
on the *U.S.S. Grissom*
In his own words as told to Peter David

Kathryn Janeway
by
Michael Jan Friedman

Her Early Life and Career

Kathryn Janeway was raised in a 24th-century agricultural park in the region known as Indiana, on Earth. Her father, Edward Janeway, was a career Starfleet officer who rose to the rank of vice-admiral before his untimely death.

During the latter stages of Kathryn's childhood, the elder Janeway spent increasing amounts of time away from home, dealing with the burgeoning Cardassian threat to the Federation—a threat that would ultimately erupt into armed conflict. Young Kathryn responded to these absences by trying to excel at the activities her father had laid out for her, becoming an outstanding mathematician, scientist, tennis player, and ballet artist in an attempt to impress and please him.

Once, after losing a tennis match, Kathryn Janeway set out to trek twenty miles through rainy woods rather than take a ride back to her home. It would not be until later in life that she learned to deal well with failure, though she remained driven to succeed in every aspect of her life.

Janeway accompanied her father to Mars at the tender age of nine and developed an affinity for the terraformed world that would bring her back on several other occasions.

As a young woman, after completing her senior honors thesis on vertebrate anatomy, Janeway discovered what appeared to be a chordate skeleton while cave-diving on Mars—suggesting that there had been vertebrate life on Mars at one time. The discovery brought her a certain amount of fame in scientific circles at an early age.

Originally, Janeway aspired to become the science officer on a deep-space exploration expedition, and even completed a doctoral degree in quantum cosmology toward that end. However, the young woman changed her mind about her career direction while serving as an ensign under Admiral Owen Paris on the starship *Icarus*.

Janeway's assignment to the *Icarus* was her first in space. In the course of it, both she and Admiral Paris were briefly taken prisoner by the Cardassians, whose actions the *Icarus* was investigating. After Janeway aided in the admiral's escape, he suggested that Starfleet would better benefit from her services as a command officer.

Janeway went on to serve under Paris as science officer on the *Al-Bataani,* but later took his advice and switched to the command track. It was at about the same time that Janeway's father and fiancé were killed in the crash of a shuttlecraft on Tau Ceti Prime.

Janeway, who had been piloting the vessel, was only injured in the crash. Still, she carried its emotional scars for some time afterward, even sinking into a clinical depression.

Her mother, Gretchen, and her younger sister, Phoebe, are credited with having brought Janeway out of that depression. Janeway also benefited from the company of Petunia, a dog she rescued from a snowstorm near her family home, and the support of Mark Johnson, a childhood friend and a member of Earth's Questor philosophical symposium.

Janeway went on to become romantically involved with Johnson, though she had never before seen him in a romantic light. Nonetheless, their relationship didn't keep Janeway from pursuing her aspirations to explore deep space as a Starfleet officer.

Her first mission as captain was a six-month venture into the Beta Quadrant. Afterward, a Vulcan ensign named

Tuvok was asked to assess her efforts as the commanding officer of a starship. He found her lacking in respect for military exercises. Though Janeway was nonetheless commended for her tour of duty, Tuvok was assigned to accompany her on her next command—to make sure she conducted the necessary tactical drills.

Janeway and Tuvok went on to become fast friends and staunch comrades. The captain came to rely on the Vulcan's clear, logical vision and technical expertise. When she was placed in command of the cutting-edge starship *U.S.S. Voyager,* Janeway named Tuvok her tactical officer.

The *Voyager* Adventures

Starfleet Command "borrowed" Tuvok from Janeway and had him infiltrate the revolutionary group known as the Maquis. However, in 2371, the Maquis ship to which the Vulcan was assigned fell victim to an anomaly in the region of space known as the Badlands.

Janeway took *Voyager* into the Badlands in an attempt to locate Tuvok, but fell victim to the same anomaly. Both she and her ship were swept into the distant Delta Quadrant of the galaxy, some 70,000 light years from the nearest Federation border.

After the destruction of the Maquis vessel, which had also been drawn into the Delta Quadrant, Janeway recovered Tuvok and accepted the Maquis crew aboard her ship. Furthermore, she invited its commander, Chakotay, to become her first officer on *Voyager.*

Janeway's courage and leadership were instrumental in the survival of her ship and its occupants as they made a long and difficult journey back to the Alpha Quadrant. One of her earliest challenges in this area was to meld the Starfleet and Maquis components of her crew.

To accelerate the process, Janeway named other Maquis besides Chakotay to staff officer positions. Prominent among these appointments was that of B'Elanna Torres, a half-Klingon, half-human female who was placed in charge of the engineering section.

Tom Paris, the son of Admiral Owen Paris, served as helmsman on *Voyager* during those difficult days. Though the younger Paris had been discredited for lying and ousted from Starfleet, Janeway valued his skills as a pilot and had him removed from a penal colony to take her into the Badlands. Though he couldn't keep *Voyager* and her crew from being thrown into the Delta Quadrant, Paris proved his mettle as a pilot and an officer, and justified Janeway's faith in him on numerous other occasions.

Captain Janeway encountered a number of intriguing and dangerous species in her journey across the Delta Quadrant. Prominent among them was the Kazon, a savage and acquisitive people divided into individual sects, each one hostile to Janeway and her crew. At one point, the captain tried unsuccessfully to forge a defensive alliance with a number of Kazon sects.

The captain also encountered the Vidiians, a species ravaged by a virus called the Phage, which gradually destroyed the organs of their bodies. To fill their increasing need for new organs, the Vidiians captured individuals of other species and used them as involuntary donors.

In 2371, Janeway and Tom Paris were investigating a world laid waste by a polaric energy explosion, when they were thrown back in time through a subspace fracture. Arriving at a point just prior to the explosion, they managed to prevent it—and thereby save an entire planetary population from extinction.

That same year, Janeway sought Chakotay's help in experiencing a vision quest in search of her personal animal spirit guide. Her quest indeed yielded her a guide—a lizard.

Soon after, Janeway got the opportunity to meet one of her heroes—the 20th-century female pilot Amelia Earhart. Apparently, Earhart had been abducted from Earth in 1937 by an alien species and brought to the Delta Quadrant, where she was preserved in suspended animation.

The captain's feelings for her father were reawakened when she allied herself with a local eccentric on an alien planet, in an attempt to recover Tuvok and B'Elanna Torres from a prison cell. When the man took a fatal wound helping her, Janeway recognized his courage by going along with his illusion that she was his long lost daughter.

In 2372, Janeway ran into the entity known as Q for the first time, when she encountered another Q with a death wish. A year later, Q returned to *Voyager* to ask the captain to have his baby, over the objections of a jealous female Q.

On another occasion, Janeway took *Voyager* through a void in space and discovered an identical ship and crew existing in a parallel universe. With the help of her counterpart, the captain saved *Voyager* and her crew—though, in the process, her own Ensign Harry Kim was replaced with the Kim of the other universe.

Janeway was extremely protective of her subordinates. At one point, she found it necessary to enter a computer program and pit herself against the embodiment of a race's fear. Some time later, the captain risked her life to save Kes, a member of her crew, from a coma—the result of Kes's encounter with the Nechani homeworld's "spirit" realm.

Late in 2372, Janeway and her crew were boarded by the Kazon and beamed off *Voyager* onto the surface of a savage planet. Using their most basic skills, the captain and her people survived the rigors of that world and went on to recover their vessel.

In 2373, Janeway had to fight for her life and that of her crew once again. This time, she was pitted against a spreading macrovirus threatening to take over *Voyager*.

Also in 2373, Janeway and her crew got their wish and were transported back to Earth—but in the wrong century. In returning to their own time, they also were forced to return to the Delta Quadrant.

Janeway experienced her first brush with the Borg when *Voyager* encountered a disabled Borg ship in the Delta Quadrant—as well as the ship's besieged planetbound survivors. Fortunately, the survivors turned out to be friendly to Janeway and her people. They created a Borg-like neural network and destroyed the cubeshaped vessel before it could come back to life.

A lifelong dog lover, Janeway grew up with a wire-haired mutt named Bramble. At the time of *Voyager*'s disappearance, Janeway's Irish setter, Molly, was about to give birth under Mark Johnson's watchful eye.

During her off-duty hours on *Voyager*, Janeway enjoyed participating in a gothic romance holonovel set in old England on Earth. In the program, which was referred to as

Janeway Lambda-1, Janeway played the governess of two children whose mother had died.

Janeway was also an accomplished pool player. She got a chance to demonstrate this in another holo-setting, a recreation of a French pool hall called Chez Sandrine, favored by Tom Paris during his Academy days.

Janeway considered coffee to be her only vice. Even though replicator privileges on *Voyager* were strictly rationed, she always had at least two cups of coffee a day.

Kathryn Janeway will be remembered as an individual who always rose to a challenge, inspired others with her unflagging optimism and ability, and never took no for an answer.

Look for STAR TREK Fiction from Pocket Books

Star Trek: The Next Generation®

Star Trek: Deep Space Nine®

Star Trek®: Voyager™

Flashback • Diane Carey
Mosaic • Jeri Taylor
The Black Shore • Greg Cox

Star Trek®: New Frontier

Star Trek®: Day of Honor

Star Trek®: The Captain's Table

Book One: *War Dragons* • L. A. Graf
Book Two: *Dujonian's Hoard* • Michael Jan Friedman
Book Three: *The Mist* • Dean W. Smith & Kristine K. Rusch
Book Four: *Fire Ship* • Diane Carey